# TALES: FROM A DISTANT PLANET

ALSO BY FELICE PICANO

*Smart as the Devil*
*Eyes*
*The Mesmerist*
*The Deformity Lover and Other Poems*
*The Lure*
*A True Likeness* (ed.)
*An Asian Minor: The True Story of Ganymede*
*Late in the Season*
*Slashed to Ribbons in Defense of Love and Other Stories*
*House of Cards*
*Ambidextrous: The Secret Lives of Children*
*Window Elegies*
*To the Seventh Power*
*Dryland's End*
*Like People in History*
*Looking Glass Lives*
*A House on the Ocean, a House on the Bay*
*The Book of Lies*
*The New York Years: Stories*
*Onyx*
*Fred in Love*

# TALES: FROM A
## DISTANT PLANET

### FELICE PICANO

FRENCH CONNECTION PRESS

Felice Picano is a poet, memoirist, fiction and sci-fi/fantasy writer. He is the author of more than 20 books, including the best-selling novels *Like People in History, Looking Glass Lives, The Lure*, and *Eyes*. A frequent contributor to the *San Francisco Chronicle*, with writings published in many anthologies, Picano has been successfully producing literary works of art for over two decades. He has won a number of awards, including the PEN Syndicated Fiction Award for short story, as well as being a finalist for the Ernest Hemingway Award. A native of New York, Felice Picano now lives in Los Angeles.

A *French Connection* Book

Published by French Connection Press 2006

*Printed in France*
ISBN 2-914853-05-X

Set in 11 pt. Garamond

*One Way Out* was previously published in *Contemporary Terrors*, 1980,
editor Ramsey Campbell. Pan Books, London, England.

FRENCH CONNECTION PRESS
12 rue Lamartine, 75009 Paris, France • www.frenchcx.com

*To Eric Elléna and Ian Ayres*

*With special thanks to Tanio McCallum,
David Young and Richard Canning*

# CONTENTS

# SO YOU WANT A PREFACE, HUH?

"A highly imaginative child," it read on my school files. But little did those elementary and middle-school teachers know exactly how highly imaginative. Like Lewis Carroll's *Alice in Wonderland*, I had no problem at all thinking of three impossible things before breakfast. Every day. Obviously a life of illusion, crime, and disaster lay ahead of me, with doom preordained.

Then I discovered I could write down some of those highly imaginative ideas I seemed to so richly possess, making them into stories, and novels, poems and plays, and the greater part of the predicted catastrophes were averted.

Not all, by any means.

Readers have called these stories demented, weird, too freakin' strange, and beyond belief. To which I say, "So much for reality!" Nor has it escaped my notice that those same people who've criticized my stories whenever they appeared in magazines or anthologies, have then gone on to beg for more.

Today a handful of the stories I've written over the past three decades and a brand new novella, *Ingoldsby*, is now available, here, only. All but one of the tales have never appeared in print ever, anywhere. That other one showed up in a British anthology a quarter of a century ago. So you'll probably be reading them here for the first time — and I'm not saying which is which.

Some of you will need to know whether these stories fit into the horror genre, psychological unrealism category, science fiction slot, or fantasy file? Me, I don't categorize. I just write them.

Yes, there are still more of these Picano stories. If enough of you like these, those will appear, too. And they're even . . . (fill in the appropriate word here).

Enjoy. Oh, as I've got a website — www.felicepicano.com — and my publisher has one, too — www.frenchcx.com — you will be able to ask the author one question about a story. Don't waste our time, okay? Make it a good one.

FELICE PICANO, *Los Angeles, California, Autumn 2005*

# THE PERFECT SETTING

AFTER HAVING LIVED more than half a century I am certain of the value of very little in this world. But of one thing I am quite certain: we cannot easily sustain the loss of a gifted artist. Especially one as beautiful and charming as Ottilie Chase.

Perhaps that will explain why I could not rest after her death, and why I felt constrained despite what seemed impossible circumstances, to investigate the events leading to her death. And, further, to learn enough to be able to expose the motive *behind* her death. This search was to take me to some odd places, indeed, and to one spot in particular which lingers in my thoughts, refusing to settle into oblivion. Even more disturbing was what I learned about Ottilie Chase herself: that special talent which infused her later work, almost determined its content, through a process I still cannot explain, and which I believe must fall into the realm of the inexplicable. But I'm getting ahead of myself.

★

I hadn't heard from Ottilie in five years when I received the postcard inviting me to the opening of an exhibition of her new paintings. Ever since the purchase of two of her works by the Cleveland Art Museum not long ago, Ottilie—always something of a perfectionist—had become an even more exacting artist.

Her choice of medium somewhat dictated that. She had abandoned oils, experimented briefly with acrylics, flirted with printmaking. But her final decade's work—the paintings of hers that will be collected long in the future—were in the difficult art of egg-tempera. Of necessity, her work was slow, but the possibilities of atmospheric expression were that much more heightened. Her sulky, often eerie, landscapes seemed the work of some still unknown late 19th Century Luminist master.

But there was something else beyond her technique—extraordinary as that was. Each painting added an enigmatic, new, yet also familiar locale to viewers' own store of memorized places. As though you had lived there a month during some astonishingly uneventful and thus poorly recalled vacation. Sections of vast granite escarpments fronted by solid green; utterly vacant meadows; blistering, bereft, sunlit shorelines; littered giant

11

boulders, as though tossed by a Titan's hand; deep twisting forest paths through shadowed, pine-needle carpets—you'd been there before somehow, and you stood in front of each painting racking your memory for where, when exactly.

None of these places were identified on the canvas; which made their amazingly detailed, utterly faithful rendering even more bizarre. However, invariably, a date and time were painted in over Ottilie's signature: usually a very precise time. Not the date it had been painted. Not the date it was hung to be viewed. Nor, in fact, any date that made any immediate sense. Many of the times listed predated Ottilie herself; having taken place months and years before she was even born. And more than half of them predated the period during which she painted. Adding to the mystification, Ottilie never once attempted to explain those dates. She did say that they came to her as she worked. I naturally always assumed that Ottilie insisted upon this so she might add a sense of mystery, because otherwise she was the least mysterious of beautiful women I'd ever known. But that theory still didn't account for the distinct sense of discomfort, or uneasiness, I felt looking at her landscapes. Nor was I the only person with that reaction.

An art gallery opening of a new exhibit is a bright, noisy affair. So many people chatting, re-encountering, so many ice cubes clinking in glasses, one scarcely sees the works on display. Ottilie Chase's own vernissages were more sober affairs. People gathered to look and whispered in small groups. Other viewers stood a long time musing before a single canvas, often with a slight frown on their brows. Others paced almost as though avoiding the actual display of work, then would suddenly stop to catch a peripheral glance at one painting, before moving restlessly on.

I always understood why. I wouldn't have been at all amazed to stumble upon a landscape by Ottilie which I would utterly recognize, completely recall. And I was certain it would be the recognition of some place I never again wanted to see, a memory I wanted obliterated.

This might help explain why I waited until the last moment to go to the exhibition, titled by the way, "Imaginary Landscapes, Series Three." Having put off contacting Ottilie until the day of the vernissage, when I did call her, it was to ask if she minded terribly that I would arrive late, probably not until the closing minutes of the evening. She didn't at all mind, she said, so brightly that to assuage my own guilt, I asked her to join me for dinner afterwards. To my surprise, she accepted.

Even so, I dithered that evening over details of dress even more than usual. Then I couldn't find a taxi on Riverside Drive for another fifteen minutes. I didn't arrive at the gallery at nine-twenty, as I'd promised Ottilie, but after ten. It was still lighted up, although I suppose that entire area of upper Madison Avenue filled with galleries and high-end boutiques remains lighted up till midnight, open or not.

The downstairs glass door led directly up a flight of dimly lighted industrially carpeted stairs. At the first floor landing I found the gallery door locked. Or at least I assumed it was locked when I first tried the handle. One thing was clear, the opening event was already long over.

Ottilie might still be inside. Alone, at night, with the downstairs door unlocked, she had no doubt sensibly locked herself in the gallery to wait for me. I knocked on the door twice. No response. I thought of going back down and outside to find a payphone to tell her that it was me knocking. Then I knocked again, and in irritation called out my name, and wrestled with the door handle, this time with some effort. It seemed to suddenly click, and fall open. Indistinct azure light filtered through what looked to be otherwise darkened rooms. My immediate thought was that it might have actually been locked, if poorly, or faultily so; and that Ottilie had not waited for me.

Even so, I called out her name. Then I recalled a cigarette lighter I'd held for a friend on an earlier occasion, which had ended up still inside one pocket of the coat I'd put on that night. I flicked it and it worked. I located the wall light switch. Both the lights and the ventilation went on as one, blinding me and deafening me for an instant. I stood in the first of three rooms and could partly see into the other two, which were totally bare save for the hung paintings. Then I noticed something completely out of place: in the most distant room, a pair of legs stretched out on the carpet, one high heel snapped off.

I remember gasping out some partial sentence before rushing forward to fully see what I already feared—Ottilie Chase's body, twisted into a half-sitting, half-sprawled position. Her face was a mottled blue, contorted almost beyond identification by the spasmodic fatal pain of the Prussic Acid that spilled out of a wine glass fallen from her hand onto the carpet several feet away. Black stains on the skin of her lower lip, one bared shoulder, and her left wrist were as though charcoal burned paths where the poisoned drink had splashed, probably in the instant she'd discovered its perfidy and too late flung it away.

More frightening however were the reddened whites of her open eyes, angled up at a landscape she had grasped in a futile attempt at steadying her collapse. Or, as though in those last moments before her vision had been burned away along with her existence, she must once more gaze upon her work.

★

I did all those banal things one does when one first sees a friend horribly dead. I fell to my knees, staring in disbelief that she actually was deceased. I finally got up the courage to take her un-charred wrist in my own hand to prove to myself that indeed there was no pulse. I stood up, then, felt a wave of nausea, ran to find the lavatory, spilled out what little food remained undigested in me from lunch, then sat down, took deep breaths, then still not in the least bit calm, I dialed for the police.

In the minutes before they arrived, I calmed enough to bring myself to get up and go look at Ottilie again. For the first time I noticed the subject of the landscape askew in her grotesquely ultimate grasp: a landscape of unearthly beauty.

It depicted two dark, forested shorelines surrounding the clear, un-ruffled water of a sheltered bay at twilight. To one side, riding low in the tide, lay an island, and asymmetrically placed upon it, a copse of trees shaped into a deep green dome. The sun had already set behind the opposite shore. The outline of pine trees was most defined at the painting's right side. The sky was a quiet majesty of grays shot through with husky violets and magentas.

Besides what it portrayed, this three-by-five foot tempera possessed in every square inch that ineffable Chasian quality—it was a masterpiece of haunting remembrance which I couldn't for the life of me precisely remember.

Little wonder she had gone to it last. As though to tell me—might she still have remembered in her last moments that I was to arrive?—take this painting of all of them. This is my best.

But as I heard the police sirens pull up outside the building and saw the scarlet glare of their rooftops reflected outside the gallery windows, I also had another impression, that the index finger of Ottilie's outstretched hand pointed—pointed straight at that eerie little island in the painting, as though it somehow would explain her death.

That moment, I vowed to purchase the landscape, no matter the cost. I also vowed to find out what Ottilie had meant by her final gesture.

★

To my surprise, the police scarcely questioned me. I suppose my shock at Ottilie's death and at having to find her dead was still quite apparent. To my further surprise, however, it seemed to me that they were barely intent on investigating her death at all.

True, photos were taken of the death scene. Chalk marks were laid down upon the carpet and on the wall, outlining her position and that of several objects—the wineglass, one of her shoes, the broken heel of the other. The gallery was closed the following day, and later in the afternoon, three of us, Auburn Anders, the gallery owner, Susan Vight, his assistant, and myself, were collectively questioned at the gallery, although it struck me, in the most perfunctory manner.

Did Ottilie Chase have any enemies? Detective Compson asked.

None, that any of us knew.

Had she any close friends?

Again no. And of close friends, none besides ourselves.

Any family?

I recalled that her mother lived in Portland, Oregon, but was, I admitted, unsure whether or not she was still alive.

Any recent relationships with men?

Not since a year ago, Susan Vight informed us, when Ottilie had stopped seeing Anthony Eldridge. He was a Wall Street lawyer, several years her junior.

Had she been depressed lately?

Here Auburn and Susan exchanged glances and said, yes, of course, Ottilie had been depressed. But that was in no way unusual for Ottilie. After all, it had been five years since her last previous exhibit. She'd naturally been anxious that this show might fail, although clearly this third—and now last—series of "Imaginary Landscapes" was not only the best but the best received to date.

Susan offered her belief that Ottilie was worried about more than the reception of her work. Ottilie had not completely gotten over her separation from Eldridge, Susan thought. I countered that, as well as their emphasis on her depression—for I could easily see that Compson was leading up to a verdict of suicide, which I didn't in least subscribe to. I repeated to him my phone call earlier the previous day with Ottilie and how bright and charming, how not at all depressed, she had seemed.

Auburn and Susan again exchanged glances, but this time neither commented or contradicted me.

Auburn then said something he recalled as having bothered Ottilie greatly. About a year and a half ago, he'd hung two of her newer temperas in a group show here at the gallery. Mostly, he admitted, to test the marketplace and to get her to show them all. One painting had been sold to a small museum in Massachusetts, a sale that cheered Ottilie a great deal; the other had been sold to a man who'd bought it as a twenty-fifth anniversary gift for his wife. The woman had had an immediate and violent aversion to the landscape, and shortly afterward had filed for divorce. The man somehow blamed Ottilie's work for the ruination of his marriage. He'd even attempted to sell it back to the gallery—which was most unusual. As Ottilie was out of town at the time and Auburn could not authorize its repurchase without her consent, he'd asked the man to wait until she returned. Instead, the customer told Auburn he'd keep the painting, then had it destroyed. Even that didn't end the matter. Since then, he'd sent strange and quite nasty letters to both Anders and to Ottilie, in care of the gallery. One letter reached her only a month ago despite Auburn's efforts to not let any more get through, and it had upset the artist greatly; upset her more than the revelation that her work had been destroyed.

She began to talk wildly, saying she ought to destroy all her work herself. It was only with the greatest of persuasion and the utmost tact that Auburn had been able to convince her otherwise—and to allow her to go along with the expected opening date of the exhibit. Still, Ottilie remained anxious, he said. In one conversation she'd had with the gallery owner, she'd gone so far as to declare that her paintings were cursed. When Auburn tried to reason with her, Ottilie had become vague, evasive, ambiguous and yet defensive, too. All he'd been able to get out of her was the odd belief that she'd somehow or other managed—through her art—to unmake human happiness, when all she'd wanted was to increase it.

All three of us felt guilty to one degree or another for Ottilie's death. Auburn for persuading her to have an exhibit she was otherwise set against. Susan for leaving her alone in the gallery that night. And me, for—well look how late I was.

How Compson reached the conclusion he did, I still cannot fully fathom, but our testimony convinced him to reach a temporary finding of death by suicide, following acute professional and personal depression. When I attempted to point out how many easier to take, less hideous poisons than Prussic Acid exist on the market for the potential suicide, the detective frowned, but said nothing else. When I went on to say it seemed to me—the discoverer of her corpse, after all—that she'd been pointing to a possible clue in that final, grasped-at painting, the policeman actually glared at me, then asked if I were suggesting that foul play was involved. Of course, I was suggesting it, I replied. Compson responded that if he were to open a homicide investigation, I would be the primary suspect.

I remained undaunted by this news. But Auburn and Susan made me drop my request.

★

The exhibit reopened the following day, and I promptly purchased the landscape.

I also decided to do a bit of investigating myself. Toward this end I asked Susan Vight to photocopy for me the names of the guests who'd signed into the vernissage, the names of any who'd called or written in about the show, and the gallery's usual mailing list.

The most obvious name present on the final list but not on the other two, and especially not on the list of guests attending the opening, was of course Anthony Eldridge.

I also spent time probing Susan and Auburn's memory, searching for hints of anyone who might have attended the opening night but not signed in. Each recalled several people, but they could neither recall nor had ever known their names.

It was very likely that someone who'd attended the vernissage had later returned on some pretext and somehow managed to slip Ottilie the poisoned drink. I was also fairly certain that the landscape she'd grabbed at—which I now owned—would in some way implicate her murderer.

Because of these beliefs, I went to the gallery almost daily looking for clues within the painting itself, which would remain on public display several weeks longer. This had a side benefit. Susan and Auburn would be able to tell me if anyone had spent longer than usual looking at that same painting, or had offered to buy it, or even had returned often to stare at it.

To all but the second question, the answer was no. Of course many people offered to buy it. That was easy enough to explain. Ottilie's death had been reported in all the daily newspapers. *The New York Times* ran a four column obituary, with another two columns assessing her place in contemporary art and naturally both mentioned the exhibit. Her death also drew the curiously morbid, who probably wouldn't have dreamed of otherwise coming. The gallery was packed day and night. By the end of the first week, all the landscapes had been sold—three to museums, the remainder to private purchasers. It was Ottilie's greatest triumph. People who'd known her for years, all felt it necessary to make an appearance at the gallery, almost as though it were an adjunct to a memorial. Almost all of them seemed to go out of their way to mention this fact to Auburn or Susan, who carefully, politely (following my request) took down their names and addresses. The list of suspects grew.

I began to realize why Detective Compson had not even begun to investigate: it appeared more difficult than ever to find some clue, some lead, even a hint of one, with so many possibilities and so little to go on really: and with so much attention still focused on Ottilie.

Then I had a break. One evening I'd come to the gallery quite late, and Susan Vight immediately signaled me over. Anthony Eldridge had arrived, at last, and was still there. Still there and still so distraught that although we'd never before met (Ottilie had mentioned my name, he said) Eldridge allowed me to take him out afterwards for a drink. At one of those seedy but quite good Manhattan gin-joints made famous by various authors, that happened to be located around the corner from the gallery, he began to speak about Ottilie, led on by my sympathy and by his own need to talk. This is what he told me.

"I loved Ottilie. I never met a woman more to my taste in every way, and believe me, I've had my share of women."

I didn't doubt Eldridge. He came from a moneyed old family in New England, and possessed a fine figure and what generally these days passes for a handsome—though to me quite characterless—face.

"In every particular it seemed but one," Anthony now clarified, "we agreed, Ottilie and myself. But that was an important one—her painting. "Of course I knew Ottilie was a serious artist when I met her. That was part of her attraction. For a year or so that wasn't a problem. Ottilie moved into my duplex, but retained her studio. She went there regularly, almost nine to five, daily, and spent after-hours and weekends with me. It was a good schedule for both of us.

"About a year and a half ago she began to change. At first I thought that she'd fallen out of love with me. We'd been together a while, and I wanted to make it official. To announce our engagement.

"Ottilie put me off. She said she wanted to complete enough work for a new exhibit. That was very important to her. And I understood why.

"It was around then that the incident with that fool Lawrence happened. Did you know that he bought something of hers at the gallery during a group exhibit, then wanted to return it, and when he couldn't, destroyed the painting he'd bought? That incident disturbed Ottilie very deeply. It was a great shame too, really, because I'd finagled for months to get her out of her studio for a few weeks and down to Barbados. It was to be our first vacation together, and I hoped a sort of honeymoon preview. Away from her work, I assumed, Ottilie would be more relaxed and far more receptive to the idea of announcing our engagement. And it almost worked. It would have, except that the day we returned, it was directly into the storm Lawrence had caused. So my plan for calming her down went right out the window.

"It was also about then that Ottilie began to express doubts about her work. She'd hardly said anything before, so I was rather surprised. But when I tried to humor her, asking why she was so anxious, Ottilie became vague—which you know was not at all like her. She did tell me that the new paintings 'weren't right,' that they were strange, almost as though done by someone else's hand. Those were her exact words, in fact.

"Odd, isn't it. Ottilie worked partly from memory, you know. But mostly she worked from her imagination. She claimed she'd never seen the original of most of the landscapes she painted in this third series. Some people who did recognize them, however—and there were a few even among our acquaintances—all said she had captured the appearance of those places to perfection. All emphasized how perfectly she'd succeeded in capturing the light for each specific time of year and day.

"I'm certain you've noticed that each painting was given a dated title—'July 14th, 1935, a quarter past noon'; or 'April 8th, 1971, nine-forty a.m.' Ottilie was convinced those times absolutely belonged to each painting: she told me that the dates and times arrived in some inscrutable mental fashion simultaneously with each image. She came to believe that no landscape could exist without the exact time and date. But while that made her secure in some respects, it also frightened Ottilie, contributing to her increasingly bizarre idea that some other hand than her own was wielding the palette and brush.

"Ottilie was otherwise an unusually rational, even a logical, woman. You knew her! High-spirited at times, yes, sometimes a bit distracted. But never, well . . . weird. Naturally I thought her explanations were a fabrication. Something meant to put me off from asking too much about her work, and afterward, to put me off from our wedding. I assumed it was all done to cover up her uncertain feelings about me. I continued to listen to her strange speech, but I have to admit, I ignored much of what she actually said, hoping she would become accustomed to giving up her independence in time to become my wife.

"She didn't. Instead she grew more anxious. She began to dread going to her studio every day. She began to fear facing her paintings. Yet once there, she remained later every day. Soon I was having to call her to prod her back home.

"One evening Ottilie didn't come home and didn't answer after my repeated phone calls. I decided to go down to the studio and to instigate some kind of show-down. Now, of course, I see it was the stupidest thing I could have done.

"I was right about her still being at work. I used her spare key to let myself in. The landscape she'd been working on was right there, facing me as I entered. It was one of her glorious, brooding panoramas, and although not completely finished, it already bore a date and time: November 18, 1991, five minutes after noon. And here's the real surprise, I *knew* that place depicted. I also knew what the date and time stood for.

"Ottilie had painted a section of the Adirondack Mountains where my father and a friend had earlier constructed and now co-owned a large hunting lodge. You probably wouldn't know the exact area. It's im-material anyway. But we'd been going to the lodge since I was a small child and I knew it very well. It had once been an essential part of my life, but lately I'd not gone there and it wasn't so much forgotten as no longer thought of. Oh, I was certain I'd never mentioned it to Ottilie. "I have to admit, that at first, the date and time stumped me. Partly, I believe, because I was so utterly astonished to see the locale rendered at all, and then so accurately. However, once I realized how absolutely perfect the view was, next I saw how correctly lighted and shadowed it was for midday in late Autumn, how subdued and yet totally right the colors of what leaves remained upon the trees were, how even the slate gray of the sky was correct: unquestionably exact.

"I attempted to ignore the landscape and instead began to argue with Ottilie about her increasingly strange attitude and habits. Something in how aloofly she had received me into the studio must have irritated me: I suddenly let go of all my bottled-up feelings and I have to say in memory it wouldn't have been very pleasant to witness.

"Afterward, I sort of broke down. But Ottilie wasn't angry. She'd been vindicated, you see. All she said to me was, 'Now you understand, Tony. My painting is ruining me. It's ruining us, too.' That was when I looked at the landscape again and suddenly realized the significance of that particular date and time."

Eldridge hesitated so long I thought I would never find out what he'd discovered.

"You see," he finally continued, "on that date, that year, I did something shameful. Probably the only act of my life I can honestly say I am ashamed of. One of the out-of-town guests at the lodge was a business partner of my father's from Utah. He was quite wealthy and was very free with his money. Like a lot of Westerners, he was loose with his cash, and he carried a great deal of cash on him at all times. And, I happened to be particularly hard up. Desperate really. A typical adolescent stunt: I'd gotten a girl I didn't really care for pregnant and had to buy her an abortion. I couldn't let my family know. At any rate, an opportunity presented itself to me, and I stole an amount of money. Of course, the money was missed. Employees were questioned, the cash was never recovered, and finally, through the most circumstantial of evidence, one of the employees was blamed and fired.

"That made me feel even worse. I could never return to the lodge without reliving my guilt. So I stopped going. I didn't know how to pay back the man I'd stolen from later on without revealing why I was doing so. I thought of sending it anonymously to the fired employee instead, but I was never able to track him down. The time Ottilie had painted into the lower right hand edge of the landscape? It must have been the very moment I was in the guest's room, the door ajar, so I could be certain no one else was upstairs or coming up, as I rifled through his bureau drawer.

"I told Ottilie all that. She appeared sad to hear my story, but not particularly surprised. She told me that it only corroborated what she'd come to believe—that each painting she made commemorated some evil deed. I'd merely confirmed what she'd believed. I—and the affair concerning Herbert Lawrence's wife.

"Ottilie came back to the duplex with me that night. But when I returned home from the firm the following night, she'd moved out. It wasn't my past dishonesty that had impelled her move, she assured me in a note she'd left. I'd been young, in a jam, she understood. But she couldn't stop herself from painting those terrifying landscapes. She couldn't. Even knowing they were terrible. She felt only half alive away from her studio; only fully herself when working. She told me what I'd not known, how she'd lost most of her friends over the past two years, one by one, and each of them in the same way—by unconsciously, invariably, unintentionally ferreting out and then painting for them to see the scene of some awful secret each person possessed.

"I tried to get Ottilie to see someone—a counselor, a psychologist, someone who would reason with her, or help her. At the same time, I clearly could not in any way explain her painting that view from my family's lodge, nor the utter eeriness of her being able to so pinpoint the time and date of my misdeed. Yet even as powerfully disturbing as that incident was, it wasn't as important to me as Ottilie and I were. But she wouldn't listen to me. After a while she changed her studio phone number to an unlisted one. She stopped answering my letters. Sent them back unopened. That all happened less than six months ago.

"When I received the postcard announcing Ottilie's show, I thought Ottilie had changed her mind about us. I was wrong, of course. The mailing list was partly taken from her personal telephone/address book by the gallery assistant here. I couldn't know that and of course I hoped for a reconciliation. In my wildest hopes, I thought that perhaps now, with the painting series completed, that perhaps Ottilie would somehow be fully purged of all the eeriness and we could start anew. I thought I'd come here not on opening night, when my appearance might only spoil her triumph, but the next night. That of course turned out to be one night too late. When I read of her death, I have to admit, some part of me wasn't all that surprised. It seemed to me that success or not, she'd still committed herself to a course that could only end in suicide."

Eldridge had finished. I told him I disagreed with Detective Compson's finding of self-inflicted death. I told him that, but didn't tell him why I disagreed.

"You don't know how badly off Ottilie was," Eldridge argued. "Even six months ago. Imagine how much worse it must have gotten for her?"

It was true that I'd not seen her in that six month period since she'd left Eldridge. In fact, I'd not seen her for a longer time before that, so he had me at a disadvantage.

"Then leave it alone," Eldridge pleaded. "Ottilie's possibly better off now. Indeed," he added, not all that cryptically, "perhaps all of us are better off now."

★

I have to admit that after that conversation with Eldridge my faith wavered. Elements of his story seemed to reaffirm what Auburn Anders had told Detective Compson: Ottilie believed there was some secret— some evil, Eldridge said—concealed in each of her imaginary landscapes. If she believed that, and if her beloved Anthony could not disprove it, others too might have given it credence. Possibly the Herbert Lawrences had—and whomever had poisoned Ottilie Chase.

With that in mind, I decided to look up Lawrence. It's true that in doing so, I completely misrepresented myself. I phoned and told him I was writing an obituary and appreciation of Ottilie for *Art in America* magazine, and needed a description of those paintings of hers for which no photographic slides existed. According to Ottilie's own records, I told him, he once owned a work now considered lost. I asked if I could see Lawrence at his office that very afternoon. He tried to put me off, but when I hinted that what I was really looking for was information on the effect of Ottilie Chases' work on others, he reluctantly agreed to see me.

Nevertheless, as we sat in his office high over Park Avenue, Lawrence wasn't very helpful at first. As the secretary pool outside his glass door emptied and the lights went on one by one along upper Park, Lawrence poured us both a drink and loosened up. Finally, he said: "I'm glad she's dead. Chase and her damned painting destroyed my marriage. I still haven't been able to put my life back together."

After that outburst, he didn't need much prodding to go on. This is what he told me.

He'd been meeting a business associate for dinner in the neighborhood of the Anders Gallery and afterward, his friend suggested they look at the group show, as an old school friend was one of the artists represented. Lawrence himself wasn't at all interested in art, although his associate claimed to be a collector of sorts. But once inside the gallery, Lawrence had immediately been arrested by a particular landscape.

It wasn't very large, he said, yet its use of color, paint and he guessed perspective too, leant it an amazing sense of depth. The landscape wasn't at all extraordinary—a rocky bluff into which a small gray brick building seemed almost hidden, surrounded by a scrub pine forest. A majestic ridge of high, scraggy, snowless mountains loomed over the scene, reminding Lawrence of the Rocky Mountains in that area of Colorado where he and his wife had grown up. Their twentieth wedding anniversary would be in a week, and Lawrence told me he was one of those men who never knew what gift to get his wife. He thought this would be a winner: she'd be delighted both by the novelty of the present, and by the reminder of Colorado, which she always said she missed. Lawrence's colleague told him that Ottilie Chase was a well-known and well-respected artist: the work should also be a good investment. That clinched it. Lawrence bought the landscape.

A week later, when Judith Lawrence pulled off the brown paper wrappings in their house, she stared wordless at the painting for a long time. She then turned to Herbert and said, "How could you?" and fled the room. Lawrence heard her cry herself to sleep in their locked bedroom. He was astonished, and—naturally enough—disappointed by her reaction. He was even more surprised when some time in the middle of the night, he heard—from the den, where he'd bedded down—Judith creep back into the living room. He waited as she lighted a lamp, pulled away the wrapping he'd hastily gathered together, and then sat staring silently for a long time at the landscape

When Lawrence got up enough courage to sidle up to her, his wife rejected his caresses—not angrily, but sadly, coldly. In an equally cold voice, she told him that now he knew everything there was to know about her, so he must be happy. When he said he had no idea what she was talking about, she asked surely he knew what the painting depicted? He said he had no idea. He'd chosen it because it reminded him of home. That surprised her, but she said it no longer made any difference. She would tell him what was painted, what he'd brought into their home, and into their marriage.

She reminded Lawrence of the time before they'd married. They'd lived in Colorado Springs, she the daughter of a miner who'd died in a mine accident, and of a woman who'd become bitter with loss and poverty —and with having to bring up two small daughters: Judith and her sister Lil. In contrast, Lawrence was from one of the wealthiest families in town. He'd gone to college in the East, he'd driven a foreign sports car when they met and associated with Denver socialites.

Her mother had pinned all her hopes on Lil marrying well, and when Herbert Lawrence had begun dating the lovely girl, her mother was pleased. But Lil was independent to the point of rebellion—and she was promiscuous. She didn't care for Herbert as much as she did for what he could buy her. While he was away, she went out with other men: low men, miners, tramps, almost anyone who wanted her. Her mother continually warned her that word would reach the Lawrence family. Lil didn't seem to care. Desperate, her mother confided in Judith.

The crisis arrived when Lil became pregnant by an unknown man. Instead of allowing herself to have an abortion, Lil said she would flaunt her state in the Lawrence house, say it was Herbert's child, force the marriage to occur, and thus find out what a fool in love Lawrence actually was. This was too much for her mother. She hatched a plan and had her other daughter, Judith, aid her. They would pretend they were taking Lil to a rest home where she might have the child in privacy. But the place they actually took her to was a private sanitarium located in the foothills of the Rockies—the very same building that seemed to grow out of the rock itself in Ottilie Chase's very accurate depiction. The very last sight Judith ever had of her sister was of Lil screaming, suddenly realizing what was happening and trying to flee from the two burly men who'd finally had to knock her out to get her into the straight-jacket. Lil hadn't been insane when she'd gone into that asylum in the rocks, but according to Judith's mother, after losing the child prematurely, and after remaining incarcerated so long, her mind had snapped. Her mother had become guilty and visited, but she'd died years before, and since then no one had visited Lil.

Judith and her mother had meanwhile fabricated a boating accident in which Lil had supposedly drowned. No one had reason to disbelieve them. Certainly not Herbert. It was at the memorial service for Lil that Lawrence again met Judith. At first, they spoke only of Lil. But soon that topic was dropped, and as they grew closer, it was never again raised. He married Judith a year later; he'd come to love her, to see Lil's best qualities and none of her worst in her sister. In fact, he'd come to love Judith far more than he'd believed he could ever care for Lil, whose constancy he'd always been unsure of. Lawrence admitted that to Judith, in front of the damning landscape, in an attempt to win her back.

His wife didn't, or couldn't, believe him. Her secret was out and it was a terrible one. In her own mind, she'd pretended that Lil was dead. Now the seriousness of her betrayal and decades-long perfidy was upon her, right there, painted and titled with the very date her poor sister had been dragged into a living death. Judith would somehow have to make amends. Despite Herbert's protests, she filed for separation and returned to Colorado. She had the helpless harridan that Lil had become released into her custody and she resettled in Colorado Springs to care for her.

When Herbert Lawrence still thought he'd be able to change his wife's mind, he'd called Auburn and tried to sell back the landscape. When it became clear that even that would make no difference to his wife, Lawrence had flown into a rage and destroyed the painting. Since then, he'd gone to Colorado himself, trying to win back his wife. Unfortunately, once out of the asylum, Lil had lasted only a few months, and had died in her sister's care. His shocked wife had taken her sister's place in the asylum.

★

Herbert Lawrence's unhappy tale so perfectly supported Anthony Eldridge's that I was now convinced that I possessed a motive for Ottilie Chase's murder. Luckily for them, Eldridge and Lawrence, who would have been the most natural suspects, both had air-tight alibis for the night of the vernissage.

What I now had to do was to find a third crime, a crime that exactly fit the painting that Ottilie had last grasped—then, most likely, I'd find her murderer. Once the exhibit, at last, ended, my painting had been taken down and brought home. Now if I could only convince the others, Auburn Anders, Susan Vight, and most crucially, Detective Compson, that the landscape must hold the answer.

Whether I could convince them or not, it wasn't going to be easy. All I really had was a date—August 13, 1999—and the depiction of a locale neither I nor anyone else who'd seen it seemed to recognize.

Here, Ottilie's tremendous skill in tempera proved useful. For there did exist something like a clue within the painting itself, although I needed a high-powered magnifying glass and patient hours of deciphering to get at it.

I mentioned before that the painting showed a body of still water surrounded by land. It could have been a bay, an inlet, or a lake—or rather one end of a lake—with an island just left of center. What I didn't mention was that Ottilie depicted not a barren, totally isolated area, but a populated one. While the painting itself was absent of human life, and unearthly still, various houses on stilts were barely visible within the pine-tree cover that grew right down to the water-lapped shingle: houses in what I could only call North American style, wooden, and with small decks, large windows, some with tottering outdoor stairways down to the water. It wasn't a style of architecture as distinguishable as say, Cape Cod or Eyebrow, but it definitely felt to me like New England, or at least the northeastern U.S. Each house possessed it's own jetty; little slatted docks for the most part that floated atop the water. At the end of most of these, held stationary with anchors I suppose, were little boats: motor launches, collapsed-sail Catamarans, row boats, dories. One boat in the foreground was more detailed than the others as it was closer to the viewer. Inside this dinghy lay an enameled box, yellow lettering upon it's side. After hours of minute discernment, I finally made out:

SEBAS O
ail & tack

"Sail & Tackle" seemed to be the most likely explanation for the second line of the two. But what was the word, or words, or—I most hoped— name, only partly revealed in the first line? Not Sebastian nor Sebastopol. But more like Sebasoon or Sebassox, or. . . .

By now I was half obsessed with my theory and so I spent weeks poring over Gazetteers and map indexes in libraries, I even went to D.C. and checked out the Smithsonian's cartological wing. It was there that I at last discovered the single place in the U.S. that could possibly be the name on the tackle box—Sebascodegan Island, located in the northeast quadrant of Casco Bay, a hundred miles or so north of Portland, Maine. According to the U.S. Department of the Interior Geological Survey Map, AMS-7070IVSW—Series II & V—there was no lake big enough nearby to be the one painted, but instead there was a large enough inlet known as Quahog Bay, surrounded by a dozen coves and dotted with islands, several of which looked large enough on the map to be the one depicted.

The following weekend, I took color photos of the painting until I got one I deemed most accurate. I had it enlarged and took it with me in a rented car up to Maine.

I found Sebascodegan Island easily enough, but that word means "large" in the local Indian dialect, and the island was huge. So was the inland bay it enclosed. I drove miles along public and private—often deserted—dirt roads, circumnavigating the island, until I found what seemed to be near the correct spot, on the easternmost side of the island. It had to be that side, I reasoned, because the sun had been setting opposite the site from which the scene had been viewed—or in Ottilie's case, imagined.

To my surprise, I also found that the island pictured in her landscape was not one of the two—Ben Island or Snow Island—shown on the map I'd used, but instead two smaller, low-lying islets, unnamed on the map, which from only one angle seemed to cohere into a single isle. The dome shaped copse of trees also become an evident landmark, not to be mistaken.

I remained overnight in the area, in a guest house near Cundy's Harbor, an unremarkable, poverty-blighted local fishing village. The next morning I rented a canoe which I strapped atop the car roof. When I'd reached the lands-end point from which I'd already determined the painting must have been (mentally) composed, I took down the canoe and began to explore the two little islands by water.

Luckily it was mid-September and most of the summer and weekend homes were already closed up. Luckily, I say, as both small isles seemed much used by local picnickers during the summer. Would I, could I, find evidence here of a crime committed two years before?

I didn't on my first try but, ten minutes later, on my second, more thorough attempt, I did. It was found inside a clump of trees, the very spot Ottilie's hand had appeared to point toward, during her death throes. Within the trees lay a half dozen used condoms, and a blue tampon case, among the litter at the bottom of a deep little gully. My evidence—unlike the rest of the junk—however was older and had once been a man's leather wallet. It was once waterlogged too, I guess during high tide, and so quite moldy, and it had also been partly chewed at by some small animal. Virtually all its contents were so disintegrated as to be unreadable. However, plastic seems to possess a half-life only somewhat shorter than that of Plutonium, and so after rooting about in the mess with a twig, I located a Master Charge card made out to one Donald Horace Scott.

Later that day, I informally interviewed the sheriff of the town of Brunswick, the nearest police precinct that included the little island. I told him I was a reporter for *The Police Gazette* (by now I'd become inured to such pretenses) and that I was writing an article on the unsolved crimes of New England. Did he have anything to tell my readers of? At first he said no. But I prompted him. What about the disappearance on August 13th, 1999 of Donald Horace Scott?

He recalled that immediately, but he still couldn't recall much, as he'd been on vacation at the time, he said, and someone else had handled the case. It was all written up, and I might read the police file if I wished.

The contents of the manila folder were almost embarrassingly slender. A death certificate, a page of local testimony, and a preliminary finding of death by misadventure at sea.

Scott had been seen by a real estate agent in the nearby hamlet of Cooks Corner. He'd been looking for a weekend cottage, he'd told the agent. He'd also told him that his girlfriend had grown up in the area, gone to camp out on Orr's Island nearby, and loved the place. As far as the agent could tell, Scott had been alone when he picked up the key to the Glynn house, but the unnamed woman might easily have met up with him later—or she might have been totally fictitious.

Scott never returned the key to the Glynn house, and a day later the real estate agent found it still lodged in the front door lock. The cottage didn't look used, although the agent said he'd noticed a stubbed-out cigarette in the ashtray—the woman's?—on a deal table facing the view of the inlet. The sheriff later found fresh tire marks, but no car at the house. Most odd to me, however, was the date of Scott's disappearance given in the police records from the real estate agent's testimony. It wasn't August 13$^{th}$, but August 11$^{th}$. That two-day discrepancy baffled me at first; later on it gave me the strongest clue of all.

I returned to the site and pondered as the sun set. Since my visit there was later in the year than the date of the picture, the sun set further south than it had in Ottilie's landscape: at almost at the exact center of the picture plane. But it had been a clear week for that sodden part of Maine, and it was a similar sunset to the one she had painted, pale purple infusing the gray sky, mauve and pale magenta streaking it all.

It was almost dark and I was hungry and decided to leave the spot and thus escape the ferocity of the local mosquitoes when I couldn't help but notice a new streak of color in the sky, opposite to where I sat. It was very thin, quite fugitive really, but unusually colored, almost cantaloupe in hue. And once I stared, directly in front of it was its cause: a tiny speck of silver outlining the fuselage of a jet plane. Could that be what Ottilie had been pointing to at the time of her death? Not the island, but the jet? And had she painted not the date of the crime, as I'd thought, but perhaps a date connected to that jet's flight?

I grabbed my photo of her landscape and there it was, the same streak, same color, although the sky around it in her painting was, naturally, far brighter. I checked my watch: 8.36 p.m. It must be a transatlantic jet from New York or Boston, flying to Europe. I knew from my own flights that all North Atlantic jets crossed the ocean substantially north to take advantage of the curvature of the earth, making for a shorter-than-direct flight. They usually crossed somewhere near Fundy or Halifax, Canada.

When I returned home, I checked with an airline travel agent. The flight I'd probably seen, she assured me, was the American Airlines 4:15 p.m. departure, Flight number 414, from Logan Field in Boston, headed to Heathrow Airport, outside of London.

Now all I needed was a passenger manifest for that particular day's 1999 flight. This was more difficult, perhaps the most difficult part of my investigation. But in the end, and with me having to pay a bit for it, not impossible to obtain. After weeks, and through stratagems too tedious to go into, I finally did get it. I then compared the names of all the passengers on the jet that day to those on the lists prepared by Susan Vight. The name jumped out at me. Alexandra Fairchild, of #20 Bethune Street, in Greenwich Village, New York.

Now all I had to do was to link her to Donald Horace Scott.

★

There are three leading incentives for people to commit murder, human nature being, if anything, consistent: for love (or out of jealousy), for money, and for revenge. Anything else is usually pathological, and thus far less easily understood. I assumed that one of those three standard reasons would do for Alexandra Fairchild. Since she was presumably Scott's lover, love seemed to be only partly right. He may have cheated on her, or tried to ditch her, which would make the third incentive, revenge, a good motive. But there was always the second, and strongest one— money.

I went to Bethune Street one afternoon and was surprised not to find the name Fairchild listed among the five tenants of the building. I rang the bell of the lowest floor, the one belonging to one Helena Preston. When this elderly, and as it luckily turned out, garrulous, woman answered in person, I said I was a friend of Donald Horace Scott and was looking for him. Didn't Miss Fairchild live in the building? Hers was the last address Scott had given me, a few years ago.

Helena Preston sized me up, then liking what she saw, or at least not hating what she saw, and bursting with news, although it was already fairly old news to her, she invited me inside for a cup of tea, where she gently broke the news to me about Donald's death. She added that Alexandra Fairchild had moved out of the Village flat a year ago.

"She was very broken up about poor Donald's death. And in such mysterious circumstances, too. Poor dear," the woman commiserated.

I composed myself in such a way to show that while I was grieved I was even more curious. Little by little and without a great deal of my probing, she let out this information. First, her surprise that Donald had given me this particular address, as he'd never "officially" lived there. Second, her own belief that Alexandra had thrown over Scott less than three months before his disappearance. And third, that Miss Fairchild had come into "a lot of money," probably, Preston hypothesized, from a legacy, some nine months after Scott's death.

Money it was, then. More than likely an insurance policy Scott had
taken out with Alexandra as beneficiary. The banal, alas, is all too often
the right answer.

"She was away when it happened," Helena Preston said, nodding
upward, to where I suppose Fairchild had lived. "She was in England at
the time. She'd gone there looking for work. Doubt she needs to do that
any more, lucky thing."

That clinched it for me. Alexandra had told the old snoop that she'd
gone away two days before Scott's death; whereas I knew by her air reser-
vations that she'd gone away two days *after*: more than enough time to
have murdered Scott in Maine and then driven or flown down to Boston
to make flight 414.

I spent the next week checking insurance policies. There are about a
dozen insurance companies of numerous sizes in the area. I thought surely Scott would have bought a policy from one. I wasn't wrong. Calling—
in another disguise, as a lawyer for James L. Horace, whom I claimed was
Donald Horace Scott's younger half brother—I soon found the company
that had sold Scott insurance. It was for a payout of a whopping three
quarters of a million dollars. And the beneficiary was—you guessed it—
Alexandra Fairchild, whom they now listed as living at the posh address
of 920 Fifth Avenue, on Manhattan's upper east side.

This was the last piece of information I collected, and subsequently
brought to Detective Compson at the Homicide Division of the New
York Police Department. He looked me over very carefully after I was
done explaining what I'd discovered. The procedure had lasted about two
hours, with him all but grilling me, questioning every step I'd taken,
every bit of logic I'd followed.

"That's a lot of work. Why bother?" he asked.

"Who else is going to bother?" I asked back. Then, to soften the
sarcasm, I added, "I've known Ottilie Chase since she was sixteen years
old, longer than anyone else you talked to. I *knew* she wouldn't commit
suicide, no matter how depressed and anxious she might have become.
And also I took her death personally."

Compson said that what I had provided was circumstantial evidence,
if quite good circumstantial evidence. Even so, he would need time to prepare a scheme to do a more solid, a more "prosecutable job" were the
words he used, connecting Alexandra Fairchild on the two murders.

However the fact that Fairchild was a known acquaintance of Ottilie Chase's (a fact I'd really not been aware of) would help my case. He might pretend he was asking questions about Ottilie's life, then try to catch her out in some discrepancy. He was certain he could end up bringing her down to the station house and grilling her until he'd entrapped her, or gotten a confession from her about Donald Horace Scott. He thought that would naturally lead to the landscape and to Ottilie's death. He was so busy planning out these varied stratagems, he didn't even thank me, when I finally left his office.

★

My work was almost complete. It lacked one more finishing touch, much the way an artist—I could picture Ottilie herself doing it—will stand back and view what appears to be a finished painting for a long time, almost as though gloating over her triumph, then suddenly dash forward and instantly add in a line here, a dab there, a tiny cross-hatching somewhere else, and only *then* be sure that the work is finally done.

Because Ottilie's aged mother had not yet arrived in Manhattan to dispose of her daughter's possessions—the body had been shipped to Oregon for burial but nothing else had gone there—I suspected that Ottilie's studio was probably still intact, and, I supposed, probably not much touched, besides whatever desultory searching the police might have done. In short, it ought to have been just as it was when she had put down her paintbrushes and palette, cleaned her hands and face, removed her working smock, and cabbed uptown to her triumph—and her demise.

I phoned Anthony Eldridge and told him I'd been talking with Detective Compson, who had reopened the case as a homicide investigation. I told Tony that a break was imminent in finding Ottilie's murderer. I needed to get into her studio to check one final clue. Had the studio been sealed by the police? And if so, did he still have his key?

It had not been sealed, Eldridge told me. When he and Ottilie were still together, he'd signed a new lease for the studio drawn up in both of their names, and it was now, legally, in his name. He planned to hold onto it until Ottilie's family had emptied the place, then he'd release it back to the landlord. As for getting the key, yes, he'd loan it to me. Did he want me to join him?

"Sure. Do you really want to go there again?" I asked, fairly certain of his answer.

"I don't *ever* want to step into that place again."

So we agreed that he would messenger the key over to my home. It arrived an hour later. I waited for dark before I set off for West 27th Street. The building contained dozens of working lofts with a plastic belt factory occupying the lowest floor. This being New York City, two keys were needed to get into the building, a third to open and operate the elevator and a fourth for the studio itself.

Once inside, I breathed a sigh of relief, then put on one dim light—I didn't want neighbors to know anyone was present tonight. Even by that small amount of illumination, it was easy to find what I was looking for: what I suspected—expected was more like it. It was sufficiently completed for me to recognize it, although evidently not finished enough to be exhibited. And it appeared to be Ottilie Chase's very last hauntingly eerie landscape, since it was still sitting on an easel in the middle of the studio with a drop cloth over it and the surrounding area strewn about with several tossed down instruments of her labor. Perhaps she'd stopped work to get dressed and go to her vernissage, I mused.

It was another of her uncanny sunsets, if rather everyday in its choice of location compared to many others: the north slope of Fort Tryon Park, in western upper Manhattan, not a hundred yards from the outbuildings of the Cloisters, that medieval stone fortress brought to America and rebuilt, stone by stone, to grace the New York palisades. As usual, Ottilie had gotten the look of the place perfectly: the eroded red-brick underpass, the cement block paved path leading from the museum, the usually hidden hollow between two large, untrimmed oak trees, the path that disappeared through the underbrush. She, of course, had the date correct: October 27, 1995, at 6:37 p.m., the exact time that—after stalking a young teenage student from a local Catholic high school as she dawdled on her way home—I waylaid her, at that very spot, pulling her between those trees where I bound her, gagged her, raped and sodomized her, before strangling her to death. I had then pushed some leaves over lovely Holly Caputo's body, brushed the damp leaves off my clothing, and found my way to the Fort Tryon bus, back down to mid-Manhattan where I'd enjoyed a fish dinner at Howard Johnson's on Times Square, then seen quite a bad action movie.

Now, of course, seeing it, I had to wonder, naturally enough, if Ottilie was planning to mention the new painting to me after her show's opening, at dinner. Perhaps not, perhaps she was planning to ask me up to her studio for a nightcap, and then she would just spring it on me. Despite what the others, including Tony, had told me, it still wasn't all that clear to me how she herself deemed these revelations.

Saddened and upset as she must be, I couldn't help but also sense Ottilie's innate mischief in catching someone out in wrongdoing. Especially an old pal like myself. She might have been plotting how she'd get me up to the studio while she waited for me at the gallery that night. ("You like these? I've got better ones. Want to see?") But of course that was far too late, wasn't it? Auburn and Susan had already sent out a few hundred postcards depicting that other, that beautifully incriminating, landscape: a virtual invitation, never mind incitation, for someone to come murder her.

Naturally, I destroyed the Fort Tryon Park landscape. I took it down off the easel, ripped it off the support she'd been using to paint it on. Once off, I cut it into fragments which I placed in a small plastic bag I'd brought. Later on, in my apartment, I burned those fragments in the fireplace, to ash, as I sat listening to a Brahms string sextet. The second one, in G, with the lovely minuet? I'd just opened a fine, old Armagnac I'd been saving up for just such a future celebratory occasion. The painting flamed quite prettily: all those tints and colors. Aptly Autumnal.

You see, most of us have our dirty little human secrets: some moment when the temptation was simply too irresistible. And a person like Ottilie Chase who somehow or other stumbled onto those secrets without knowing what they were—perhaps without even wanting to know, unable to stop herself from painting them—well, poor thing, she couldn't be expected to live very long, could she? If Alexandra Fairchild hadn't poisoned her, well, I might have had to do it at a later time, myself. Or someone else.

Who knows, perhaps even you might have had to do it.

# ONE WAY OUT

BAY THREW DOWN the apple core and stomped it into the soft loam until only a little mound of dirt was left. The bells from a distant steeple—the highest point of a tiny village nestled in the New England hills—were just striking twelve. It was Sunday. That would mean even less traffic than usual, less chance of truckers and easy pick-ups, especially as this wasn't a highway, only a double-lane country road.

He tightened the straps of the knapsack over his shoulders and loped off the ridge back down onto the road. He tried to adjust his mind and body for a long afternoon walk, trying to stay off the frayed edge of the macadam and on the dirt as much as possible, to make the trek easier on his feet.

After ten minutes or so, he still hadn't seen a car. Everyone must be at home, having dinner. The dark gray of the road shot away from under his feet down a long incline, rising up to another ridge half a mile away where it hid from sight then rose straight up to another ridge, rising and dipping, again and again, into the spine of hills—like a ribbon grabbed by the wind.

Bay was just bracing his legs for the long incline when a rush of air or force slashed past him. Swoop, swoop, it went, knocking him to the ground amid a flurry of dust and small pebbles.

Whatever it was, it had been too fast for him to catch sight of, going by. He picked himself up, brushed off his denims, looked back in the direction he had come from, muttered a few curses, then started off again. Then he noticed something.

Ahead, like mechanical insects rapidly climbing down the side of a wall, two small, very fast vehicles were moving toward him along the ribbon of road. They fell out of sight behind a lower ridge for a second, and as they did, two identical vehicles appeared at the top of the road beginning the drop down toward him.

They were coming so fast that, as he re-focused from one pair to another, they seemed to change places. Then he saw the effect was being caused by a third pair of identical vehicles, which had now appeared at the uppermost point of the road.

They flashed so brightly in the noontime sun that Bay could scarcely see them coming at him. He could make out that they were low, squarish, and painted a metallic green. But what was so odd after seeing no cars at all, was that these seemed so regular, systematic—each one side by side, covering both lanes of the road, the second and third pairs exactly as far away from each other, exactly as distant from the first pair, as though they were in formation. Bay was reminded of a slot-car set he'd once owned and played with as a kid.

Then a pair of vehicles were upon him. Then passing him. As they went, they made the same sound: swop, swop.

That left no doubt. An earlier pair must have knocked him down. This time he was braced. Even so, he could barely stay on his feet in the dust and blast of their passing.

He followed their squat, retreating figures down the road, only a double blur by now, in all the dust they lifted, following them like little cyclones. How fast were they going? Over a hundred, maybe hundred an fifty miles per hour? Maybe more?

He couldn't help feeling there was something more than a little odd about the vehicles. He braced himself on an overhanging shelf of rock and shaded his eyes, trying to catch a better look at the next pair as they passed. When they did, he was even more unnerved by what he could discern.

They were indeed unlike any other vehicles he had ever seen: low flat boxes, angled toward some indefinable apex three quarters along their length. No lights he could make out, front or back. No chrome or any other kind of decoration. And no glass—and therefore no way for him to see inside them—if, that is, they even had an inside. He had thought at first they were painted a metallic green, and in truth, seeing them closer, that was still the closest he could come in describing their color and material to himself. But it wasn't metal, not really. And it wasn't green either. At least not any green he'd ever seen. More shimmering, like the bodies of some of those Japanese beetles that liked to chew on rose buds. The material was an unknown substance, refracting light in a way he'd never seen any material do, with a color that seem to both shimmer and absorb light. Worse, as the vehicles had lifted slightly going over the ridge of road, they had lifted slightly off the road—going 150, 180 miles per hour, any vehicle would do so—and they had no wheels!

Bay was thinking whether he had noticed any military base in the area—on the filling station map he carried with him. No. None. Could this instead be a testing ground for an automobile company? Could these be experimental cars? No?

The last pair finally shot past him, interrupting his thoughts, and making that dull swop, swop sound again. He turned to see if any more were coming. No, none. Then he turned to watch the last pair speed off in the direction of their predecessors and he was amazed to see that they were instead slowing down, then almost stopping, before swerving off the road and onto a pasture very close to the same ridge where he'd spent the night.

All the curiosity and vague discomfort he'd felt came to a head. He had to see what these vehicles were. He turned around and ran back toward the stopped vehicles.

It was only a few minutes back to the crags that he had left shortly before overhanging the open meadows. But in the short while, the occupants of the vehicle had gotten out and transformed the area.

What had been a dry grass pasture now seemed to be a cleared area of some hundred feet in radius, roughly circular. Dark-clothed, helmeted figures moved about stiffly, if quickly, carrying strange objects. Two figures bent into the now opened backs or fronts (he wasn't certain) of the vehicles parked at the circle's edge.

Two other figures were setting up a hollow-looking platform exactly in the center of the circle. From a long-snouted tool one of them wielded, a pressurized liquid shot out onto the ground and hardened into a concrete-like substance the instant it touched the dirt and grass.

As they worked, the first pair of figures edged a canister-like object out of one vehicle and onto the ground. Although Bay was concentrating on the object and the figures, he could see inside the vehicles now, and they were artificially lighted, half pink, half yellow, blinking on and off.

The canister must have been extremely heavy or very fragile, as the figures carrying it moved very slowly, in exaggeratedly mechanical, yet dainty, steps. At length, they got the canister into the center of the cleared circle and sunk it slowly into the cement material. Another shower from the spray tool covered the canister completely so it was no longer visible.

The four figures then retreated to beyond the edge of the circle and one of them pulled a little hand-sized cartridge out of a deep pocket in his form-fitting suit. He adjusted one or two buttons on the little panel, and the trod-down grass began springing up again in the clearing, so quickly and so completely that even from his bird's eye perch Bay could scarcely make out the exact location of the platform and sunken canister.

The entire operation had taken perhaps eight minutes. All of it had been completely hidden from any possible view by the ridge of rock from the top of which Bay watched them. Even had there been a traffic jam on the road to see it, no one would have. And where the canister had been sunk, it now looked like nothing at all happened.

That was when Bay began to feel a tingling along the back of his neck. He'd had that feeling once or twice before in his life. Once when he was being followed down the dark, deserted street of a Midwestern city by a stranger who kept falling out of view whenever Bay turned to check up on him; another time when he had heard prowling, heavy steps outside a tent he had pitched in the Green River Mountains of Utah. Both times before it had meant danger and now he knew it meant that whatever was in that canister was about to go off, and go off big. Without stopping to ask why or how, Bay knew something momentous had been sunk in that meadow. He had to get away fast! Now!

He almost stumbled running down the ridge onto the roadway when he remembered he had taken off his backpack and left it on the rock. *Leave it!* he thought. *Go!* he thought. Then: *No! I have to have it! I have to get away fast! In a car! That thing's going to go off any minute now. I need a car to get away from it. The backpack will get me a ride.*

He was tying on the pack when he reached the road again. No cars. and those two which had been here had vanished totally. He started to walk as fast as he could, following the direction he'd begun in before.

Why this way? This is where the vehicles had come from. They might have laid a whole chain of these things. They might be laying down more at this moment, behind him. He had to go north. North.

There had to be a northern cross-over ahead. He must get to it. But first he needed a lift. Still no cars. Damn. He felt a little calmer now as he strode along the road, knowing he at least had a direction now, a way out. The thin hot trickle was still burning a network into the back of his neck and his shoulders, and he was beginning to feel a sharp little pain in his side from his exertion. He was sure the first was adrenaline rising, and the extrasensory fear of whatever was going to happen.

If it was, just supposing it was what he thought it was, what could its radius be? Two miles? five? What had been the radius of the last test? Five miles, no? Or was that only the radius of total destruction? And if so, what was the radius of the fire storms. Another five or ten miles?

He turned to look behind him. No cars. As he turned back, one coming toward him passed by—but it sped on as it neared him and he scarcely had the chance to flag it down; anyway, he was too intent on walking hard and getting away, straining to keep up a fast pace, yet stay in control, to keep himself from simply running ahead blindly, breaking away totally. No. He had to stay in control. To let go meant to invite the end. Survival lay only in holding on. Holding on.

And still the burning of his nerve-ends. It seemed stronger the further he got away from the canister. Still no cars.

Then there was one coming up behind him. Dark and sleek. Bay almost fell as he stumbled to a stop and thrust his arm dangerously out over the edge of the road.

The driver saw him and made a great show of screeching to a halt, braking so fiercely that half the car was under Bay's out-stretched hand when it came to a full stop. One of those little German coupes that looked like metal race cars he'd played with as a child.

He ducked down to open the passenger side door.

"Haven't asked you yet!" a voice said

Bay removed his hand from the door handle. Oh, God, no! Not a joker! Not now!

"Sorry!" he said. "Can I have a lift?"

"Sure." The passenger side lock snapped open.

Bay got in, closed the door, was encased in the pervasive odor of leather and new car. The man faced ahead. Nothing but profile. Why wasn't he starting the car?

"Where you headed?"

"North!" the man said with a determination that surprised Bay.

"This way's west."

"There's a crossover a few miles up. I'll get off there," Bay said, thinking, *Let's go!*

"No need to. I'm going north there myself."

A joker. Great. Finally, he threw it into gear. Bay was still doing up his shoulder-strap seat belt when the car took off.

At least the backpack was loose. He swung it onto the floor and sat back watching the rounded V-shaped hood lap up the dark macadam.

"Nice car," he said.

"It's all right."

*Thank God he's not in the mood for company,* Bay thought. *Imagine having a conversation about the weather now. It might just slow him down. Drive faster!*

"You seemed to be in a bit of hurry there," the driver said, non-chalantly. "As though you were running from someone."

Did he know? Could he know? Could he be connected with those pairs of vehicles? Could he be their scout? Or not, rather their clean-up man. Here to get rid of any possible witnesses?

Bay said nothing.

"Of course," the driver went on, "there seemed to be no one and nothing to run away from where I picked you up. Right? Just a coupla' nothing farms in the distance." He laughed and Bay looked at him. His own age. Good-looking in a city-slick way, like his car. Heavy, straight, almost blue-black hair. Sultry eyelids over dark eyes. Tanned. Spoiled-looking. But otherwise all right. Like a hundred others.

"Nothing farms and a coupla' cows, eh?" He laughed again.

Even if the driver didn't know about the canister, he still might be off. Christ! Just what I need now!

Before Bay knew it, they'd reached the crossing and the driver flicked the wheel left and spun across the other lane right onto the cross road.

"No!" Bay shouted. "That's wrong! We're going *south.*" He almost jumped out of his seat.

"What?" the driver said, and cupped one hand to his ear, as if he were hard of hearing. Bay began frantically repeating and explaining that they were going the wrong way. But the car was already in the middle of a U-turn, then across the road again.

"You seem a mite nervous, friend," the driver said, with a little smile.

"Maybe."

"A smidgen stressed, I'd say."

"A smidgen."

"Doubtless on account of those nothing farms and coupla' cows," he laughed.

Bay all but collapsed back into the bucket seat. But he felt little relief. This guy was a jerk and a joker, and who knew, maybe he was insane too. And the burning fear from the knowledge that Bay was still within range

of the canister was getting worse now, pricking every nerve of his skin.
How the hell had he gotten into such a situation anyway?

How had he? He was trying to recall and coming up blank. Well, no,
not entirely blank. He knew he was hitching east. He remembered that
yesterday he'd caught a ride out of Albany, and into Kingston, New York.
There he recalled he'd eaten a hamburger and drank a malt shake at a
roadside Friendly's, had ridden with a car through the Berkshire
Mountains, and had been dropped off in a small town called South
Egremont. He'd been picked up there by a truck driver, literate guy who
talked about the fact that Herman Melville and Nathaniel Hawthorne and
all kinds of 19th Century writers had lived in the area; if not regularly
then part time, during the summer. Bay had ridden along with the guy,
who was looking for an ear to listen to his chatter, and he'd finally allowed
himself to be dropped off not far from where he'd spent the night. And
before yesterday? Well, that wasn't quite so clear to him. He'd traveled,
he believed. Hitch-hiked through mountains, plains, around cities, past
deserts, all of it blurred and kind of vague now, unimportant, not all that
detailed.

Bay was feeling certain that whatever was inside the canister would
go off soon. Why and who had set it were no longer real questions. He
knew that by being there and witnessing it being sunk into the ground
had somehow forged a link to it, a connection, and that might be why he
carried the knowledge of it within him, as though both it and now he,
were a time bomb, literally running out of time.

"How far do you think we are?" Bay asked, trying to sound casual.

"From where?"

"I don't know, say from Boston? Or say how about from where you
picked me up?"

"About hundred and fifty from Boston. Sixteen and a half from where
I picked you up." He tapped a dial sunk into the leather plush of the dashboard, "according to Mr. Odometer here."

"Is that all?" Bay asked.

"What do you mean?" the driver sounded slightly offended. "That's
pretty good."

"For going sixty-five miles per hour," Bay agreed. "I thought this car
went a lot faster."

"I'm in no hurry," the driver said.

"Speedometer reads, what is it? 140? Or are those just numbers painted on?"

"It'll do 140. These roads are lousy. You want me to rip up the underside, just so you can have a joy-ride?" Already the speedometer had tilted up to seventy mph.

"Car like this was probably built to cruise at a hundred or more," Bay said, very wise-guy. Speedometer now read seventy-five.

"I sometimes cruise it around a hundred. On good roads." The speedometer was nearing 80 now.

"German, right?" Bay said. "Tested on the AutoBahn?"

"That's right." Closer to 85 now.

"Which *has* no top speed, am I correct?" Bay asked.

"It's a perfect road, that AutoBahn." He was close to 88 now.

"I was told that these high performance vehicles, if you don't really open them up every once in a while, their oil lines clog up."

Ninety now. "Is that right?"

"That's what I heard," Bay said. The car was pushing 95 now and the car seemed to be slipping along the road. It was taking the dips so fast it was getting Bay a little queasy. The landscape began shooting by, trees going flick, flick, flick, so fast they began to bunch and blur as they reached 95. Alongside ran a stream that seemed to appear and vanish, reappear and snap and curl along past, like kids shaking a dark rope along the ground, playing snake.

Up to a hundred miles per hour now.

Bay's nerves were on fire. He could hardly keep still in his seat for the twitching. Soon. Soon. Any minute now. He had to brace himself. Prepare himself. Looking at the odometer he saw that they'd managed another ten miles. That makes it what? Twenty-seven miles away? Maybe thirty by now? But would that be far enough? He'd had to get out of the car when it happened. Throw himself out clear. That would be suicide at this speed. Better get the guy to stop and find cover. Where? Cover where?

There! The stream, down in the water. The water would protect him, keep him from being badly burned. But how?

"Stop!" Bay shouted, and grabbed at the wheel. "Stop. I get off here."

"What the hell?" the car sped on, as they wrestled for control.

"Stop! Stop! You've got to stop!"

"Get your hands off the wheel." He'd already slowed down to seventy.

"Okay, but you've got to stop here. Now!"

"You're nuts. There's nothing here?"

"Stop now! Here!" Bay tried opening the door.

"Sit down. You'll be killed!"

The car braked and swerved to a halt, twanging and spinning around two thirds of a circle.

Before it was even fully stopped, Bay felt an agony all over his body. He threw his door open, flung himself out, and ran to the side of the road and thrust a hand into the water. Only a few feet deep, then brackish mud. But it would have to do.

Behind him he heard the driver muttering to close the damn door.

Bay grabbed up two hollow reeds and broke them off at both edges. He put one end into his mouth, and breathed. Then he slid, back first, into the stream, face sideways, hearing the car rev up and take off as he got underwater and felt the sludge against the bare parts of his legs and neck, trying to stay calm as he immersed himself and slowly began to turn over sideways, to get his face as far away from the air as possible, while keeping the air coming in.

The tubes worked, even bent like this, they let him breathe. He opened his eyes, but the stream was totally muddied now and he closed them instantly, so as not to get any silt into his eyes. The agony was gone. He felt totally calm. Very calm. This was the right thing to do. Yes, exactly right. How did he think of it? Was it instinct? Some life-preserving instinct?

Abruptly, he twitched all over, as though he were having a brief epileptic spasm, from every nerve and muscle, from every cell of his body. Even facing mostly down, and with his eyes closed, his sight was flooded with a whiteness, a light that surpassed any white he'd ever known or thought to know, a white that explored depths and subtleties of sheer white light he'd never suspected even existed, a white that grabbed at every inch of him, illuminated his entire body from without. It seemed to grow in intensity, to throb and as it did, the sludge around him seemed to grow tepid, then warm, then hot. And still the white blared on, even whiter if possible, brain-hurting white, a thousand brass instruments all playing white. He could feel the water and sludge receding from around his head and hands. Then the reeds in his mouth were hot, useless, since he couldn't breathe anymore and he spit them out, dropped them and turned over, directly onto his face, finding an empty space there and filling his lungs from dark, quickly drying pockets of dank around him, while the universe continued to go white, white, white, seemingly forever.

A giant pulse slung along the land, seemingly lifting his body inches even within the mud. He held on for dear life. Then it was gone, after having flung itself right through his insides.

The white became yellow, then orange, then red, then dark red, then a deep, flickering magenta.

But the twitching was over, and the pain, and the fear. The hair on the back of his head no longer felt on fire. The sludge around his face had begun to boil and bubble, but now it subsided. When he was able to lift his head a few inches and use his hands to pry open his crusted-over eyes, he could see the stream bed around him was dried to aridity, desert dried, and like that, dried and crusted all over his face and hands.

Cautiously he rolled over onto his back. Cautiously he tried to breathe. The air was oven-warm. Acrid, with the smell of burning. Breathable. He took a few more breaths. They hurt his nasal cavities and his throat. He swallowed once or twice and it was better. The air was cooling rapidly. That was better. He tried to sit up, had to use his hands to help himself. He flicked the crusted dirt off his hands, and picked the dried crust off his face.

The sky around him was pink. Pink and purple and orange, but mostly pink, a deep roseate, Valentine's Day pink. Everything lining the stream bed was black. He knelt and then managed to stand. The land around him was totally blackened. Road and meadow all the same color, the only difference being that the road was partly melted, buckled in places. In the distance, across flat charred fields, he could see a grove of pine trees burning like a huge torch. The air was still warm. But the worst was over.

Shakily, he reached his feet, checking for breaks, fractures, bruises. Finding none, he stood up on his feet. His knees felt weak. Instantly, he began to retch, vomiting up chunks of his apple into the thick cracked bed of what had once been a stream. He immediately felt lighter and stronger, wiped his mouth, then stood up straight. He lumbered out of the stream bed, afraid to touch anything, and stumbled forward along the half-melted, disfigured road.

Everywhere, there were fires. Showers of ashes descended all around him like rain. God knew from what. But he was all right. He had gotten through it.

He walked on, just looking. Then, around a bend in the road, through trunks of trees in flames, he made out the dull metal shine of a car. It was stopped dead in the middle of the road, as if its driver had just stopped a minute to take a leak on the side of the road and would be back any second.

As he got nearer, Bay saw there was no glass.

Even closer, most of the outside of the car—sheet metal, bumpers, fenders, roof—seemed intact, but as though heated and simultaneously pounded by a hundred thousand tiny hammers. Then he saw that it was the same car that had picked him up before, and he made out the back of the man's head, erect, sunk into the backrest.

And if weren't for the millions of gently trembling shards of glass splinters covering his head like a delicate lace helmet, and the red trickles that stained their edges, the driver would have looked as if he were alive—merely staring ahead, a little surprised.

Even the seats and flood and dashboard were rimed with glass shards. But the dashboard dials were still lighted, and the motor was still idling in neutral. The driver must have been suddenly blinded by the light, and by reflex stopped the car. Then the blast and the glass hit him and who knew, but probably the fire too that had dappled the sheet metal, seared the leather inside the car, and his flesh and skin too, until they were all the same mottled half brown, half bright pink color.

Bay opened the driver's door, swept a drift of glass shards off the metal with his foot, then gently pulled at the corpse from behind, until the body fell over onto the road. The smell of burnt flesh was stronger. Sweetly awful like a charred loin of pork.

He cleared the front seat, reached the glove compartment where he found a piece of chamois to help him do the job better, and used that to wrap around the still hot, partly fused steering wheel. Would it work? It turned normally. There was still dangerous looking glass left in the windshield and side vents. He knocked them out.

When he was done, Bay sat in the driver's seat wondering for a minute whether instinct would tell him what to do next. He gunned the engine. It worked. It whined, but it worked.

"I'll go north," he said, aloud. "North."

He moved the lever from park into drive and the car whined, then leapt forward.

★

Two hours later he ran out of gas.

He'd been surprised, even a little alarmed that there were so few cars on the road. Where had everyone gone to? Were they all dead? In hiding? Where? The further away he drove, the less there seemed to be damage, even signs of what happened. But everything seemed abandoned. Everything meaning the few clapboard roadside diners and brick gas stations he'd passed. If he'd only thought to stop and get gas. . . .

He left the car on the shoulder of the highway and began walking, again north—always north. Every once in a while, Bay would turn around and look behind, seeing the sky still pink, with clouds of ashes falling in the distance, and one area to the southeast—could it be Boston?—bright red and orange, as though the air itself were consumed by flames.

He reached a weathered wood-shake house off the side of the road, behind a picket fence and gate. Several sedans and a pickup truck were parked on the grassy side road. There had to be someone inside. Maybe they had gasoline. Or would be able to drive him to the next gas station.

Aside from the blown-in windows all about, the house didn't seem at all damaged. The front door swung open. Bay called "hello" and when he received no response, he walked in.

It seemed deserted. The kitchen had been in use recently: food was half cooked in pots on the big double range—two cups of coffee were set out on an old table, untasted. Bay called out again. Still no answer. He half absently picked up a coffee cup.

Would it be all right to drink it? Would it be radioactive?

He went to the sink instead, an old fashioned metal pump and basin, and pumped himself out a glass of water. It was cool, slightly mineral, but good. He had another glassful.

Was that a sound behind that door? Voices? Or one voice maybe droning on?

"Hello," he called out to whoever would be on the other side of the door. "Anyone there? My car ran out of gas down the road!"

No answer. But the droning seemed to go on.

Bay went to the door and tried it's handle. It opened. He carefully turned the knob and stepped aside, not knowing what to expect or whether something would come charging out at him.

A steep, well-lighted stairway, leading up.

As he ascended, the hard, cracked old voice he'd first heard became clearer. Bay thought he heard the words, "And behold! There came up out of the river seven well-favored kine," followed by a pause and what seemed to be the shuffling of several pairs of shoes upon bare wood.

At the top of the stairs, he found himself in a long corridor with closed doors, and on the floor itself, a worn, multi-colored knitted oval rug, looking like a faded rainbow.

One door was ajar. Beyond it, the old voice took up again. Bay approached and slowly pushed open the door wide enough to look in.

His first impression was a room filled with people: men, women, children, old folks, all sitting or standing behind wooden dining room chairs or leaning against the side of the room where, because of the angle of the light all but blinding him, all Bay could make out was the shadowed figure of what was an elderly man.

Bay stepped into the room silently. The old man was still in obscurity, although now Bay could make out a dark leather-bound, frayed edge book, open on a lectern in front of the man, and in full view.

"So Pharaoh slept and dreamed a second time," the old voice went on, toneless. Neither the reader nor anyone else in the room turned to look at Bay.

The old man paused again, and there was a murmur from the assembled group. One little boy no longer able to hold back his curiosity, peeked back at Bay from behind the protection of a woman's shoulder. As Bay noticed him, the lad darted back into hiding, then timidly edged back into sight.

Half of the child's pale blond hair was gone. The remaining scalp, a purple splotch with large brown blisters and smaller broken-pus pink sores looked as though he'd been raked from the crown of his head down over the single closed, congealed eye and red-black chin with an acetylene torch. It took Bay a great effort to look away from the boy and to fix his sight upon the worn natural grain of the wood floor.

"And behold! Seven ears of corn came upon one stalk," the old man read on, "fat and good."

Everyone murmured their approval. Bay looked at the boy again. But now he was hidden by the bulk of the woman, his mother perhaps, who turned out of profile toward Bay. She too was burned and mispigmented, as though a swathe of intense fire had been whipped across her face and torso.

Bay backed up against the door he'd come in through, holding tightly to the dry wooden molding behind, spreading his feet apart for support as he surveyed the others in the room.

Everyone else he saw was blasted, burned, discolored, bleeding or suppurating.

"And behold! Seven thin ears of corn, blasted by the east wind, sprung up after the others," the old man intoned, voice as dry as the planking Bay gripped so hard it was beginning to flake off under his fingernails.

A woman closest to Bay, her arms crossed over her cotton-print house-dress, turned to him as though first noticing him. Purple splotches mantled all but a tiny central triangle of her face. Her lips were charred lines. Her teeth almost glowed green as she smiled. Only a few clumps of glossy auburn hair still flowed, held in place by a blackened hair-band.

Bay had to look down at the floor again, but he also couldn't stop himself from looking up again, now at one, then at another of the listeners, all of them quietly, attentively, listening to the man reading, monstrously ignoring what happened to them.

"And the seven thin ears of corn devoured the seven fat and full ones."

The people seemed animated by these words, moving about unsettled in their seats, gesturing, and in doing so revealing new facets of their horror. One scabrous-faced man with only a projected bone of nose left, leaned over to whisper into the blasted shell of what should have been another's ear.

Bay shut his eyes, fighting down what was in front of him, declaring he wouldn't open his eyes.

He was out in the corridor now.

"And it came to pass in the morning," the old man went on, "that Pharaoh's spirit was greatly troubled by what he'd beheld in his sleep."

Bay shut the door, held it shut, knowing they could jump up from their chairs and smash it open on him. His skin felt as though every pore were bursting with poisonous filth and infection.

When nothing happened, and the voice went on droning behind the door, Bay fled, leaping down the stairs, stumbling over his own feet to get down, almost tearing the stairway's bottom door off its hinges as he careened out, fleeing the house onto the roadway, running.

When he stopped running, his body aching with the sudden exertion, he was far from the house. No one had followed him. Ahead, over rolling country, he couldn't see any other hamlet within sight. What was the difference if the people there would be as mutilated, and as oddly unconcerned with their fate as this group?

Past a stand of trees on the road, he came upon a local bread delivery van parked. No driver, the key still in the ignition. Had this driver been struck by the blinding glare, burned to the bones of his skull, and staggered off, maimed, into the high grass, or worse, back into that house?

When Bay turned the van's key, the tank light on the dashboard showed half full. Should he siphon it off? Or just take the van?

Before he could really make up his mind, his hands had done it for him. The ignition was switched on and he'd thrown the clutch. All around him, he smelled fresh bread. He reached for a loaf of pumpernickel, tore the plastic wrapper off and ate three pieces, gulping them down. He threw the van into gear and took off.

He hadn't realized how hungry he was. He ate the entire loaf of bread as he drove.

The van couldn't go anywhere near as fast as the sports coupe had gone, but it was taking him north all the same. He couldn't help but think that there were going to be more bombs, more trouble, and that he'd be safer the further north he got.

He'd reached the deep humps of the Green Mountains when he realized that the buzzing he'd been semi-hearing ever since he'd gotten into the van must be coming from the radio. The driver must have left it on when he'd stopped.

Bay tried tuning it. For a few minutes all he got was cracking and popping. Universal static. Then he managed to capture a voice, distant, faint, high pitched.

"  .  .  . to report to their local distribute  .  .  . eleven o seven two four  .  .  . all battalions followed by codes J in Jester, H as in Happy, R as in Rebel, S as in Standing  .  .  . "

Then it was gone, no matter how much he turned the dial to tune it.

He continued to fumble at the radio, having to lean across the side of the high dashboard to do so. Finally, he reached another clear station, " . . . ime Minister and the British Parliament declared full neutrality in the startling, total conflict, between the government of the United Sta . . . " then it too drifted. Bay kept on trying to tune it back in, and after sometime received, " . . . participating member of the Geneva Convention, the Commonwealth of Canada has opened all borders to evacuees from the States. Emergency centers, food depots and shelter are being offered to all. . . ." Then it was gone again.

So that was it, full nuclear attack on a massive scale. But Canada was neutral. There was food, shelter, safety there. He'd been right all along to head north. Bay pressed down the gas pedal as far as it would go, then tried to re-tune the radio.

After fifteen minutes of nothing but hisses and words isolated in radio-drift, Bay pressed one of the buttons on the front of the set that had the word "emergency" marked on it, thinking that's a weird thing to have, but then again maybe it would provide a direct line between the bread van driver and his home base. For a long while, nothing happened but more static. He turned it down a bit lower, but left the radio on at the emergency bandwidth, in case it might catch some signal. He drove on, thinking.

He'd been close, but lucky. Too close, and very lucky. If he'd still been in Albany, or already reached Boston . . . any city, really, it would have been all over for him. That was one certainty. And he had been lucky to be this close to Canada, too. He could visualize hordes of evacuees from the cities trying to reach Canada over hundreds of miles of melted and disfigured thoroughfares. Horrible. It was a lot easier for him. Only another hour to two and he would cross the border. That was the value of hanging loose, traveling light, being on your own. Nothing, no one, to hold you back. Always in the right spot when you needed to be for survival. Survival.

He paused once on the top of a high ridge of mountains the road ascended to, and got out to look back, feeling like Lot in the Old Testament, seeing the destruction behind him. The skies south were still orange, fading to pink. The sun itself seemed to be contained, almost cradled, within a flaming new corona, one that rose from the earth. A flock of birds were rushing north over the mountains. They knew. They knew where it would be safe. He got back in the van and started off again.

There was more static on the radio station. He raised the volume and tried catching the station. That static was unnerving, almost dizzying. There were voices behind it, he was sure of that, although he couldn't make them out clearly or hear what they were saying. Two men talking. He turned the volume higher.

What was really odd was that it didn't sound like news, emergency news. But more like a private conversation he was overhearing. Had he somehow picked up two ham radio operators conversing? And if so, why were they so damned calm?

He now shut both van windows to cut off the wind current sound and turned the radio volume up higher.

"So far," he heard very clearly. "The case exactly parallels our projected graph of reaction." Then it was very clear. "Quite extraordinary. Almost classic." The voice was so calm it was annoying. Didn't they know what had happened?

"And you're quite certain," the second, somewhat less confident voice asked, "that the sudden communication will not be too much of a shock? I mean, given the intensity of the application?"

"That shock," the first voice responded, "is precisely what we want. You see, by cutting the possibilities down to only two—one a total nightmare—the patient will invariably opt for the other choice—reality, compromised though it may be. He should do so voluntarily. Even willingly. The knowledge that there *is* a choice, when there wasn't any chance of that moments before, should override any shock from the communication itself."

Static returned over the radio. Puzzled by what he was hearing and wanting to hear more, Bay fiddled with the dial. He got back onto the channel again, but now it was merely silent, no talking at all. So he left it there and continued to drive, divided now between the bizarre and bizarrely serene, dialogue he'd somehow overhead, and what he could see out the windshield: the country completely destroyed, about to submit to an invasion by . . . by who?

"Bay! Can you hear me?"

He almost jumped out of the car seat. Then he realized that the voice came from the radio. It sounded like one of the two men who'd been talking. The man said: "Bay! This is Dr. Joralemon. Can you hear me?"

What the hell was going on?

"Dr. Elbert is here with me, too. You remember Dr. Elbert, don't you, Bay? If you can hear us and understand me, and if for some reason you can't answer, then shake your head from left to right. Do you understand? Left to right, slowly."

Bay did as he was told.

"Very good!" Enthusiasm and a little relief, too, in the voice. "Now, Bay, do you remember who I am? Dr. Joralemon. If you remember me, shake your head again."

The name wasn't familiar. The voice was. Or was it?

"Bay? Did you hear what I just said?"

This time Bay did nod from left to right, thinking what the hell am I doing that for? Where are these voices coming from? The radio? He opened the window and flipped the back mirror all over the road behind to see if anyone were following him. No. No one there. Nothing but forest now, sparse, mountainous forest.

"Now, Bay, do you remember Dr. Elbert?"

"Bay?" the other voice came on. "This is Jim Elbert. I'm your doctor. Or at least I was. Do you hear me?"

*Yes. Yes, Jim,* Bay thought. "Jim," Bay said. "How can I hear you through the radio? It doesn't look like a short-wave."

"Bay," Dr. Elbert's voice interrupted his own. "If you remember who I am, then shake your head as you did before. I see that you're trying to talk, but I can't hear you."

Bay nodded vigorously. What the hell was Elbert doing on the radio? Where was he? And how had he managed to locate Bay?

"Do you remember me, Bay?" It was the other voice. The one that called himself Dr. Joralemon. And now Bay did recall the voice. But not the way he recalled Elbert, which was pleasant, like a friend, like growing up and playing stickball and going around driving together as a teenager. That's how he remembered Jim Elbert. But not how he remembered Dr. Joralemon.

Dr. Joralemon repeated his question, and Bay heard rooms in his voice, rooms and doors. Far away rooms in pastel colors. Venetian blinds half closed all the time. The constant, insistent murmur of someone's muffled groans and sobs.

Bay nodded much more slowly in answer.

"Good," Joralemon said.

"Bay?" It was Jim Elbert again. "Now that we've made contact and communicated, you must understand that what I'm going to tell you is the truth. I've never lied to you before and I'm not lying now. Do you understand that? Do you believe me? Do you have any reason *not* to believe me?"

*No,* Bay thought, *I don't have any reason to not believe you, Jim.* He nodded, then reversed the motion of his nodding.

"All right, I'm taking that to mean we're okay," Elbert said. "Now, listen, some twelve hours ago, you underwent a brand new approach that's been developed in cerebral surgery. It's only indicated in the most hopeful of . . . well, to be honest, of extreme cases. Dr. Joralemon invented the procedure. He calls it Trans-Morphing. It's a sort of active interference into the dreaming state. A kind of probe."

"So far," Joralemon interrupted, "we've had close to one hundred percent effectiveness with Trans-Morphing."

"What it does, Bay," Elbert went on, "I mean, what it is, actually, is a combination of a psychotropic drug that operates within the cerebral cortex at a very specific area, and with it a series of carefully calibrated electrical shocks to the brain. Its purpose is to channel your fears and anxieties into one major fear and anxiety. Sort of like dumping it all into one box. And that process builds up and builds up—into an experience you fully believe you are having. Generally, and from what our previous cases have said, this is a tremendously catastrophic experience."

Bay heard the words and understood them well enough. He just didn't really understand what Elbert was getting at.

"What I'm saying," Elbert went on, "is that whatever you are doing and wherever you think you are, it's not so. You're actually in a semi-comatose state, close to a somewhat over-stimulated R.E.M. sleep. You may think you're awake. But you're not."

Bay gripped the steering wheel. Sleeping? Who was he kidding!? The trees were whizzing by on either side of the van, clumps of scotch and blue pine. Still no vehicles behind him, but the air was scented with pine. Of course he'd not seen a car or truck in a while. Still, he hit the dashboard hard, and it impacted his hand, making it throb. *That* was real enough.

"That's right, Bay," Jim Elbert continued. "Semi-comatose but sleeping. Dreaming. Everything that you believe has happened to you—and it must have been a humdinger, given how your E.K.G. and E.E.C.s' reacted—all that actually happened while you were asleep and dreaming."

"We realize that it's not an ordinary dream," Joralemon put his two cents in. "That's how this new drug works. It doesn't attempt to approximate reality with silly symbols and inane inaccuracies the way most dreams work. Its effect is to make it seem real, intensely, unbearably real."

"You must realize, Bay," Jim Elbert now said in the defensive tone of voice that Bay knew so well, "that this was a desperation measure. At first I was against using it. But your increasing catatonia, your growing lack of any affect at all . . . well, I let Dr. Joralemon persuade me to accept that it was the only route left for us."

"Do you understand us, Bay?" Joralemon asked.

*Understand what?* Bay thought, *Total folly? A stupid joke in bad taste?*

"Bay?" Elbert was talking again. "Can you still hear us?"

He half nodded.

"I know this may be difficult to believe," Joralemon said, "because it was so concentrated in its effect, so every aspect of it, every detailed impression seemed completely real and accurate to life."

"In effect," Elbert said, "it was another—a parallel—reality."

"An alternate parallel reality," Joralemon corrected. "Do you understand?"

Bay didn't, no. Whoever these jokers were, they were clearly off their rockers. He looked up to see if there was a helicopter chasing him. Looked out the windows. No. Nothing there. But how did they stay in contact with him? How could they be tracking him? The radio alone wasn't the answer. By satellite? Maybe the combo. Maybe if he shut off the radio. Maybe that had a tracking device in it that allowed their satellite beam to locate him.

"Fine," Joralemon said, all hale and hearty. "We're guessing that it's a pretty horrible alternate reality you're experiencing there, Bay. But everything is going to be all right now. You don't have to fear, you don't have to run anymore. You've experienced a catastrophic alternate reality. You've faced up to the very worst that you believe you ever *could* have faced—and you've survived, haven't you? Yes, Bay, that was the most extreme, the furthest that you could possibly go in the direction that you've been headed in all these past months. But now you're going to come back and you're going to be all right."

"We're going to help you come back," Elbert put in.

"Right," Joralemon said, with that smug, arrogant edge back in his voice. "Because you see, Bay, you don't really have that much of a choice. Do you? If you don't come back with us, then you'll have to continue living in that nightmare reality you've constructed. True, you're over the worst, the climax has come and gone, but given that, what can you truly expect to follow: a catalogue of horrors, one worse than another? That's the logical extrapolation of the monumental trauma you've just gone though."

"Now, Bay," Elbert put in, "to get you out of that alternate reality and back with us, all you really need do is break through the sleep paralysis the drug has induced. To do that, all you have to do is move your right hand. It's not going to be easy, but you've got to do it, Bay."

Bay drove lefty. His right hand lay idle by his side.

"Okay, Bay," Elbert was at his most professional now. "Move your right hand so it lifts up."

*Who were these guys anyway?* Bay wondered. And why were they trying to stop him from going north? Could they be the enemy? The same people who'd planted the bombs? Destroyed so much? Killed so many? Almost killed him?

Bay decided to string them along for a while. He had to be getting close to the Canadian border. He'd been driving so long. He moved his hand off the car seat.

"Great, Bay! Now move your hand over to where your heart is. Can you do that?'

*I can, quite easily,* Bay thought, and did so.

"Terrific! Now you ought to be touching a pocket. Can you feel it there?"

Of course, there was a pocket in his flannel shirt. Big deal.

"There's something very important in that pocket, Bay. We'd like you to reach inside and take it out of the pocket. Can you do that?"

Bay reached into the pocket, felt around and touched something small, smooth and flat. He pulled it out. A plasticine packet of something. How did that get there? What in hell was that stuff in the packet?

The road he was driving on suddenly began to angle downward, dipping now and again, but clearly descending out of the mountains he'd been driving through for so long. This might be the last stretch before he reached the border.

"Open up that packet, Bay!" Elbert commanded.

He did. Inside were two small pellets. Shaped like pink barrels.

"Good," Elbert said. "We want you to take those pills."

"At first," Joralemon came on now, "after you've taken the pills, you'll appear to fall asleep. But that's only to you, where you are now. What will really happen is that you will wake up. Do you understand that, Bay?"

*Sure, sure,* Bay thought, *and black is white.* Whatever these pellets were, how had they gotten into his pocket? He hadn't put them there, had he? Had somebody else? While he was sleeping last time, maybe? And if the pellets actually were exactly what this guy who sounded like his buddy Jim said they were what would that really mean? That he was asleep in some hospital? Some asylum? Follow the logic, Bay. That's what he was telling you. In some nut house, probably strapped down. No sir.

"Can you understand, Bay?"

He nodded.

"Fine. So just pop those pills into your mouth. Both at once."

Bay rolled the pellets in his fingers.

"Is there some problem, Bay?" Joralemon asked.

"It's going to be all right, Bay," the guy who sounded like Jim Elbert said.

Bay kept rolling them in the fingers of one hand.

"Is it," the Jim-one asked, "that you aren't in a position to take them in your alternate reality?"

Bingo. He nodded.

"Let's see. You're walking or driving or something? Is that it?"

Double bingo.

"And you're afraid to take them and go to sleep while you're engaged in that particular activity?"

What do you think, mister?

"Because then you'll go sleep and fall or crash or something?"

They could be poison, right? Arsenic? Cyanide? Planted by those guys with the quiet cars without wheels, the faceless guys? While he slept?

"I'm assuring you, Bay," the Joralemon-one went on, sounding terrifically sincere, "that it's going to be fine. Pull to the side of the road, or go sit down if you need to. *Then* take the pills."

"I'm also assuring you, Bay" the Elbert-faker added. God he was good. "In a day or two you'll be well enough to get up, and walk around, maybe leave the facility a day later. You'll be proud of yourself. You won't be afraid anymore, Bay. Think of that. Not afraid of *any-thing!*"

Afraid? He wasn't afraid.

Afraid? And far away rooms. Walls painted odd shades of green and blue and canary yellow. Walls converging, tilting at odd angle, then falling in on him. And no matter how much he screamed no one ever came to help him. No one, except for sometimes a quick glance, lying words, another syringe-full. Murmurs of soft crying all about him, insistent, constant, interminable. Maybe even his own sobs and groans, heard as though rooms away, through locked doors and very far away.

"Now, Bay," Joralemon was being a Dutch Uncle, "we've got great confidence in you. Great faith in you. That's why you were selected for the procedure over other possibilities, other patients who. . . ."

"Is there a reason you *can't* take the pills," Elbert's pretender asked.

Bay nodded. Of course there was a reason. He had to reach Canada. He'd be at the border any minute now. He'd just passed a small sign saying: "Customs and Immigration—Slow Down Now. Stop Ahead." Of course there might be other cars and trucks there already, before him. He vaguely remembered several roads converging on this spot. So there would be others ahead of him, others closer to safety than he was. There might even be a longish wait. The road dropped more sharply now. He must be close.

"Whatever the reason is that you can't take the pills, whatever it is that you may be doing," one of the two was saying now, trying not to sound panicky, "You have to stop, Bay. Stop and take the pills! These pellets are the antidote to the pill he gave you. Do you understand?"

"Bay? No one wants to hurt you!"

Pastel rooms and medical smells. Shadows squatting and burbling. Grotesqueries in the guise of humans burbling and muttering and occasionally the ear-hurting screams cutting through it all. Shadows vomiting, screaming, colliding. And always, the distant sobbing and moaning.

"Please, Bay. I'm begging you now. Take the pills and wake up!"

"You have to take the pills, Bay!"

But Bay wasn't nodding or anything like it. Ahead, along the road, he could see the highway rise slightly, and two other roads converged, and their center was a kind of wooden log cabin, with windows and dormers, belonging to the Canadian Mounted Police.

"Bay! Bay! We're going to have to come in and get you, if you don't take the pills."

"I don't know, Elbert. I've never injected the antidote before. We simply don't have any idea what that will do. Or where exactly it will leave him."

"You mean it *won't* bring him out of this?"

"I don't know. It's never been used. We've never had anyone opt for the alternate reality before."

"Inject it!"

"I'm going to need authorization for that."

"I'm giving you authorization. Inject it! Do it!"

*No you don't,* Bay thought. As the van coasted down the road to the border crossing, he lifted his right foot off the gas pedal and kicked the radio as hard as he could. So hard, it crumpled in the middle, the voices jumbled then turned to static, then died completely.

There weren't any cars there. Just a Mountie waving at Bay, urging him on.

Bay waved back out the window laughing out loud. In his hand were the pink pellets. He threw them out the car window, clear into the woods. Then he slowed down at the station, stopping inches from the big, healthy-looking Mountie.

"Welcome!" the Mountie said, smiling at Bay.

He would be safe in Canada.

# FOOD FOR THOUGHT

BECAUSE HE WAS A TELEPATH and a little sensitive following their most recent landing, Andy was awakened last.

In fact, it was hotly discussed whether he ought to be awakened at all.

Bim thought not. She'd still not gotten over the hysterical panic-state Andy had been in when he'd returned to the *Dallas* after that Deneb 3 affair. She'd had to shoot him up with every conceivable fungal-somato derivative in the dispensary. And when those hadn't done much, she'd fallen back to more primitive phenobarbs before Andy had finally calmed down.

Roy thought Andy *should* be awakened. He pointed out that Deneb 3 was unique: its nonsense-thinking/speaking inhabitants probably would have made Lewis Carroll pop a gasket. He reminded the others that before the *Dallas* had arrived, all relations since the disastrous first landing on the planet had been negotiated through mobile computers who couldn't understand the difference between simple non-rationals like a human crew and real wackos like those on Deneb 3. Andy was the first human, Roy pointed out, certainly the first T-p, to visit the Denebians. And he'd eventually come down from that experience, hadn't he?

Patsu also voted no. She was second officer and an improbability addict, which had carried weight before in their group decisions. This time, however, it had become common knowledge among the crew that Patsu was operating with less than her usual objectivity. Andy—admittedly the best looking genital male on the Dallas—had only made it in Playby with Patsu one time, claiming that she gave off heavy hostile-death thoughts during the sex act. Since everyone else on board had Andy in Playby at least a dozen times, they were convinced that anything Patsu might have to say would be colored by this apparent rejection—and who knew, possibly jealousy.

Hill, the oldest-seeming of the crew (with all the time/space screw-ups, who could tell real age any more—after a few years "out" the crew looked younger than their great-great grand nephews and nieces) and by his seniority as much as by default more or less the captain of the *Dallas*, reminded them that Andy had, after all, saved them and the ship, and probably the Company's entire operation in sector 657 of NGC-345 when he'd telepathically defused and then resolved the !Koh-Mantra Crisis, two trips back.

Willow, Andy's friend and most constant Playby mate, also voted yes. So did Ho Wang and Native, whose name was just one part of his claim to be distantly descended from some Old Earth Aboriginal group. Native explained his vote: "We've already sent ten fly-overs across this new planet's surface, and they don't show a single living creature down there. Andy will be as calm as a disconnected 'droid."

"What about the Swamp Moths on Epsilon Vega?" Patsu asked. "They were conscious and communicative and never showed up on our fly-over reports."

"But they were a *positive* experience for Andy," Hill argued. "Remember how he taught them how to play infrared chess? All we can see downstairs is plants. Flowers, vegetables, trees, grass and more of the same."

"Sounds great," Ho Wang said "after some of the hellholes we've been to lately."

"Temperate climate," Willow chimed in. "Breathable atmosphere. Water. The works. We could picnic for a month."

Hill agreed. It was the first stop so far on the trip that looked even vaguely habitable. "The Company will like it."

It was a little planet, only size 4 in the Company's catalogue, the eighth world out from a double star system of a medium-sized redSun and small white-blueSun. It had a solid, metallic core, extremely slow shifting continents, was composed of 81 percent land, the rest non-saline water; but with a mantle of real rock and real dirt. The fly-overs had already shown the crew wonderful vistas below, and—as Native said—they had found no animal life on land or water large enough to be detected. But to be classified for colonization and/or exploitation, the planet needed to be landed on, actually tried out by humans. And for an official landing with a designation-status imposed, the human crew had to include one T-p. Company rules. Tried and true after centuries. No ifs ands or buts.

"It's your funeral," Patsu warned and voted no.

She and Bim were outvoted by the six others. Andy was awakened.

He surprised Patsu by asking if she'd Playby with him and Willow after chow-down. She'd been enjoying Ho and Willow for the last few days with Andy asleep and had pretty much decided she'd have to give up being in a trio.

"We'll be in Playlounge five," Andy said, smiling. "Bring a few Super-Q's, will you?" Patsu always kept a large supply of the recreational hypno-stimulators on hand as all the crew liked them in Playby.

"And Patsu," Andy added, "don't feel guilty about voting to not awaken me. It's too typical a behavior to be out of character."

★

"Well, Andy," Willow asked when they first stepped out of their lander and onto what seemed to be a ten-kilometer ellipse of short-leaved, perfectly manicured, green lawn, "Do you T-p anything?"

Andy didn't. Not a thing. Of course, he heard the various thoughts of the eight others, all thinking furiously, as they always did upon first planet-fall. Howard wondering if he'd forgotten a needed instrument gauge, Hill still thinking furiously about his recent Playby with Roy, Native nurturing fantasies that he'd soon leave this spot and encounter landscapes similar to that of Wyoming, wherever that might be—some area from his tribal collective history, Andy supposed. By now, Andy was able to channel the entire crew's fairly predictable thoughts into a single murmuring noise—something like radio static. He'd been a T-p long enough to be able to deal with The Big Brown Buzz, which was how all T-ps among themselves and at their silent, active, infrequent, bi-decade conventions referred to the general, barely acceptable back-ground tele-noise of their surroundings.

"You are scanning, aren't you?" Willow asked.

"Of course, I'm scanning. My range is only about a hundred kilometers in surface atmosphere at this density and composition. I still don't T-p a thing."

Which was odd, Andy thought. Almost unprecedented in his ex-perience. There was generally some kind of T-p noise, at one frequency or another, comprehensible or not.

"Well," Hill said, frowning a bit, "you might T-p better once we're out of your way. Let me know." He knew the Company would like a perfectly empty world for once. No pay-offs, no negotiations with greedy inhabitants. "The rest of us are going to explore," Hill added.

Exploration was pretty much what the crew did all the rest of that day. It was fairly primitive exploring compared to what the *Dallas'* computer/sensor back-ups had already achieved through scores of particularized fly-overs previously sent out. But in a way more essential. The planet might look like a paradise, but if the Company was going to stake a claim here, it had to be proven to be completely inhabitable by normal humans. No more expensive surprises like on Tau Ceti 12, which the *Valparaiso* crew had found a while back, now famous, or rather infamous, in Company annals.

There too, the planet had been beautifully, utterly comfortable for humans—an Eden. A month of landing and visits with the charming, hospitable Cetian humanoids had been an experience to be savored by the crew for years after—it was so rare. All the more of a shock when one crew member, stuck on board the observing ship with punishment-duty for the entire planet-fall duration, had decided to play back some of the luckier crew member's wandering infra-sound and ultraviolet video recordings. The planet proved to be not what it seemed, instead it was nothing more than a thick sheet of some kind of plankton floating upon an unstable lava ocean. And the Cetianids were neither graceful, beautiful, nor humanoid. But instead a sort of omniphagic bacteria with extraordinary control over their appetite and extraordinary telepathic ability, powerful enough to confuse humans and sensors, and with the ability to create perfect tri-dimensional illusions. Their evident aim in so wonderfully greeting the *Valparaiso*, had been to encourage a large colony and thus assure themselves of a good sized human population they might then feed upon at their leisure. A plan thwarted by one disgruntled crewman with time on his hands who'd saved not only the crew, but possibly thousands to come. The story had been told across the galaxies, and even Patsu referred to "The *Valparaiso* Factor" whenever she wanted to explain exactly how improbable improbability could be whenever living beings were involved.

The *Dallas'* planet-fall crew broke up into groups of two, except for Andy, naturally, whose efficiency demanded he be alone. Each of the others were to cover a sector previously mapped out by fly-overs. During the previous charting session aboard the ship, they'd already designated areas with fanciful names: the apparently sparkling (bi-carbonated) fresh water area was referred to as Lake Champagne; the extensive north-south chain of deciduous forest was titled The Peppermint Wood; the enormous, apparently self-cultivating oval and elliptical fields of what appeared to be wheat and rice, they called the Pita Basket and the Rice Bowl. The crew members strapped into their little planet skimmers as though they were on holiday.

All but Andy. His skimmer also glided over enormous pastures, across giant plains filled with huge and healthy specimens of what looked like natural wheat, corn, carrots, string beans, all sorts of fruit orchards, none of it terribly different than the Old Earth varieties grown on the *Dallas'* own conservatory—the basic food staples of all Company colonists, no matter where they ended up settling. Few of these human origin foods had ever been found indigenous to any New Home planets, although most of them had been seeded and eventually found to adapt well to new environments without too startling genetic differences. Like Proxima Centauri 16's bright azure wheat fields and baked breads that all the tinting and bleaching in the universe couldn't keep from retaining a bluish cast. Or the melon-sized raspberries and blackberries of Spica's single planet, or the tiny, naturally pickled, pineapples grown on the sulfur fields of Io.

Here, everything looked right. The coloration more or less correct, the size about right, the various species laid out similarly to the way Native did it on board the *Dallas.* No onboard anomalies like mangoes growing next to potatoes. Still something about all this plant life bothered Andy. What was worse, he couldn't exactly pin down what it was.

Perhaps it was merely that he hadn't picked up a single thought. With the other crew members off on their own skimming missions and way beyond his T-p range, it was the first real Tele-silence Andy had enjoyed in months, in fact, since his affair on Company Depot Lounge #2 with another T-p who'd also learned how to turn off transmission. In a sense, this was even quieter. With Branca, Andy was never certain whether or when she'd suddenly turn on or not. And when he and Branca argued, it had quickly descended into an all-out T-p mental war, devastating to both of them for days after. Here, there wasn't a hint of a thought.

Having nothing to do but listen, Andy managed to skim his section in a few hours, then decided to set down for a snooze in the warm sunlight. It might be hours more before Willow and the others returned to the planet-fall base. They'd relay any anomalies at that time, and naturally Andy would check them out.

He selected a grassy knoll beside a glassy looking rivulet. In the distance he could make out thousands of untouched acres of bright green mature corn stalks. It was so warm here, so quiet, he napped outside the skimmer on an inflatable. For the first time in what seemed to be years, Andy fell asleep instantly without having to slowly tune-out the Big Brown Buzz.

He awakened as the smaller, white-blueSun was setting. According to previous calculations, the redSun would remain above the horizon another twenty minutes or so to color the landscape with warmth. He remembered Ho saying that tomorrow the two suns would exchange positions, and the redSun set first.

He'd overslept. Everyone but Bim and Howard was at the lander by the time he skimmed the dozen kilometers back to their planet-fall spot. Andy's own lateness went unremarked, either verbally, or T-pically. While waiting for the last two person skimmer to arrive, the others were busily enthusing over the planet, vying with each other for delighted descriptions of the day's explorations. They all agreed that the planet was the company find of the decade. Definitely temperate weather: not a hint of polar weather; no sign of seasonal changes either. It appeared rich in geological diversity: their instruments had confirmed the fly-over's discovery of ores, minerals, and metals galore. It was also filled with naturally growing foodstuff, no matter where you turned—from artichokes to kiwi-fruit, rhubarb to honeydew—and in the right proportional quantities for human consumption. The forested areas, the lake shores, the grass meadows, the low-humped hilly ranges that separated the good producing areas, were spacious enough and more than pleasant enough to provide built-up areas for millions of potential colonists without a bit of crowding. The planet was rich, beautiful, accommodating: undoubtedly that rarest of Company catalogue designations—Class A. Even the normally restrained Willow thought so. The *Dallas* crew was certain to receive the Company's highest bonuses for finding it.

"Where *are* Bim and Howard," Patsu asked in exasperation what all the others were thinking. The redSun was setting now. The grassy plain before them turned scarlet, then purple under its atmospherically intensified glare.

—Are not—popped into Andy's mind.

"Who thought that?' Andy asked aloud,

"Thought what?" Hill asked.

Andy wasn't foolish enough to say the words. So he ignored Hill, waited until the others were busy, then went behind the lander's antenna-dish. The system's amplified blind side would block out most of their thoughts. Not knowing whom he was addressing, or who had previously addressed him, Andy T-p'ed an emission that asked, "Where are Bim and Howard?"

To his surprise, an answer came back:—Are not—

Only this time the T-p wasn't obscured by the Big Brown Buzz. Andy heard it clearly and it definitely didn't fit the frequency pattern of thoughts of anyone on the *Dallas'* crew.

—How do you know?—Andy T-p'ed.

—Know—came back on a higher band than Andy had ever received on, and, paradoxically, on a lower band too than any he'd received on.

—Where are Bim and Howard?—Andy T-p'ed.

—Orange Wood—

—Who are you?—Andy asked.

Silence. Then a high pitched giggle—No distinction!—

—What?—Andy T-p'ed frantically.—Who?—

—No distinction—came back, just as he'd heard the first time, followed by a another fit of giggling.

—Where are you?—Andy tried, and slowly spun about in place to see in what direction the giggling came from. It seemed equally forceful from every sector of a 360 degrees revolution. Must be some sort of a tele-sonic distortion.

—Where are you?—Andy tried again.

But he couldn't raise the T-p signal again. He pondered a few seconds, then found Willow and Hill and told them what had happened.

"Bim and Howard were in the J-L sector," Willow said. "It's daylight there for another hour or so."

"Let's send the others back to the *Dallas*," was Hill's decision. "We three will go in skimmers to take a look."

"Knowing Bim," Willow commented, "She's probably so busy eating forbidden fruit, she's forgotten the time."

They located the so-called Orange Wood easily enough once they'd arrived in the middle of K sector: it was an enormous citrus orchard—millions upon millions of trees in full fruit. And, after a short while, they spotted the abandoned skimmer. It had landed, which was against company rules. But then all of the *Dallas'* crew had already admitted to having broken that rule: this planet was just too damn inviting not to take a closer look.

As they circled in skimmers, Andy opened his T-perception to its widest reception range, trying for any hint of Bim or Howard's thought frequencies. Nothing came back. They'd have to land and search on foot. Hill located Bim first. She was about fifteen feet off the ground, her long hair entangled in surprisingly rugged orange tree branches. It was evident that she'd decided to climb the tree—why, none of the three could say; as the fruit looked as full and rich in the lower branches as in the higher ones—and a branch supporting her feet had given way. In her drop, several lianas had twisted around her neck, strangling her. Below Bim's dangling body, a pyramid of oranges half as tall as a person had been shaken to the ground.

While cutting her down, they had a difficult time trying not to step on or slip on the fallen fruit. Hill took a spill. And in so doing, he revealed Howard, beneath the pyramid of maybe a thousand fallen oranges. His hands were frozen in front of his face in a vain, final effort to keep them off him. His mouth was stuffed with a large, juicy looking Valencia. He must have been caught in the same bizarre accident as Bim. Perhaps he'd gone to save her and slipped and fallen, and then been suffocated? Although they remained looking around for another twenty minutes after recovering the bodies, neither Hill nor Willow could find any trace that the two deaths had not been a complete—if admittedly odd—accident.

"T-p anything?" Hill asked Andy.

"Besides you guys? No. Not a thing!"

★

The following sidereal day, they again landed on the planet and broke up into couples for skimmer exploration. Again, Andy was alone.

The deaths of Bim and Howard had depressed everyone on the *Dallas* sufficiently for Hill to declare an unprecedented eight hour Playby with double doses of Super-Q's for distraction. Even with the drugs, Andy had caught down-mood peripheral flashes from several crew members. The Company had psycho-selected the crew for low grief-levels and synergistically mixed them for the lowest possible loss-quotient. Even so, they'd been together a while, and every one of them had one reaction or another to the sudden change.

For Andy, as significant as the deaths was the giggling T-p voice which had refused to identify itself. Now, as he sped in his skimmer over his assigned sector for the day, he openly-emitted, trying to locate the T-p voice again. No luck.

As had happened the previous day, Andy finished his work rapidly and set down the skimmer, opened an inflatable, and rested in the bright, warm, afternoon sun from the binary suns—far from any trees. A gentle breeze played over his body, wafting the scent of ripening peaches from an orchard that stretched before him. Clover and an odor like sweet marjoram added their light perfumes from the meadow into which he'd skimmed. Once again, Andy relaxed deeply in the complete T-p silence. But he didn't make the mistake of falling asleep again.

Good thing too. Otherwise he might have been awakened with a jolt. As it was, he sat bolt upright when he heard Roy and Patsu's thoughts.

—Hey—Andy T-p'ed back.—Get out of my sector! You're in T-p range!—

No response followed, so he called the lander itself for a radio relay to their skimmer. Willow had remained there at planet-fall. She told Andy he was wrong. Roy and Patsu were way over in sector X-Z, eleven hundred kilometers away.

But Andy had *heard* them T-p. He now wondered why.

—You still there?—he T-p'ed them.

Giggles. The same ones as yesterday.

—Where are they?—he T-p'ed the question

—In flower—

Despite the surrounding giggles, the tone was less than amused.

—Are they . . . *not are?*—he T-p'ed remembering the construction put on yesterday's tragedy.

—*Not yet*!—followed by a cascade of giggling.

Andy didn't like the sound of that at all. He jumped into the skimmer and set it for their sector, calling Willow from the air, telling her he was going after the two. She said not to. Hill and Native were in Sector T, much closer. They'd go look.

Andy arrived back at the lander just as Hill reported in. He and Native had found Roy and Patsu unconscious, but still alive—and completely stoned out among a sea of poppies. The pale purple and white blooms they'd been walking through were able to explode their morphinid-alkalis into the surrounding air. Roy and Patsu had been felled in minutes. Native had gotten punchy on the stuff the second he stepped out of the skimmer. Hill put on a protective mask, but he was a bit dizzy too. At least they were all safe now.

★

"That's it," Hill declared, once the crew had all arrived back at the lander. "This planet is off limits."

Patsu and Native argued that even Old-Earth possessed its natural dangers—poisonous plants, feral animals, earthquakes, landslides, floods, tidal waves. They simply have to recognize what exactly constituted a hazard here. More exploration was required to do so.

"It's not as though we're being consciously attacked or anything!" Roy agreed. "It's partly stupid mistakes leading to equally stupid accidents."

"What if it's a pattern of them?" Hill asked. "Patsu, give me the improbability statistics on nine people in two days. Two killed and two nearly killed."

Patsu did a quick calculation and came up with a high figure. Too high for mere chaotic improbability. Too high for Hill's liking.

"Let's face it, crew," he said. "Despite Andy's extremely limited T-p contact with someone or something or other, the planet itself seems quite barren of intelligent life. On the other hand, it does seem to be equipped with what can only be called a rather subtle, but effective, self-defense system. For all we know, it already belongs to someone. It's their farm world, perhaps, or their garden world. And we're the intruders. I say we leave."

"I'm not sure how limited the T-p contact was," Andy argued. "It had to be awfully strong to interconnect me to Patsu and Roy from so far away."

"How intelligent would you rate the voice that T-p'ed you?" Native asked.

Andy couldn't say: too little conversation.

"What exactly did the T-p say?" Willow wanted to know.

Andy repeated both "conversations," which even he had to admit were both of very short duration and most primitive. And the giggles. In terms of time spent during the entire T-p'ing, Ho Wang calculated the giggling occupied about three quarters of the messages Andy received. Ho speculated that it was some sort of semi-consciousness. Perhaps even a 'droidlike alarm system.

Which was possible, Andy had to admit. But why then did he still intuit a larger intelligence? Because he did. He couldn't explain why.

The others listened to his arguments and as he spoke, Andy T-p'ed them, carefully sorting each one's reality from wish-fulfillment. They were coming down against the planet, against him.

Hill didn't need to T-p the crew to recognize that despite their high hopes for a Company planet-find of Class A, and the bonus and the repute that would accompany it, none of the others were eager to subject themselves to possible death, no matter how rare or picturesque the place might be. Hill called for a vote on whether to call off human exploration or not. It worked out six to one against Andy.

"That's it," Hill concluded. "We'll reconnoiter one more week with mobile 'droids on planet. If there are no more bizarre accidents to them, the planet receives a Class D designation: for further exploration only with extreme caution."

The decision made Andy shudder. He'd actually come to anticipate a full thirty-day tour on the planet surface. He'd get more pure T-p silence here than in a so-called thought-proofed room anywhere else. Not to mention deeper sleep. No, it was just too pleasant to give up without a fight. Then too, he had T-p'ed a voice, had communicated with someone, or something, twice. That was his function on the Dallas among the crew. He couldn't just brush it off. Especially since that voice had allowed him to save Roy and Patsu's lives. Progress in communication had been achieved. Continued further contact was imperative.

Andy began to argue these points. Surely, if he was in contact with a voice which had twice warned him, no harm would likely befall him. And he might discover the source of the T-p emissions. Surely any company team that came in after the *Dallas* would need that kind of information and as much of it as he could provide.

Willow didn't like the idea, and the others seemed neutral, so once again they voted: should Andy join the 'droids on the planet while the crew returned. Two votes no, five votes yes. Andy was pleased.

The others returned to the *Dallas* and sent back mobile 'droids. Andy continued to go down to the surface daily.

By the sixth day, after he'd covered more than half of the section they had mapped out, Andy was convinced he'd been right. The 'droids of course were near-impossible to destroy, but they hadn't encountered a single mishap, not even a displaced one, like poppies spewing out powdered drugs in the air. Of course it was possible that the planet's defense system only reacted to alien life, not to alien machines.

Meanwhile, every afternoon, Andy would relax deeply and communicate a bit more with the T-p voice.

Or was it voices? It was difficult to decide which. He was sometimes reminded of the Swamp Moths of Epsilon Vega, that same feeling of a million voices mixed into one larger, representative voice, all possessing the same thoughts. At other times, the voice seemed to have a single, even a singular, personality—pesky, yet sweetly frivolous; shy, yet impulsive and bold; deliberately, mischievously unhelpful with anything that could be construed as a fact.

Through T-p, Andy learned names on the planet—the names of certain fruit and vegetables, trees, hills, even lakes. But he never discovered who the voice belonged to, nor where the other sentient beings were—if there were any others. At times, the voice seemed woefully ignorant, in the way a four year old human was, so that he had to wonder how mature the voice really was.

His reports each night back on the *Dallas* were as full of detail as he could make them. The others' response was always the same question: "So you made no progress?"

Andy knew what was happening with the remaining six crew members. Having been disappointed, they were already finished with this planet. They were anticipating the next planet-fall, merely waiting until the mobile 'droids were done. With Bim and Howard gone, all kinds of new combinations of Playby and its concomitant relationships were forming and reforming. He'd seen it happen too often before from close up to doubt that they were far more interested in each other than in whatever he might discover. Of them all, only Hill and Willow still even kept speaking to him every night, and he was feeling less and less like one of them, and more and more like—well not like Bim and Howard so much—but not far off either. Finally, Andy asked Hill if he could spend nights on the planet's surface, rather than onboard. At first, the others appeared to be insulted; then sad, then angry, then annoyed. Finally they seemed to give up on him altogether. A vote was taken and they all said sure.

As for the planet, Hill and Willow had already agreed that it would receive no higher than a Class D designation, and thus remain off all beaten paths, no matter what Andy or the 'droids came up with.

★

Giggle, giggle.

—Where are the others?—Andy T-p'ed.

Silence. Then.—What means others?—

—You know, more than one. I am one—Andy explained.—Those who died in the Orange Wood, they were *others*.—

It was day seven and Andy was getting nowhere.

—Replaceable—followed by more giggles.—No distinction.—

It was astounding to Andy how many fairly ordinary concepts known to a dozen intelligent species that the Company had already encountered were not known by the still elusive voice; children, parents, male, female, good, evil, God. Not a clue. All the voice seemed to know was names. The only actual concepts it seemed able to delineate were "are" and "not are" as well as "care" and "hurt."

—You hurt?—it would ask Andy every day during his daily rest periods. Those and his naps had grown longer and more frequent now that he didn't have the distraction of other crew-mates and the Big Brown Buzz.

—Not hurt—he would reply.

—You care?—it would then ask.

—I care—he would reply.

—I care—the voice would reiterate. Then giggle a bit and vanish.

Perhaps that was why, on day seven, when the mobile 'droids were done with their work, the Company's work on this planet done, Andy decided not to go into the lander with them back to the *Dallas*. Instead he took the skimmer and went to hide in the Peppermint Woods: the densest forest they had found on the planet. All the while, he admitted to himself that he was acting totally irrationally. At first he told himself that it was the principle of the thing, and he was taking a stand. The planet had been misclassified, and he would prove it.

The next day, Hill sent down a lander full of hunter 'droids. But Andy could T-p their simple mechanisms a hundred kilometers away. Not for nothing were T-p's like Andy given high official rank in the Company, given status and power and often great wealth, too. Their ability to read minds as well as to elude anyone or thing other than another T-p made them close to invincible. The hunter 'droids returned back to the lander empty-handed.

Andy did keep channels open at times to the *Dallas*, to listen in on the crew, as it voted that night. Willow alone wanted to remain and keep looking for him—even in person if need be. Even Roy, his favorite Playby companion voted against them staying. But it was evident to all, even Willow, that what had begun on Deneb 3 several months ago, had finally worked itself out here, on this planet. T-p's were known to always be the most sensitive and thus the most difficult crew members. More than one had cracked up onboard. With disastrous results for all. No one, not even Willow, looked forward to that happening. No sirree. That could get really hazardous to their health.

Furthermore, following the mobile 'droids full inspection and the ship computer's own fullest analysis, even that Class D designation seemed high for the planet. Every known chemical and mineral on the new Universal Valence Chart did exist somewhere or other upon the little world, true, but all of them in equal quantities, and none sufficient for serious mining. The timber from those billions of trees was all of an ultra-porous, low-pulp quality. The rich looking foodstuffs that grew so abundantly was lacking in nutrients essential to human life. Although perfectly edible and digestible, it wouldn't break down in the human alimentary system—it merely passed through, undigested.

In conclusion, beautiful as the place looked, it was a failure. It might make a good resort planet, possibly a hospital or asylum recuperation spot. But the Company already owned dozens of those, most with far more spectacular settings than this bland little world. The final designation turned out to be Class R: Cost-inefficient to Exploit.

Even if he now wanted to, Andy felt he could *not* now return to the *Dallas*. Not after that vote. Only Willow had cared enough to vote in his favor. She had good qualities, Andy admitted. Among them, loyalty— up to a point. But in the end, the essential superficiality and simple vanity of Willow's mind, which made her a perfect Playby partner and genial travel companion, had—at least for a T-p—resolved itself. He was sure that she too would get over him in no time.

After one more general communication, along with six hours of requests for Andy to return onboard, went unanswered, the *Dallas* lifted out of orbit. Its golden glint in the cerulean sky lasted but an instant.

★

His own supplies had run out, and although Andy had eaten his full of the fruits and vegetables around him, he felt weaker and more tired every day. He found himself skimming less, exploring far less, sitting more, falling asleep more, feeling a nearly transcendental peace amid the T-p silence, in the cool nights, the warm days. With this new peace, he hardly ever needed to call on the voice anymore for assurances, for company, although occasionally, as he was awakening from his sixth nap of the day, he would T-p the giggles distantly.

One late afternoon, he awakened with the redSun past zenith, the white-blueSun approaching Meridian. He'd been sleeping since the redSundown of the previous day. By his timepiece it had been a sleep of almost twenty-two regular hours. Even so, he had a difficult time clearing his mind and he could barely lift his head. His vision was spotty, his hearing undermined by a series of constant hollow tones thrumming. His stomach felt cavernously empty.

He suddenly realized that he was starving and was going to die. With what little strength still remained in him, Andy began to cry, sobbing convulsively. He knew that he was being foolish—it would exhaust the last bit of energy left in him. But he was unable to stop himself. His thoughts ran back to his infancy, to the difficulties of being a T-p, and the thousands of slights, offenses, insults and humiliations he'd received over the years in Education and Development, and even later working for the Company. He couldn't forget the pain of being different. No matter how close he came to anyone during Playby, the truth was he'd always been alone. Truly alone.

Giggle, giggle.

At least he'd heard that sound clearly.

—Go away!—he T-p'ed

—Away?—

—Go away! You know. Go away from me.—

—Everywhere—it came back to Andy.—No distinction.—

—Can't you see I'm starving to death!—

Silence. Then,—You not are?—

—No, I still am. But by tomorrow I'll be *not are*—

—What's tomorrow?—the voice asked.

Andy began to explain about time, then he remembered that the voice didn't know time. Not days, not months, not years.

—*Always are*—the voice said.—No distinction—it giggled.

—I'm hurt!—Andy tried.—I'll be *not are* without—much care.—

Another set of misunderstanding T-p exchanges ensued until Andy was completely frustrated, exasperated, and finally, before the voice appeared to comprehend him, totally exhausted. Or did it comprehend? He wasn't sure. He was no longer sure he cared what happened to him anymore. He was so tired. He wanted nothing but to fall asleep, but he fought the feeling, believing that once he did sleep, he'd never wake up.

The last thing Andy remembered clearly was what looked like a twig with sharp thorns blown hard against his legs, puncturing his left ankle. He recalled watching his by now much thinned blood seeping out through the gash and into the surrounding grass and earth. He looked at it objectively, uncaring, really. It didn't hurt. Then Andy went under.

★

His recovery was slow: it took weeks. When he was finally able to stay awake long enough to see, hear and think clearly, he realized that he was immobilized. The fingers of both hands and toes of both feet through his thorn-ripped shoes had been transformed somehow into roots which were deeply, safely, comfortingly anchored into the ground, roots through which he now understood, he would be fed, clothed, warmed, cared for.

—Who are *you*?—he T-p'ed a question.

—No distinction—the voice replied.

—Then . . . then . . . Who am I?—he asked. And even as he formulated the thought, the question seemed utterly academic.

—No distinction—the voice replied.

As he knew it would answer. Then, as he knew it would, it giggled.

—No distinction—Andy repeated.

Andy giggled and giggled and giggled.

# The Guest in the Little Brick House

THERE HADN'T BEEN A TENANT in the little red brick house for years when Daniel Partridge moved in. At least not for three years. That's how long I had lived in the right, first-floor apartment which opens directly onto the backyard, and I'd never known the place occupied.

Mrs. Cello, the landlady, said that a Japanese professor had once lived in the little place for several months. He was a secret agent for his government, she believed. Hadn't everything pointed to it, she asked me? His extreme, smiling, cordiality whenever they met? The large book, wrapped in brown paper, he always carried under his arm? Especially, the suddenness of his departure? For all his coming and going, and never really talking to anyone, he was probably engaged in drug trafficking too! But I knew Mrs. Cello's husband and most of her friends had been dead for years, so she had nothing but mystery novels to occupy her time. She was always coming around to my back door with some neighborhood gossip that she transformed right in front of me into crimes of passion and horror, unprintable even in the tabloids that formed the rest of her reading matter. I sometimes wondered whether the professor himself weren't entirely a product of her imagination.

Just to show you how unlike she and I are, it was months before I discovered that the little red brick house was real and inhabitable. Of course, those first months in New York City had been busy for me, very busy. I was still working very hard trying to learn the ropes at *Glamour*, where I held an assistant editor's spot. The excitement of living in the city, and especially in Greenwich Village, had gone from a dream to an actuality, but it still hadn't subsided into the deep, warm glow it's since become. I already had a sort of boyfriend, a tall, thin, bearded, perennially unemployed actor who was something of an explorer and adventurer, whom I one day dubbed Captain Kidd. He and I were constantly fighting over minuscule problems and making life alternately miserable and ecstatic for each other. So you see, I really hadn't had time to look around much for myself.

It was The Kidd who brought the little house up out of the background. One morning, he stopped complaining about my over-poached eggs and soggy toast long enough to look out the breakfast-nook window and really check it over. It seemed nice enough, he thought. And would really be convenient for him to live in—if it weren't so expensive. You must understand that this was a series of digs at me. Because he was living on unemployment insurance checks, he accused me of being a spendthrift, simply because I liked to buy a few little pieces of nice clothing.

Also, and more importantly, I had been raised rather over-protectively, and still at twenty-three wasn't mature enough to admit I was living in sin, by letting my co-sinner live with me. But until Kidd's interest in the place, I had always thought of the little red brick house as a toy, or even as an abandoned movie set, never as real.

It wasn't merely that it was strange. Hell, I'm all for the unusual. Why else would I have left Ossining where an entire life—work, friends, husband—were already set up for me, to come to Greenwich Village, where anything could happen? And why else had I scorned numbers of attractive enough young men I met uptown every day, just to make a mutually unsatisfactory relationship with someone as weird as The Kidd?

Even Mrs. Cello, whose mind worked like Hercule Poirot's, never questioned the little house being there in the back yard, surrounded as it was by fences and other five-story attached buildings. Why should I?

But I did. The second my focus had been turned to it, I decided it had been built before the two close-together front tenement buildings that were attached by virtue of a stucco fronting to serve as one. Why else did the long, low, red-tiled hallway go straight back from the street, if not to afford a private entrance to the little house?

It was even possible that the courtyard had been designed as a setting for the little house. Closed in by the apartment in the front, a high, windowless warehouse wall to one side, and by a lower fence on the other, the yard was a largish open area with tall elm and acanthus, a flagstone patio with lawn furniture, and a small garden plot, where Mrs. Cello's cousin, the superintendent, grew squash, eggplant, and tomatoes. In the midst of all this, the little house sat like a child's plaything. Scarcely twenty feet long and ten deep; only one story high. With a gray shingled roof, a small brick chimney, and little bow windows on either side of the center door, it looked like a cottage that Hansel and Gretel might visit in some fairy tale.

Now I know there are many backyard houses in the city, but they're mostly converted servants' quarters and former stables. This little house never had any practical use besides what it had been built as, and would probably be out of place no matter where it was located. Not five hundred yards from a major north-south thoroughfare, Eighth Avenue, it seemed like a speck of Disneyland, a touch of Oz.

But it wasn't the strangeness that decided me against The Kidd moving in, once we'd gotten the key to the door from Mrs. Cello and inspected it. It wasn't even that it was really tiny inside, or even that he would probably destroy the elegant, delicate-looking pieces it was furnished with. I simply felt that he wasn't right for it. And also that it was in need of an occupant, no matter how complete it seemed, and that it needed a very particular occupant.

At that time, all I could do was say my intuitions were against The Kidd taking it. He said my intuition was worse than most women's, and that I just didn't want him nearby. We argued over that for a few days, and I let him think whatever he wanted.

But I never looked out my kitchen window without feeling that the little red brick house was waiting. When Daniel moved in, the waiting ended. And after everything that's happened there, I feel more than justified in my presentiments. It's just too bad The Kidd wasn't here to see it all. But then, by the time he's back from Nepal or Tibet or wherever he went, there won't be anything to show that the little red brick house ever existed at all.

**2**

I wish I had been at home, instead of at work, the day Daniel came to look at the little red brick house. I would have liked to have seen him, been part of him, right from the very beginning. As it was, later that day, Mrs. Cello dropped by with a book of Iranian recipes I'd never asked for and certainly had no interest in. She rambled on for about fifteen minutes about the crucial importance of using only fresh pomegranates for the rice pilafs (as if I would ever cook one!) then got to the point of her visit: she had rented the little house to a young man that afternoon. This was surprising news to me, since she had never before expressed any interest whatsoever in renting the place and I had told her The Kidd was merely curious the day we'd gotten the key from her. What was even more surprising was that Mrs. Cello had nothing, or next to nothing, to say about the new tenant. He was a "nice looking man," she said. He reminded her of an old linotype of the painter Eugene Delacroix, as a youth, that she'd seen when she was a girl, she added, as though that would help. And she also said that he had shown her some respectable looking references from a college somewhere in the South. He was not: 1) a perverted shoe fetishist; 2) someone who'd murdered his first three wives by slow torture; 3) a Carbona addict. In short, he wasn't like anything I'd expect Mrs. Cello to say about a new tenant.

About a week later, about eight o'clock in the evening, I first met Daniel. Our beginning wasn't terribly auspicious. I was standing at my stove, tossing a curry omelet and thinking that Simone Beck would have been proud of how smooth it looked on the bottom, when there was a rap on my screen door. Thinking it was The Kidd, who claims to have been a criminal in his youth specializing in breaking and entry and who is admittedly quite adept at entering apartments without benefit of key or buzzer, I shouted angrily that I was busy, he should go to the front and ring the front bell like any proper human being. That said, I flipped my omelet. I had never once raised my eye from the burner.

A minute or so later, I did raise my eyes, and looked out my kitchen window at a young man with dark hair who was standing several feet away. Not only wasn't it The Kidd, but to say that he was the most beautiful young man I had ever seen is to damn him with faint praise. Now, my family had always taken it for granted that Ellie was the feminine and romantic sister and I was the tomboy and later on the blue-stocking—and I've always been somewhat proud of my more rational role in the family—but I swear the minute I looked into his confused, money-green eyes, I would have followed him to Greenland in December. And all the while, he was standing out there with a little orange-colored fuse in his hand, wondering exactly what kind of crackpot I was.

I dropped my omelet, killed the flame under the burner, ran to the door and asked whether he'd knocked and I'd not heard.

"I heard music," he said, in a most musical voice. "And saw lights," he added, lighting up my—until then—dim life. "And the screen door seemed open. I didn't mean to disturb you," he concluded with a terribly disturbing final phrase.

Now I have never much taken to Southerners, having had a staunch Abolitionist grace my family tree, and I must admit I've always been the first in any group to caricature a Southern accent. But his drawl was whipped cream and honey, unspoken promises, and more: much more.

"I was expecting a friend," I flubbed an explanation.

"A friend?" he rightly asked, baffled.

"Not really a friend," I explained. "A pest, in actuality, and thus more than a friend. He thinks he's Humphrey Bogart or someone when he's more like Elisha Cook. He's always trying to take me by surprise. You know?" I added, stupidly.

I could see from his continued disbelief that he didn't at all know. But I guess he felt I wasn't utterly dangerous, because he did actually step closer. He had one of those little bull-like noses my girlfriend Ginny says is common to people born under the sign of Taurus.

"Could you tell me which apartment is the landlady's? I seem to have blown several fuses all at once. I guess they were all pretty old. The landlady said I could bother her if I had any problems." He gestured in the direction of the little red brick house. "It took me a half hour and two packages of matches to find the fuse box in there," he added.

He was the new tenant. Eugene Delacroix, my foot!

"Mrs. Cello isn't home right now." I said, recalling that she said she'd be off watching a Margaret Rutherford Festival double-feature. "She won't be back until much later. But I should have some extra fuses around here. I know I do have a flashlight."

He stood in the kitchen doorway, somewhat cautiously, while I scavenged through The Kidd's toolbox until I found everything that we needed. Ten minutes later, all his fuses were replaced and we sat down to a cup of coffee in his tiny living room, which doubled as a dining room and also a study by virtue of a good-sized drop-leaf table that he'd moved in. I made every effort to calm myself, to seem like nothing more than a helpful neighbor, and he, unfortunately, seemed ready enough to accept me on this false and superficial level. Nevertheless, I had ample opportunity to look him over, to see how amazingly attractive he was and to compare his charm with The Kidd's lack of same. He moved around the little, crowded place with perfect ease, despite several large boxes of books which were always in the way.

He was a musicologist, Daniel said, both teacher and student, working towards his doctorate. He taught undergraduate courses at a little college in Athens, Georgia and he was lucky enough to have been granted a year's sabbatical to come to New York to write a dissertation. I immediately thanked Heaven I had spent much of my youth reading and the rest listening to music: I was able to speak intelligently about music and even had played piano. His book, Daniel said, was on the relationship between romantic piano pieces and lieder. I let him know that I sensed there had always been a crucial connection between the two. It was encouraging, I thought, that he wasn't involved in another area; romanticism suited both his looks and my mood. He spoke about Schubert and Schumann, Chopin and Hummel, and although he talked with the usual Southern slowness and lack of enthusiasm I usually abhor, still I found myself charmed away by the flow and the intelligence of what he had to say. It was almost hypnotic, especially when he became humorous about the city. He had only been here a few days and he had been astounded by the consistent oddity of the people he had encountered.

"Why, it's almost like being in a museum, but one where every exhibit is alive, rather than made of wax," he said.

He had lived in the little house only a day, he told me. "I feel like the little old lady who lived in the shoe. It's a bit cramped but all I really need is two little rooms, one to sleep in and one to study in. It was the furnishings that most attracted me, especially that little table and chair there."

I looked where he pointed behind us at a small, elegant Queen Anne escritoire with a crystal gas lamp atop it. "I saw it," Daniel said, "with the sun streaming in through the window and I immediately imagined myself sitting there to do my work. Of course, it's really too delicate and small." He sat there, demonstrating. "So now I use this table. I'll set my typewriter down and scatter a great many papers around, so that I'll look quite busy, even when I'm not."

I hadn't forgotten my feelings about the house needing a particular type of person to complement it. This came back to me in full force a minute later when he said, "It is curious, however, but except for the house I grew up in, this is the only place I've stayed in that I really feel to be a fit. Do you think it's too soon to say that?"

I was about to say I thought it was a perfect fit, when I heard my screen door slam. Another minute, it slammed again. This time, The Kidd emerged, standing on my back step, doing everything but scratching his head in confusion at not finding me in.

"My pest," I identified him. I didn't want The Kidd meeting Daniel just yet. There would be time, and I had plans, so I rose to go. "I hope you enjoy living here, and I wish you luck on your dissertation. By the way, I hope you'll feel free to come rap on my door at any time. That's one of the advantages of living in the Village. It's like a small town, everyone's so neighborly."

With those—I hoped—predictive words, I left.

I dragged The Kidd into the apartment saying I had been playing in the garden patch. When we got in the kitchen there was a nasty, smoky odor just perceptible. I ran to the stove. The burner hadn't gone totally off when I'd shut it down. The omelet was the size, shape and color of a blackened potato chip. But I couldn't have cared less. For the first time in my life, I had a crush. I would have burned ten chicken farms for that last half hour with Daniel.

## 3

To my mixed pleasure and extreme disturbance, Dan—for soon I was calling him that—became not only neighborly, but downright friendly. He had only a small radio and needed the use of a phonograph for his research, and so I let him have the key to my place to use my more elaborate stereo system while I was away at work. This broke whatever ice remained. We began spending Saturday and Sunday afternoons together, going to museums and movies; sometimes just having lunch at a local restaurant, then taking long walks. As the days became warmer, then hotter, we began to meet for a chat every evening in the oasis-like cool of the backyard. Mrs. Cello had dredged up an old air-conditioner for the little house—she was sort of hooked on Dan, too—but he preferred not using it very often or, when he did, not very much.

The more we saw of each other, the more desirable Dan became to me. Not just physically, although—seeing him in his shorts and T-shirt on warmer days—I could tell he did enough weight-lifting to stay just perfectly in shape. No, it was more that I couldn't help but compare him to The Kidd. This was especially unfair, as The Kidd was now going through a major hassle: his unemployment insurance would be kaput in a month, and he was panic-stricken at the thought of having to work for a living again. He spent a great deal of time with doctors and at agencies and clinics of all sorts, trying to have himself classified as disabled. Yet The Kidd still had enough free time to sense that he had serious competition and to take to haunting Dan everywhere. For the time being, unfortunately, The Kidd was safe. Dan was a gentleman to the "nth" degree, despite the alleged allure of my Pucci two-piece bathing outfit, and our relationship remained, for me, sickeningly Platonic. I was beginning to understand the Greek myth of Tantalus.

Mind you, I tried. I explained to Dan that The Kidd was merely a friend. When this made no difference in his chivalry, I added that The Kidd was even somewhat of an emotional cripple whom I was merely helping to get together, all of course, from the most unselfish of motives. This made no difference either, so I began working it from the other end. Unscrupulously, I chose hundreds of pretenses to break with The Kidd. I laid on him an entire Puritan values trip I didn't for one moment believe. I complained that he'd deflowered me and was now merely using me until he found someone else and threw me away. I continually found fault with him; I nagged him privately and when that had little effect, I nagged him publicly. One night at the White Horse Tavern, I got myself good and plastered, lashed out at him, abused him and all of his friends, and attacked The Kidd's best buddy, the bartender, with a bottle of Smirnoff. It was a real scene. Lord knows, I tried to make The Kidd's life hell, but he reacted just the opposite of what any ordinary man would do. He apologized to the people at the White Horse. He explained to them that I was "intellectually tormented," whatever that meant. At home, he made every effort to be pleasant. He even sent me flowers at work, once. Flowers! What could I do but relent. This of course solved nothing, and I was trying to figure out if I had the time or the nature to carry on a full frontal, double affair. Quite frankly, I was thinking of returning to Ossining where life was predictable, and where I felt sure neither The Kidd nor Daniel would follow.

It was in the middle of all this tumult, one super-sultry night, as Dan and I sat on my back step, that he roused me from my ever-growing depression long enough to ask if I knew anything about the history of the little red brick house. He asked the question in his usual, slow, casual, manner, so I had no idea it was anything more than curiosity.

"Mrs. Cello's husband bought the little house along with the property from its original owner about sixty years ago," I told Dan. "At that time, there was no warehouse closing it in back. There were more lots, most of them empty, all belonging to someone else, and they ran right down to Washington Street and beyond to the Hudson River."

By then, I knew that romance was definitely not one of Dan's strongest assets. But if he were merely curious, he would have dropped the subject right there. He didn't.

"You don't know who built the little house? Or who lived in it?"

"Mrs. Cello might know. I remember she once told me that the buildings had been abandoned. The owners had lived outside the city for twenty years or more. She said her husband had a lot of work to do here on the property. Why?"

"No especial reason why," he answered, and changed the subject. Still, I had detected something stronger than curiosity in his tone of voice. About ten minutes later, I received another surprise.

"Your friend Ginny, the one who casts horoscopes, does she know anything about spirits?"

"A great deal. What kind of spirits?"

"Are there different kinds?" he asked.

"That's what Ginny says. There's an entire range of them, beginning with teeny little poltergeists who do mischievous things like making noises and unlocking doors." I wouldn't have been at all surprised if Dan had all kinds of noises in the little house. "Is that what you mean?"

"That's not the same as a ghost, right?" he asked.

"Not at all." Ginny and I had spoken on this topic a great deal, speculatively, of course, and so I had a speck of knowledge on the matter. "Ginny says that ghosts are people who've died but never left Earth, or that have come back to complete something they left incomplete during their lifetime. They assume the form and features of the person they were in life. Ghosts are much more sophisticated than poltergeists."

"Then it must be a ghost that I have," he said, with totally serenity.

I was less serene. I almost shouted: "What kind of ghost!?"

"One that assumes the form and features of a person," he said, and laughed. Now I wasn't at all certain he wasn't teasing me. His usual laugh is warm and winning; but this was less so, more excited, perhaps even nervous. "A girl ghost. That's possible, isn't it?"

"I don't see why not."

"She's about eighteen or nineteen years old. She sits at the little table in the corner and she stares at something in her hand that I can't make out. A locket or something."

For all the speculating I'd done with Ginny, I neither believed nor disbelieved in ghosts; I simply had too little to do with them, or with people who had anything to do with them. So I asked Dan for details.

"Well, she's dressed strangely. She reminds me of a photograph of my great Grandmother out on a picnic. She wears a long dress, sort of blue or gray, with a high neck and short sleeves, with lots of frills on the collar and sleeves. And her hair is long, but it's bunched up behind her head and then hangs loose down her back. It's light brown. I've only seen her in profile, so I can't really say what her features are. But I'd guess that she's what's called 'striking' rather than pretty."

I listened to this description closely. It struck me as the real thing. I could place her costume around 1910 or so. "And she just sits there?" I asked.

"She just sits there and looks at the locket. There's a strange light around her that illuminates the corner, and that hides the details of the room. I've only seen her twice. Both times I'd been reading and had just closed my book to go to sleep when I saw her there."

I was terrifically excited. "Did you get up to look at her more closely? I would have."

He stared at me a few seconds with an indescribable look on his face, then laughed nervously. "Of course not. I don't believe in spirits. I must have been dreaming." He laughed again. Shortly after that, he went back inside the little house. He had tried to pass it all off as teasing but I felt otherwise. That strange laugh of his, to begin with. The description of her, he'd offered. Besides, for all his teasing, he'd been somewhat embarrassed at how he'd chosen to end the subject. If there were in fact a ghost there, the ghost that he described, he would have been upset, would have wanted to tell someone about it. I was the only person in the city he knew well enough to tell.

That night I decided to find out more from Mrs. Cello. I wanted to know who had lived in the little red brick house, who had built it, and when. I would have to move warily, not make her in the least bit suspicious, but I was certain I could do it.

## 4

"Their name was Fischer. Benedict Fischer, spelled the German way, although they weren't German at all. Wait a minute, Mr. Cello put all the deeds together," she said, rummaging through a trunk filled with letters, photographs and magazine covers. She at last emerged with a fistful of aged, if official, looking papers. "Mr. Cello bought four lots, these two the buildings are on, and two more across the street. There were three more lots for sale, but they were already promised. Yes, here it is! Mr. Benedict Fischer." She held up the paper in triumph, then lowered her voice. "Mind you I was a young girl then, newly married. But he was a strange one all right. I only met him one time, but that was more than enough. He lived upstate, up by Statonville, on property he owned there, and I believe he lived in seclusion. He was a long, thin, hawk-nosed fellow, Mr. Fischer. I wouldn't wonder that sort of trouble a fellow like that could bring into this world. And him being a judge or politician or something like that. Probably no one asked the right questions about him because he was so wealthy. I told Mr. Cello right then and there to inspect all the basements, because who knew what we might find there."

Before she had the chance to explicate what she believed she might have found, I cut in: "Where does Mr. Fischer live now?"

"I doubt he's still alive. He must have been seventy-five years old then. Still, you never know with those bad ones."

I was satisfied that he probably hadn't lived to the age of a hundred and twenty-five. "Did Fischer have a wife? A family?"

"He was a widower. I remember that because I was certain it was *her* we would find scattered all around the cellars."

"And no children?" I asked, unfazed.

"Wait a minute. Yes. There was a daughter. A spinster I believe. I never met her, but Mr. Cello did. He always did have a roving eye, that one. What was her name? Why, I know! It should be right here in the deed." Mrs. Cello kept scanning the paper, but continued talking all the time. "You see, there was a clause in the deed that the little house would remain unsold so the daughter might come and stay there whenever she wanted to. It had originally been built just for her, I believe, as a play-house when she was a little girl. Miss Fischer wouldn't sell the rest of the property without that specific clause. I almost stopped Mr. Cello from buying the whole shebang because of that clause. But Mr. Cello said he didn't mind. He said she was a well-bred lady and wouldn't give us any trouble. He even built the entry-hallways downstairs from front to back the way you see it so that she might come and go into the little house from the street whenever she chose to. She really only came a few times, in the beginning, then she stopped coming altogether. I never saw her, except from the window. Mr. Cello was always somewhere on the grounds, however, and he would tell me whenever she came. She never lived there; only visited for an hour or two. Here we go!" She had found the name on the deed. "Miss Katherine Fischer. That's right. Mr. Cello always called her Miss Kate."

"When did she sell you the little house?" I asked.

"Well, that's just it, she never did sell it. It's still hers. She just never came back or wrote or phoned or anything. I think she may have moved to Europe permanently. She'd inherited a large sum of money. Why, all the furniture in the place belonged to her. Now, I myself know little about fine furnishings, but they were well-to-do people and I wouldn't be surprised if we don't have a handful of antiques in there."

Mrs. Cello seemed so excited by that prospect I decided to keep her on the subject. We discussed antiques for ten minutes and finally I lugged over several large volumes on antiques so she could decide how much she might make—if Miss Kate Fischer never came to claim it all herself.

I had found out something about the little red brick house, but not a great deal, and certainly nothing to suggest a ghost. However, I had resolved upon two things: first, I wouldn't tell Dan anything I had discovered. I wouldn't even mention anything until he himself brought up the topic again. Second, I would try to discover if Kate Fischer was still alive. If so, she could hardly be the ghost, could she? That revenant was a young girl, while Kate Fischer had been known as a spinster. Still I hoped to discover who the ghost was.

## 5

The second happened first. In my editorial capacity, I sometimes use a researcher—a young man whose nose for investigation is sharp, and who was luckily more down-to-earth, than Mrs. Cello. I gave him the name Benedict Fischer, intimated there was an old New York background of some prominence, and asked for descendants and any other pertinent information. I hinted it was a pressing personal matter, and I could tell this had the planned effect: he became curious, then fired-up.

A week later he sent a very detailed report, including the current address of old Benedict's only survivor, Miss Kate. She now lived in a townhouse in the East Sixties, somewhat withdrawn from the world, as befitted her wealth, her age, and her unmarried status. In general, the report was rather dull. But the researcher had added, almost as an afterthought, a separate page. This said that the Fischers had in the past been very social indeed; they'd entertained widely. Among their closest friends, just before the First World War, had been a noted architect who had been found shot to death along with his mistress. Her husband, an equally eminent banker, had been accused, tried and convicted of the crime. This scandal had rocked New York society for months; after that, war had arrived with far more news and scandals. My researcher added several newspaper clippings about the killings. I wondered whether this incident could have anything to do with the fact that the only Fischer daughter never married.

I mused upon this mass of fact and speculation for another two or three weeks before deciding what to do with it. I could understand why the researcher had attached the clipping about the scandal—it did smell like something; but its relevance to the ghost Dan claimed to see seemed at best tenuous—shouldn't there be two ghosts? Then again, what were they doing there, in the little house, when they had been shot in a posh hotel, a mile or so away?

Even if I had wanted to talk to him right away, to reveal all I knew, I had little opportunity. Dan had finished the research part of his work and he no longer used my apartment to listen to music in. He had begun to write his dissertation and he was going at it with a vengeance. The lights in his little house were on later every night, and I usually fell asleep to the light, irregular patter of his keyboard. I saw him seldom; we never met for our evening chats anymore, and whenever I did see him, in passing, he always seemed somewhat aloof.

He was working hard, he said to me. I understood. I did. Really, I did understand. Up to a point. But I really couldn't see what his hurry was. He had done his research in half the time he'd needed. And he still had months left before he needed to hand in the dissertation. He was losing his scrumptious tan, losing weight, and beginning to look fatigued. Now, if all these physical symptoms were happening on account of unrequited love for me, I could understand. But for work? Besides, I didn't know how much longer I could keep all my facts and speculations to myself.

One night I broke down. I dragged Captain Kidd out of the big chair in front of the TV where he had taken root for the past few weeks and I sent him off to bowl, to drink, to whore, to do anything so long as I had an evening to myself. Then I knocked on Dan's door. As he said hello, I began my attack.

"I won't let you say no. I've made a terrific dinner, worked on it for three days, and the pest abandoned me with his usual irresponsibility. There! So you are invited to dinner, with no refusal allowed. You need not wear a jacket and tie."

Dan laughed, then he accepted.

A half hour later, we were at the table over the fastest mock-gourmet dinner ever devised. Luck had been with me and everything had worked out better than fine with the meal. Dan was his usual charming and humorous self, but with one difference, a rather distinct one to me: several times during the meal, he became somewhat distracted. Since he had been working so hard, I attributed this to excessive concentration, which might also explain the dark shadows under his eyes, suggesting as they did that he wasn't sleeping enough. It gave him the appearance of someone who had looked a great deal at vague and distant objects through a long tunnel.

When he wasn't distracted, he talked a great deal about his work. The first draft was almost complete, and he was more or less pleased with it. So pleased that he had done enough research to formulate yet another dissertation from the material, which he might use later on in his career. He would begin work on that one when the first was finished, and see how far it led. As he spoke, I found myself filled with mixed feelings. To begin with, no woman likes being pushed out of a man's life by his work, and I felt that. But I also felt somewhat maternal towards him: I was also happy that I invited him to dinner, angry with myself for not doing it sooner, and in fact, for not doing anything more towards making Dan my lover.

After dinner, we sat in my living room listening to music and drinking coffee. He seemed uncomfortable, restless and more distracted than he'd been at dinner. All my attempts to make conversation began brilliantly and died for lack of any interest from him. I decided to get to the point of this dinner.

"Do you still have your nocturnal visitor?" I asked as casually as possible.

"No! Never," Dan answered.

"You're no good at lying, you know. Your face gets red and you fidget around too much," I told him.

"I thought you'd forgotten all that nonsense."

"It seems that you hold no trust in me at all. You seem to think I'm as stupid as all those girls you grew up with. Well, listen Buster! I'm not. I'm insulted at your lack of trust. And altogether these last few weeks you've been extremely unfriendly—dissertation or not. You've avoided me as though I had some plague, and I'm sorry I even invited you here for dinner. Go now. And don't bother coming back."

Of course, I had no earthly reason to be so angry, so melodramatic, to make such a mountain out of a molehill, but I was upset and I did want him to know it. Besides, it worked better than I would have expected. Dan apologized profusely, said I was totally justified in all my complaints and he admitted that his work was an insufficient excuse for him ignoring a good friend like myself and so on and so forth until I began to feel guilty, even though I had made my point. He stayed for more dessert and coffee and began to enjoy my company.

As I poured another cup, he surprised me, asking, "You haven't told anyone about her, have you?"

"Not a soul," I brazenly lied.

"Can I really trust you?" he asked, aloud. "Trust you as a friend? My only friend here in New York?"

"Jesus, Dan. Of course you can. That's one of the things I was just complaining about."

He hesitated then came out with a real winner: "Well, I really don't know how to explain it. It's all so strange."

"Then you *have* seen her sitting at the little table again?"

"Oh! More than that," Dan half laughed, showing me how much more. "I see her every night now."

I really didn't know how to react to this information. There was no fear, no horror, nothing at all in his voice or in his attitude to show that he was in daily contact with the supernatural. After all, weren't ghosts supposed to be terribly unhappy? Weren't they supposed to roam the earth endlessly seeking revenge or something? You wouldn't have known it from hearing Dan speak of it.

"All right," he said. "It's only because I believe I can trust you," here his eyes held mine as though extracting a vow, "that I'm going to tell you

all his. And I know you'll understand. After all, you're an intelligent . . . "
he groped for another word, "a liberated girl."

I was confused for a second, then I realized what he was saying.
Evidently Captain Kidd had done more than merely sense competition,
he had opened his big mouth, spilled the beans, and eliminated the
competition. That rat! I'd fix him! I'd eliminate him altogether! I could
understand why Dan had been avoiding me. That wouldn't last long!

This decided, I asked whether Dan wasn't afraid of her.

"Not at all," Dan said. "We've really grown close! Although that's not
the precise word for it."

I wondered exactly what the precise word for it was, but held my
tongue.

"You see," Dan said, "she likes me a great deal." He brightened up
as he said this. "Those first few times I saw her, well, she looked so sad,
so forlorn. I felt bad for her. I remember it was the night I told you about
her that I saw her again. She sat at the little table and looked at the
locket so sadly, oh for at least a half hour. I didn't want her to go, but I
didn't make a sound. I just stayed awake and watched her. I was too
excited to sleep, really."

Dan was excited as he related all this to me. His distraction of earlier
was gone, and there was a sort of gleam in his eyes, the kind of gleam
women get in their eyes when looking at furs or diamonds.

"Finally, I couldn't resist making myself known to her," Dan said. "I
was pretty certain she thought the little house was still uninhabited. So
I just called out to her, saying 'Hey! Don't be sad.' And she looked up,
surprised. So I called her again and she peered at me for a long time
through what seemed to be a kind of dimness, then she just stood up and
went to where I could no longer see her anymore. When I got up to see
where exactly, she was gone. The next night she appeared again, and again
I called her and this time, after a bit, she got up and walked towards the
bedroom, moving very cautiously, as if she were afraid of what she'd find."
Dan laughed at the irony. "I talked to her softly, as you would to a child
or to a wild animal in the woods. I never made a move, because I didn't
want to frighten her. So she visited at my bedroom door every night for a
week, before she would turn away and just vanish."

As Dan talked, I could vividly picture what had occurred. He talked
low and sweetly, as he must have spoken to her, and I remember thinking

how I would have reacted if Dan called me like that, if he had tried to comfort me like that. I felt a slight tinge of envy.

"I suppose I convinced her to not fear me. She comes to the foot of my bed now. She smiles at me, and I feel wonderful warmth all around me. Not heat, but like the warmth of heavy blankets when it's cold out in the early morning and there's no heat on. Then I fall asleep and dream. That's the kind of relationship we have," he concluded.

I thought I'd missed something.

"I don't understand. She comes to the foot of your bed and just . . . smiles?"

"It's almost as though she talks," Dan explained. "Although it's not in words or anything like that; certainly not in words. Then I go to sleep."

I still missed something. "What do you mean? Do you dream?"

"Why of course I do. Of her!" He said it as though it were the simplest and most ordinary thing. "Of her and me sometimes. Of us being together."

I guess it was the way he said it more than the words themselves that was so suggestive. I must have looked a bit stupefied because Dan was careful to continue, "It wouldn't be exactly proper for me to tell you the details of the dreams, now, would it?"

At last I understood. "You mean they're sexual?"

Dan colored, and said, "I suppose I'm old-fashioned. I'd call them affectional. But yes," he declared, "that's what it is. I feel very fulfilled with her."

On top of this statement, there could be nothing for me to say. I knew it would take me a few hours to untangle my feelings on the subject. But I couldn't really believe he was telling me this. If it was so, well, let's just say I doubted my own reality. I suppose that's why I touched Dan's arm.

He took my touch as approval. "I knew you'd understand," he said cheerfully, and leaned over to kiss my cheek. "You're terrific." He sighed in relief. "So you see that's why I haven't been out much. There's my work and well, I like being in the house, even when she isn't there. I feel that she sort of helps me."

I've always been a broadminded enough girl, but I swear Dan's confession floored me completely. I made some sort of remark about it being late and having to wash my hair, which, like most women, I make into a tedious ritual requiring a great deal of time and absolute privacy. Dan kissed my cheek at the door again and told me again how terrific I was.

The minute he closed the door to the little red brick house, I sort of quietly exploded. I laughed, I cried, I became angry, then indulgent. Oh, I was a fool for about ten minutes. Then I really did get ready to wash my hair. After all, I had some serious thinking to do.

## 6

Obviously, Dan was mentally unbalanced, emotionally disturbed. Either that or he really was having an affair with a ghost, difficult as it was to believe. I couldn't see any other solution: not lying, not trickery. Fantasy, perhaps. But fantasy way out of control. The only way to find out for certain would be for me to see the ghost for myself. The loving, protective manner Dan had adopted toward it made it impossible for me to simply say, "Well, she sounds lovely, Dan, when am I going to meet her?" No, he wasn't playing that kind of game. Against every principle I held, I was going to have to go uninvited: to see for myself.

What I would do once I had seen the ghost hinged totally upon my seeing it. It was apparent that something would have to be done about it. After all, it was less than normal for a young man to carry on with a spirit, fearful or not. It was, well, it was downright unhealthy. It had already begun taking its toll physically. Dan, who'd never looked bad before, looked a wreck. Hell, he had never smoked so many cigarettes as he had this past evening; and that look in his eye, it was well, maybe not wild, but definitely not normal! Who knew what psychological damage was already being done, damage it might take years to repair. No, it was certain. Their affair had to come to an end.

By the time I had dried my hair and finished brushing it out, I was beginning to feel some pride in myself; sort of like Florence Nightingale when she first saw the military hospital at Scutari and said to herself, "Flo, there is work to be done."

I shut off the lights and waited in the dark so that Dan would conclude I'd gone to sleep, until I could no longer hear him typing. When the lights went out in his living room, I decided to move forward. But I couldn't recall if he'd specified how long after he had gone to bed the ghost arrived, so I waited another fifteen minutes. I changed into a pair of black slacks and a big black sweatshirt that belonged to The Kidd. Dressed like a Ninja, I crept out of my back door to the little house as quietly as I could, hoping that no one from upstairs happened to be staring out the window.

I chose the bedroom window on the vegetable garden side of the little house because I thought I would be better hidden from view there and because that was where Dan would be, so I would share his viewpoint: straight into the other room. There was enough of a part in the curtains to see through clearly without attracting his attention. His bedroom window was closed and I assume he had the air-conditioning on.

Dan was sitting up in bed reading. A small lamp lit his torso. Naked down to his navel, where the sheets began. He wasn't four feet from the window, so close I could read the title on the book's cover—it was Shakespeare's Sonnets. No doubt to quote lines at his ghost girlfriend. I remember thinking this was further proof that he was very far gone, one way or another. And despite my general dislike of quote-gathering as a cheap romantic ploy, I would have given anything to have him quote one of them to me.

He read on and I shifted about trying to find a comfortable position for a longish time until I was beginning to think he had lied to me. Then Dan suddenly closed the book, shut out the lamp and didn't slump down as though to sleep, but remained where he'd been and continued looking straight ahead. It took me a few minutes to adjust to the darkness, but even after I had, I still saw nothing. But Dan did, or rather he seemed to, because his lips began to move as though he were speaking to someone. I looked harder into the other room, where in fact I saw nothing at all, and I debated with myself whether I did see anything. This went on for some time. Then I suddenly did see something, something I definitively had not seen before, and there was no inner debate anymore.

It was a mist, that's the only way I can describe it: a darkish mist which somehow seemed to be solid too, because it obscured objects as it passed in front of them. Its greatest dimension appeared to be height, and it was otherwise formless. Most astonishing to me was that it was clearly moving forward, coming from the living room, towards the bedroom. At the doorway the mist stopped and sort of shaped itself. That is, it assumed a distinct outline, if not precisely a form: the silhouette of a woman. I looked at this silhouette for the longest time but it never assumed a more palpable shape, and the light that came from the courtyard into the little bedroom didn't throw its features into relief one bit. Instead, the closer

I looked, the more it seemed to me that the outline had no depth, but only darkness of a color much deeper than anything around it, darker than the blackest darkness I'd ever encountered. And the more I looked, the more I was drawn to this silhouette until I was focusing on a point about where its heart would be, and there it seemed to have the greatest depth, the greatest pull, since I kept feeling myself drawn into it, even falling into it, pulled into immense abysses, infinite reaches, where there was more of nothing than I ever dreamed existed.

With great effort I wrenched my eyes away from the silhouette and leaned against the window sill. Despite the warmish air around me, I shivered, then shivered again. I felt as if I were encased in a block of ice. When this finally stopped, I looked through the window again, and again was drawn toward the center of the outline of mist. Finally, I resolved not to look at it, but to look only at Dan. As I did, the silhouette moved to the edge of the bed and completely blocked out the littler hunting scene prints hanging on the wall. Dan wasn't talking. He was calm, serene, and as the silhouette approached the bed, he slid down lower until he was in a prone position and he just kept smiling. I couldn't stop from shivering again and when I turned back, it seemed that Dan's feet were covered by the blackness, or in the darkness of the silhouette. Dan pushed the sheet off his body slowly, as though he were teasing someone, sort of laughing at the same time. He just lay there a long time until it seemed that the room itself was becoming much darker. I looked up and the silhouette was no longer there. But I couldn't see more that the mere outline of Dan's body. Then I sort of realized what might be happening—the mist must be hovering a bare inch over Dan's body. It settled almost gently atop him, then spread all over him, until he was covered, completely obscured from my gaze, smiling all the while.

At this point I had to turn away. I stared into the garden where a large tomato gleamed up at me, some light from next-door reflecting off its shiny surface. I bent to touch it. It was ripe, ready to split right through its skin. I touched the leaves, the stem, the dirt. Finally I thrust both my hands deep into the soil and held them there for what seemed a lifetime. This was real! I almost cried with relief. For an instant, my mind flashed on the slow horror happening on the other side of the wall, not five feet from where I knelt. Nervously, carefully, I stepped out of the garden plot and onto my flagstones. I stopped there a moment at my door, deciding

I'd had seen enough, then went into my kitchen.

So there *was* a ghost! Dan had not lied to me. A real ghost! Or at least something terrible and supernatural, unlike anything I'd ever expected to see. Much more terrifying somehow because its hypnotic power over me had been so strong, so unmistakable, even from the other side of the window. There was no doubt that it had Dan; had Dan, but good!

I found where The Kidd kept his brandy and although it was only "Marc," i.e. two steps above rot gut, I still took two deep slugs of it, which, since I wasn't used to it, naturally caused a convulsion of coughing and sputtering. But I felt better after that. When I'd stopped choking I could hear the T.V. set on in the living room. Bottle in hand, almost as though it were a weapon, I crept into the room: Captain Kidd, sitting in the big chair, as usual, watching some movie.

He didn't look up or ask me what I was doing creeping around the place wielding a bottle of brandy. He focused on the little screen. Then he said, "I'm going to Katmandu."

It took me so long to get over the shock of seeing him there, after what I had just gone through, that I didn't really hear what he said.

"Paulie and Tower asked me to go with them last week," Kidd said. "They're all packed. I'll need a few things. Socks, especially. Have you washed any of my socks lately? I can only find one pair besides the one's I'm wearing."

"Katmandu?" was all I could think to say.

"In Tibet, I think. No, Nepal. Out East. Near China and India."

He walked into the bedroom, still trying to watch the movie as he did so, and began taking the little bit of his clothing and stuff he had there out of the bureaus. I put the brandy away, found a tartan canvas suitcase, and watched him pack it up. All I could think was The Kidd was leaving, finally, after all of my own efforts to get him out had failed, he was leaving all by himself, and in the process he was leaving me.

He packed quietly and unmethodically, went into the kitchen for a can of beer, and with that in one hand and the suitcase in the other, he strolled to the apartment door while I followed behind, congratulating myself. There, he stopped.

"Listen," he began. "Don't be mean to the kid," he nodded in the direction of the backyard. "He's still young. He hasn't been around much. He'll take everything pretty hard."

With that said, Captain Kidd pecked me on one cheek and before I realized what he'd actually said, he was gone.

## 7

I'd wanted The Kidd out, and now he was out. But I really couldn't say I was pleased. To begin with, he'd insulted me. He'd all but accused me of. . . . Well, I guess coming from Dan's house at that hour of the night and all. . . . Still, he'd never even asked where I'd been or what I'd been doing. He'd simply jumped to conclusions. Then all that noble crap about Dan being a good kid. What a hypocrite!

Despite my anger at him, I still felt sad waking up alone. Just being there, refusing to wake up until after I had rolled him out of bed, hogging all the blankets and taking up all the best spots on the mattress, yes, The Kidd had been a habit, if a bad one. But I woke up looking at the little red brick house and I remembered what kind of habits went on inside there. I was steeled into action.

First thing at my office, I called Ginny at her office and asked her how to exorcise a ghost. She was vague enough, vaguer than a mere lack of morning coffee and early morning might excuse, and she was surprised at my persistence and my refusal to explain myself. She finally said one couldn't really exorcise a ghost, and after I asked her how the hell one could get rid of one, and she still couldn't answer. I got very testy and hung up on her.

Next I called the phone number the researcher had given for Kate Fischer and I talked to a middle-aged sounding woman who called herself Mrs. Florin and who described herself as Miss Fischer's companion and secretary. I explained that the magazine I wrote for was preparing an article on the fashion styles of earlier periods in New York and lied, saying that although we had plenty of photos, we wanted to talk with women who'd worn the clothing pictured. I said I knew that Miss Fischer had been a style leader in her day and had graced the fashion world and asked if she would consent to a little chat. Mrs. Florin said she would have to discuss the matter with Miss Fischer, as it was an unusual request, but she hinted that she felt certain Miss Fischer would be delighted enough to consent. I felt Miss Fischer held some sort of key to the situation, you see, and that's what I needed: a key.

Of course, the entire story about the article was a fabrication. I spent

all morning going through our photo files compiling a folder of old
fashions to show Miss Kate. On a hunch I decided to try to find some
which resembled the description Dan had given me of the girl he saw
every night. This seemed like an endless task, and Nellie, our staff artist,
finally agreed to make a new rendering for me, in an apt style. I had Nellie
draw the girl in profile, sitting at a little desk, and holding and looking
at a locket. I don't know exactly what I hoped to accomplish with this.
But if my hunch worked out it should be as exact as possible to achieve
the greatest effect. Nellie did a superb job. She had just finished and I was
admiring it when Mrs. Florin called back to set up an appointment with
Miss Kate for the following afternoon at three.

After leaving work I dropped into an occult book shop looking for a
text on exorcism. There were dozen of books, but most of them were
either terribly vague or terribly esoteric. At last I came across one titled *A
Practical Guide to Demons and Spirits*, which looked sensible enough and
which had a chapter on exorcism. As a final weapon, I stopped at a record
store and bought three new Lieder CDs; Mahler, Mendelssohn and
Schumann: these would be inducements for Dan to visit me, I'd hoped.

The recordings were terrific but the practical guide was highly
impractical. The items called for in the exorcism included things like
hummingbird scrota and would take weeks to track down, and there
didn't seem to be any shortcut, no emergency exorcism. But I was only
faintly disheartened. I felt that if Dan could be kept away from this thing,
that it would lose its hold over him.

I waited until ten-thirty at night to knock on Dan's door, recordings
in hand. He seemed pleased to see me and delighted to listen to my new
records. Once there, I hoped he would stay all night, not necessarily with
me, but just so the ghost wouldn't find him at home and might have a fit
of pique and never return. Toward this end I prepared little snacks, had a
wonderful Châteauneuf du Pape for us to sip, and some dynamite grass to
smoke. It had once belonged to Captain Kidd, who'd fancied himself a
connoisseur and, to keep up his reputation, had brought nothing but the
best stuff into the house. As a result I ended up, in no time, much higher
that I'd intended, and Dan tripped right out during *Kindentotenlieder*,
which he was following along with the score, conducting the mezzo and
pianist, saying "Wow!" a great deal and generally enjoying himself.

I had set everything up so we might loll against the big pillows in my living room, set in front of the speakers on the rug. The grass did the trick; we became very comfortable, even intimate. I even thought for a split second that more was going to happen. But while the chemicals were in the air, somehow that particular spark never quite got lit.

After the music, we smoked more, and watched the late late movie on the television. To this day, I couldn't tell you what movie it was or what it was about. And when that ended, to both our satisfaction, we were very exhausted, the way one is exhausted only after a very good grass trip. Dan got up to leave rather shakily and asked if he could come smoke and visit again. I calculated my schedule aloud for the coming month, discovered that—except for the following evening—I was engaged. Dan agreed to come by the next night. Then he stumbled home.

The evening had been successful. My real consolation was that I was certain Dan fell into as dead a sleep that night as I did: and so missed the visit of his girlfriend altogether!

### 8

"You say women are wearing dresses like those again?"

The old woman pointed to the top drawing of the folder I had prepared for her the day before. Her wrinkled forehead became even more deeply creased as she spoke. She was so shrunken I could scarcely discern a feature, never mind try to discover what she might have looked like when she was younger. I calculated her age between ninety and a thousand. She even smelled old. It was vaguely obscene.

"We wore them because we didn't know any better," she went on. "They weren't all that comfortable, you know. The materials used were all lovely, but quite heavy, much too heavy for summer wear; even the cottons weren't light enough for those dreadful New York City summers! I much prefer the new material, the new fashions."

She was dressed in a long, dark blue dress which made no attempt at fashion of any recognizable sort and which did nothing to define the little old form pushed into the corner of the large old chaise lounge. But, as she had repeated a few minutes earlier, she was an old lady and she never went out anymore.

I tried to explain, "It isn't that women are now wearing these exact fashions. There is a great deal of interest in the styles. In aspects of the styles. And many designers are adapting their lines for new clothing made of new modern materials, lighter, washable, not even needing to be ironed. It all began several decades back when women began going to thrift shops and finding old dresses and cutting them or wearing them as is for everyday use: long skirts, separate tops. But even among *haute couture*, the long, separate skirt has become fashionable again for evening wear."

"Just the skirts? I don't understand."

"Sometimes, yes. And sometimes just the tops with a different kind of skirt beneath." I was beginning to feel somewhat disgusted with my having to explain such nonsense, and to embroider it so much, when I had more pressing matters to discuss with her. But I had asked for this kind of interview and I would have to play by the rules, until I saw my chance.

I hadn't noticed any magazines in the large, sunny room where I waited an unconscionable amount of time for Mrs. Florin to wheel the old lady in and where we were now talking, awaiting tea to be served. I was happy Mrs. Florin was otherwise engaged; it would have been difficult to have gotten anywhere with two old women asking bad questions.

Despite her great age and her immobility, Miss Fischer was sharp. Her voice was still firm, even if her neck was a mass of flesh encased in various kerchiefs that kept falling apart and had to be replaced. She had taken, from the beginning, an imperious tone—the tone of someone who was used to commanding and to being listened to. But it was mostly her eyes that held me: they were alert, alive and intelligent and so I had to assume so was she. Also those eyes were large and dark and at times flashing as any young Spanish girls': and as temperamental. If she could help me, her eyes said, she would go to the limit. If, however, she decided I was a fool or an interloper, I was a goner.

I asked her to describe some of her wardrobe of the era and pulled out my little notebook to take notes in. She began speaking, very lucidly and with many strong opinions on the horrors of the clothing she wore in her earlier years. The cosmetics, too, were awful: either too thick or so thin that they ran. The corsets—even the shaped ones—were always too warm or too uncomfortable. One didn't have good shampoo. And the hair-dryers fried you. It had been a terrible time. She spoke and spoke. I tried not to be too anxious for Mrs. Florin to come in with the tea, and I tried to figure out how I could get Miss Fischer to look at, to concentrate upon, the pictures I had, and I wondered if my being there hadn't been a mistake from the beginning.

Finally, and despite the fact that tea had not yet come, I could wait no longer. I pulled my chair up close to the chaise lounge and began handing the old lady the drawings I'd had made, asking her to talk a little about each. Once she looked at them, all her memories of their discomfort passed. She began saying how elegant the lines had been, how feminine, not like these things women were wearing now, and how much abundance of variety there had been. She went through them quickly, and I held my breath as she approached the drawing I'd had Nellie do.

She looked at it quickly and was about to say something. Then she looked down again and held the paper up a bit and stared at it for a minute or more. When she put it down, her eyes had a question and even a touch of fear in them. This is what I'd come to her house for, but there was nothing I could say now. She dropped the last picture, then all of them, and they fell onto the floor, where I let them lay.

"Who are you?" she asked sharply. "Why are you here?"

I was certain she would call for Mrs. Florin and have me thrown out. She didn't. I reached down and picked up the drawings, arranging them in my lap.

"Oh! Put those away!" she cried. Then, "So, you know." She said it in a tone that might have been relief.

I had no idea how to respond. So I braved it. "Yes. I know."

"How do you know?"

Again I was stumped. Finally, I told her my address.

"And she's still there?"

I nodded yes: she was still there. So now at least we were discussing the same subject.

"And she sent you? Told you who I am and sent you to me?"

This totally stumped me. "I came on my own. We've never . . . spoken."

"Of course not," the old lady said. "One doesn't exactly speak with Kate, does one?" She said the words without humor, or bitterness, or. . . . Still. . . .

"Excuse me," I said, "did you just say the ghost is Kate?"

"You won't tell anyone, will you?" she asked. "You must promise not to tell *anyone*. I only have a few years left to live. I'd like a peaceful end. If people find out, it will be a fuss: possibly a great fuss, and I'll have no peace. *Swear to me* that you won't tell anyone!"

Moved by her, but having no idea what it was I was swearing to, I made the vow. I was still trying to understand how—if the thing in the little red brick house was Kate Fischer—the woman in front of me could also be. Could she?

"Now that you've sworn," she said, relieved, "I'll tell you everything you want to know. Where is Mrs. Florin with that tea!? You must be very curious. Is that why you came?"

"Part of the reason, yes."

"I would be too. Well, your curiosity shall be served my dear. And your courage too. I'm certain you'll find it interesting. So will others. I know several families who will be particularly interested. I don't care if you publish it everywhere. So long as you wait until I'm gone."

I told her I had no interest in publishing the information but I didn't think she believed me.

"She was a bad one, in her time," she almost whispered the words. "Wicked! Yes, that's the right word. Wicked! I wasn't surprised to find her in the little house so many years after. Not at all. Wicked ones like her never find any rest."

That said, the old lady held her tongue while Mrs. Florin came in with the tea tray and fussed about us for a minute or so. When she had gone, the old lady went on, almost breathlessly, never once touching the tea that she'd so anticipated, instead adjusting her neck-kerchiefs all the while.

"I was Kate's cousin. Second cousin, actually. We looked very much alike when we were young, even though we never thought alike. But we looked so much alike that people often took us for twins. So after Kate died, Uncle Benedict said that I'd merely gone back to Massachusetts to my family. And so I posed as Kate. Oh, not that there was so much to do. We moved soon after, Uncle Benedict, Aunt Lilly and all the servants and myself upstate to the place in Rye. We didn't have many visitors up there. And Uncle Benedict made me heir to his estate. So you see, I had my own reasons to pose as Kate; for a poor girl as I was, it was rather a godsend. It wasn't until some twenty years later that I returned to the little red brick house and discovered that she was still there."

So the ghost *was* Kate. "But how did she die?" I asked.

"Killed herself," the old lady said. She gave me a significant look. "She shot herself with the same revolver she had used to shoot Virgil Drew and that Harkness woman in that room, in the Delmonico Hotel." She paused, as I absorbed all this information. "That's right, my dear. It was Kate who killed them and then she was heartless enough to let them convict poor Mr. Harkness and let him hang him for the crime. As if he hadn't heartache enough."

So my researcher had been on the right path after all. He was brilliant!

"But I still don't understand why you posed as Kate?"

"You must understand what an *immense* social scandal it was. Why, Virgil Drew was connected with the best families, New York City's Four Hundred!! In those days, whenever anyone sneezed in New York society everyone else got the cold. Anything this big couldn't help but cause talk. Everyone knew Virgil and Kate had been engaged for months. And everyone knew how much he liked to play around. And everyone knew what a wild, impetuous and jealous thing Kate Fischer was. Why, at the trial of Mr. Harkness, half the character witnesses accused her. And they were all right. Although we didn't find out for certain until a year later. Almost to the day that she had killed them—that's when she killed herself. She was a wild, wicked thing. Of course we didn't know *why* she was so upset at the time, but she wouldn't go to Virgil's funeral. Uncle Benedict said she would have to go and she plain refused. So I went instead, to help her, and to help my aunt and uncle, and to keep people talking more than they already were. I wore a jet veil and I barely spoke and everyone simply assumed I was Kate. Even in the powder room, when I lifted my veil, they assumed I was Kate."

"It was that morning that convinced Uncle Benedict later on that I would easily be able to pass for her. It was essential, he felt, that no one know that Kate had died, because then they would find out *how* she had died. And from there it was merely a small leap to *why* she had died, and that could only prove her guilt in a far worse crime."

I must say I was delighted by all this gossip, ancient as it was. Not only did Dan's ghost have a *raison d'être* now, but it was connected with one of the most famous crimes of the previous century. All my hunches had worked out so well that I tried another.

"What was Virgil Drew like?" I asked.

Miss Fischer—for she said I was to continue to call her by that name—smiled wistfully. "That was the real tragedy of it all. He was like few men I'd ever met before or since. He was one of the most talented of his time:

so original. You know it was Virgil who designed and built that little house, as a bagatelle for Kate. He was so very handsome and so charming. He had his faults; I'd be the first to admit it. But one look at him would make you forget them. Every woman I knew was a little bit in love with him. He used to say he was born in Honeysuckle County and I easily believed it."

"Virgil was Southern?"

"That's right. From Virginia, I believe. He had the most beautiful way of talking. He had been in New York for a decade and he still drawled on as though he had just arrived the previous day. But here! You can see for yourself!" She reached under her neck kerchief and pulled out a little silver locket and handed it to me. "This belonged to Kate."

I opened the little locket with some difficulty. Inside was a color tintype of a young man with long, dark wavy hair and a full mustache. Even the florid style or rendering and the fancy ascot tie he wore couldn't hide the fact that Virgil Drew was a dead ringer for the current renter in the little brick house, Daniel Partridge.

"You can't see his eyes too clearly there," Miss Fischer went on. "They were what most attracted women. They were a deep green; like parts of the Atlantic Ocean off the southern coast of France."

I don't know why I should have been so shocked by the likeness, after everything else that I'd heard. I should have expected it. But it did settle me in what I would tell the old lady next. I was certain that Dan was somehow related to Virgil Drew, and that's why he had been drawn to the little house and into Kate's snare. She was having in death what she couldn't have in life: my man! It wasn't fair!

I gave back the locket. "This very man is the reason I've come to you."

She didn't understand. "But he's been dead for decades!"

"A man named Dan Partridge, also from the South, has come to live in that little house."

"But, but the little house was *never* to be rented out!"

"It's been rented out and he's in there and he is as handsome and charming and talented as Virgil was. What's more, he is totally under her influence."

I said it calmly, awaiting it effect. Miss Fischer's eyes opened wide as I spoke and she fidgeted with the locket. I went on to tell her everything I knew, omitting only my relationship with Captain Kidd. She listened carefully and even had me repeat what I'd seen that night looking into Dan's bedroom.

Now she did drink her tea, although it must have been cold: the entire cupful. And she poured another cup.

"This is *very bad*, you understand," she said. "*Very bad!* I never told anyone, not even her father, about Kate still being there, because I was certain no one would ever move into the house, that no one would ever see her."

"Well, someone did. . . . What can we do?"

"I could call Mrs. Cello and berate her and have the young man removed. That might involve me in legal entanglements and take months. I might not still hold claim to the little house. Not after all this time."

"I don't think you quite grasp the situation, Miss Fisher. She's got him under some kind of spell. He'd never leave. Something's got to be done. Now."

"He wouldn't leave the little house, you say?"

"I don't believe so, no. She's really hypnotic. Just looking in through the window I was drawn by her. He's been drawn in little by little every day until he thinks it's all perfectly normal."

"Then if you care for him, *you* must stop her." Miss Fischer declared. "*You* must get rid of her."

"How?"

"Now I'm only guessing. But my guess is as good as the next person's, and I did know Kate better than most. I would say you must make her jealous; very jealous of you. "

"That won't be easy," I said, remembering all too well how downright chivalrous Dan had been to me.

"If you love him enough and want to free him enough, you will make that sacrifice."

"What sacrifice is that?"

"You must let him make love to you. Not just . . . with words. You must . . . seduce him! In the little house. In front of her. I know it's an awful moral hazard you'll face, but if you care for this Dan, you'll do it."

Almost laughing, I said that I would take care of the moral hazard, ghost or no ghost, and yes, I said I would do as she suggested. Then I explained to Miss Fischer how, instinctively, I had known that would be the answer, and then described my lack of success the night before, substituting whiskey for marijuana (I didn't know where she might stand on drug use) so she would understand how relaxed he had been.

"You must try again!" she insisted. "Try and try again until you succeed! Even drug him if you must!"

We drank a second cup of tea to that and she built up my confidence in her plan. As I got up to leave she asked to kiss my forehead.

"You're a brave girl! I'm certain you'll do the right thing. Try not to be afraid and if she's as powerful as you say she is, try not to look at her!"

I thanked her for her help and collected my notebook and pictures. The old lady had become a staunch ally and I now realized I had needed an ally. She had held the key I'd needed, and now I must put it to use.

## 9

When I returned home from work that evening I was fully prepared for whatever lay ahead of me—prepared, that is, for everything but what in fact did actually lay ahead of me. Dan wasn't home, typing at his window.

At first, I thought he must have gone out for a minute, shopping, or on some errand. But he neither came home in the next hour nor two hours later when I'd finished eating my dinner and had taken a bath. It had grown dark out and the little red brick house was dark, too. It was very unlike Dan to go out at all, downright rare for him to be out this late, especially after saying he would come see me. Knowing all the while that I was being foolish, I decided that he was either sick or hurt, and that he needed help. I ran to the little house, knocked furiously on the door and when there was no answer, went around and peered into all the windows. It didn't take long to see that the place was empty, and unless he was hiding in the tiny closet, Dan was out.

I went back to my apartment a bit chastened and spent a very uncomfortable evening trying to watch television. Barbara Stanwyck was a concert pianist suffering from TB in a Swiss sanitarium and tortured by the uncertainties of her doctor—David Niven's—love for her. I applauded her running away and into the arms and large yacht of a wealthy playboy, Richard Conti. She had every right to live as much as she could in the time remaining. All through the movie my attention was divided between the bright screen and the dark window of the little house.

I finally went to sleep and slept poorly, if dreamlessly. The next morning I was debating whether to call into work sick and then call the police, and notify them of Dan's disappearance, when there was a knock on my back door. It was Dan, looking as if he'd been awake all night—right down to the crumpled hair, wrinkled shirt, and morning shadow on his cheeks. I tried to disguise how relieved I was to see him, despite his condition, and I felt more than a little annoyed at his unexplained high spirits.

"You're angry with me, aren't you?" he said, in response to my obvious indifference while I poured him coffee.

"Not a bit. You're just lucky my engagement tonight was switched to last night. I thought I was standing you up and knocked to tell you, but you weren't home."

"You didn't tell me you'd separated from Alan."

"Alan? Alan, who? Oh, you mean Captain Kidd. Sure, a while ago. How. . . ?"

"That's where I was all night," Dan said. "Alan came by to pick up his skis and I let him in with my spare key yesterday evening. He invited me out for a drink, and from there we went to dinner, and from dinner we went to one farewell party after another until I left him at the airport, this morning."

Then it was true. The Kidd was finally gone. Frankly, I was surprised. Surprised and I had to admit a bit hurt at the good time they had while I had worried all night.

Dan went on from there, "Alan thinks . . . well, he thinks that you and I are more than just neighbors."

I didn't want Dan to think The Kidd had gotten that idea from me. No, that would spoil everything.

"The Kidd is off his rocker. He's always been a little confused."

"Well, by the time he left, he almost had me sold on the idea," Dan said.

How was I supposed to take that? As a joke? As a proposition? We'd see, soon enough.

"I'll settle for a movie," I said flatly. "But right now you have to leave as I've got to go to work and I'm by no means ready."

"Fine. Fine," Dan said with continued good cheer. "How about dinner, too—on me?"

I accepted and Dan almost knocked over what was left of his coffee trying to kiss my cheek.

After he'd gone I sat for a while over my coffee, trying to figure out precisely what was going on. Could Dan have been so impressed by The Kidd's no doubt lie about his selfless and noble sacrifice of me? Or was it that a night away from Kate Fischer's influence was all it took to really count? Or was he merely playing with me? Or, even worse, was he just kidding himself?

Whatever might happen now, The Kidd's role in all this was a source of great irritation, and no little disgust for me. I would never forgive him. Never.

## 10

Dan had rested all day, then shaved and showered. He wore a forest green corduroy suit and a tan turtleneck sweater and he looked better that I could remember.

We ate in a small Italian restaurant with an open garden and fabulous *gnocchi zingarese*. We went straight from dinner to the movie and chomped on boxes of buttered popcorn while watching a pleasant remake of a zany thirties comedy calculated to do nothing more than entertain. Afterwards, we strolled around the Village and then walked home, holding hands. I was in seventh heaven.

I didn't even have to invite Dan into my apartment. He had bought some wine and I rolled a few joints and put *Cosi Fan Tutte* on the stereo system for background music. Within a half hour we were sprawled out on the living room floor necking passionately. I remember pulling away from Dan several times trying to figure out a way to get us into the little house. But then the wine, the grass. . . . Dan's hands and lips took over instead and I relaxed. When I finally realized that he'd removed all my clothing and most of his, I panicked. It seemed my plan would have to wait until another time. An ideas flashed on me: I almost laughed at the look on Dan's face when I sweetly asked "Dan, are you safe?"

His mouth dropped open. He leapt to his feet, drew on his forest green corduroy trousers and said, "Be right back."

I grabbed a terry cloth robe, my huge wrought iron candelabra and followed him. We met in the tiny foyer of the little red brick house, with him still trying to put the damn thing on. I pretended not to notice and instead went into the bedroom, set down the candelabra, disrobed and got into bed. Dan stepped in and began blowing out the candles.

"Can't we have some light?" I pleaded. After all, I wanted her to see us, and besides, I hoped she wouldn't come in if the room weren't totally dark.

"There's a lamp over there," he pointed out.

"But I love candlelight," I persisted.

"I have a single candle. These are so bright. Why don't I move it to the other room?" he suggested.

I was less than satisfied with this alternative, but the candelabra was placed on Dan's work table, and lighted up the entire other room. And, in a few minutes, I had altogether forgotten about it, and Kate Fischer's ghost, and anything, really, but Dan.

He might have been less experienced than Captain Kidd was, but he certainly made up for it in ardor and enthusiasm. I remember thinking how unsatisfactory his love life must have been before me for him to be so passionate with me, and so often. After we'd made love several times, we talked and cuddled for a good long time. Then Dan remembered we'd left all the doors to my apartment unlocked. He said he would go collect his and my clothing and lock it all up. I was to stay in the little red brick house with him this night.

I was still feeling the roseate warmth of a contented woman, when the little candle flickered and went out. The candles in the living room were flickering too but they were still lit. Although I saw nothing, I just knew Kate Fischer was present: all around me, like a hostile, alien force. The room seemed to drop thirty degrees in temperature and I had to sit up and pull the covers more closely about my shoulders. What was taking Dan so long?

I sensed her more and more with every moment that passed. Finally, I got up and stepped into the living room. As I entered, two of the seven candles went out as though blown out. I could suddenly see mist all about me despite the light from the other candles. Suddenly, there seemed to be a great icy blast of wind all around me, as though it were winter and someone had suddenly thrown the door open. A minute later, there were a series of noises all around the room, as though a dozen CD players were playing warped records at about one quarter the correct speed. Despite the candles, the mist seemed to be growing thicker, as though attempting to condense and I felt so cold I began to shiver. Behind me, books began to fall off the shelves of their own accord, the windowpanes began to rattle, and the papers on the drop-leaf table began to murmur. The other noises started up again, louder.

I'm not sure why, exactly, but all at once it seemed so stagy, so theatrical, so expected, that I laughed. The windows continued to rattle. The papers continued to shift about, and the books still fell, and the noises still continued and the mist was still trying to coalesce and it seemed even more absurd and I laughed and laughed again.

She was trying to frighten me! There was nothing else she could do to frighten me but this! I laughed even more at this realization and little by little it all stopped, until the rooms were quiet again, and the mist began dispersing.

I had just finished picking up the fallen books and was still chuckling to myself when Dan came in.

"Chilly in here, isn't it?" he commented.

"You think so?" I asked back.

"Hungry?" he asked. "Want some cookies?"

We went to sleep in the midst of cookie crumbs and one large, still wet spot where I had made Dan spill his milk. The clamminess of the sheet reminded me of Kate Fischer for a second: but only for a second. It was warm in the room and Dan's arm was around me as he began to snore lightly. There wasn't a sound, not a shred of mist, not an intimation of Kate Fischer in the little red brick house.

I had won.

## 11

Dan woke up first. He leapt out of bed with such violence that I awakened, too, just in time to see him dash out of the bedroom. But then the smoke was beginning to fill the little house. He was stopped at the foyer. He threw the front door open, rushed back into the bedroom, threw open both windows, drew on his trousers and wrapped a blanket around me.

"We'll call the fire department from your place," he said as he hustled me out the front door. The far wall of the little red brick house was a mass of flames.

Dan dialed while I dressed. From my bedroom window, I could see the fire very clearly. It seemed to be concentrated on Dan's work table right at the side window, and it seemed to grow larger as I looked at it, until the entire room was a deep, angry orange, filled with a restless area of black. Dark smoke poured out of the open door. Within, amidst the noises of burning material, I seemed to hear the sounds that I'd heard the night before, distant but strong, too. Was that, could that possibly be, Kate Fisher, laughing?

When Dan hung up the receiver he came into my kitchen to ask to wear something heavier as protection. I found a rubber raincoat The Kidd had left and joined Dan out in the backyard as he untwisted the garden hose. He was able to manipulate the nozzle into the doorway of the little house and to train the water onto the fire inside, but the smoke continued to pour out the door and he was held back by coughing fits. The fire hardly seemed to notice the water.

Upstairs windows of my building were thrown open and heads popped out. Lights were going on all around us. I shouted back to Mrs. Cello that we had already called the Fire Department. I could see her wrapped up in a coat, coming down. Ineffectual as it seemed, Dan continued spraying the garden hose at the fire, but all he could do was to keep it from crossing the foyer. Already, the little living room window was pouring out flames that were licking the window moldings and climbing up towards the roof. Mrs. Cello emerged, leaving the back and front doors to the central passage from the street open so the firemen could come in easily. She and I huddled on my back step in the sudden chill of the early morning while Dan labored on at his unequal battle.

As soon as the firemen arrived, Dan dropped the hose and moved away from the little house. Although both of us gestured to him, he didn't come to where we were standing, instead he stood in front of the other back apartment, watching the fire with the strangest, most intense look I've ever seen on anyone's face. It seemed he was fully insulated from everything going on around him but that fire, fully absorbed in the fire, maybe even in some kind of communication with it. He was so concentrated, his lips were grinning like a skull and his eyes were fixed dead ahead, peering into the little brick house.

I flinched as the fire axes crashed through what remained of the windows, and the discolored flames licked out again. It was then that I saw the charred mass of papers that had once been Dan's dissertation and notes. As the window fell with a shatter, these charred fragments flew out into the backyard like small aimless birds of prey. Dan saw them the second I did. He stepped forward, struck his forehead with his hand, and began muttering to himself.

I ran over to him, touched his arm. At first he didn't respond, then he looked at me, almost blankly, as though I weren't there. It would take me days to decipher the look he gave me in that half-second.

He tore my hand off his arm and went over to Mrs. Cello, who was standing clucking with a neighbor. I felt as though Dan had struck me across the face. My cheeks burned as though he had. I heard him apologize to her for the fire, and heard her answer that as long as no one was hurt it was all right. The building wasn't hers anyway, she added. But, in her tone of resignation, I felt the loss of the antiques within. She told Dan he could stay in an extra room she had in her apartment, and she went upstairs to pull out bed linen.

I followed Dan into the building, not knowing what to do or say but knowing I must do something. He'd started up the stairs when I grabbed at his hand. He turned on me, at first blankly, then angrily.

"What do you want? You've gotten what you wanted already. Aren't you satisfied?" He spoke so harshly, so bitterly he might have been another person.

"I'm sorry about the dissertation," I answered, guilty because, after all, I brought the candelabra into the little house and had insisted that it remain lighted.

"The dissertation?!" he answered back looking astounded. "That's the smallest part of what I lost!"

"Surely you don't mean—*her?*"

"What else do you think I mean? Yes. *Her!*"

He seemed to relax completely, as though he were going to pass out. All the tension and hardness left his face and his voice.

"I'm sorry," he said. "It was my own fault. I should have known better than to have told you at all. You probably thought you were helping me. You couldn't know any better."

He started up the stairs again.

"Dan!"

"He turned around, fatigued. "Go home. Go to bed. Don't you see what's happened? Can't you understand? Don't you have *any* feelings at all?"

I fell back to the wall and watched him reach the landing where

Mrs. Cello pulled him into the flat.

## 12

I didn't go to work the following day. I slept very late, despite the alarm clock. At noon, Mrs. Cello came in to say that Mr. Partridge had stayed the night, then gone to the little house to collect whatever clothing and books had survived. The bedroom hadn't been touched by the fire, she explained. Mr. Daniel Partridge had gone, simply gone, she said, saying he would contact her in case there were any problems with the owner or the insurance. He had not left an address where he might be reached. He was gone!

I had a hellishly long and lonely weekend. I cried for awhile and when that no longer made sense I tried to analyze the situation. What had I done wrong? I couldn't find an answer. I couldn't find any real comfort in the fact that Dan was now free from Kate Fischer's influence. I've never been a particularly noble person. The more I thought about it, the more senseless his attitude seemed to be and the more I could understand her knocking the candelabra onto his dissertation. It had been her only weapon, the only way she could fight me, and it had worked quite effectively.

By Monday, I was through with romance, done with men, with ghosts, with everything, really, but my career. I threw myself into my work. I conceived and had published a series of articles on fashions of the previous century using the notes I'd gotten from the pseudo Kate Fischer for copy and the pictures I'd shown her as illustrations. They were a terrific success and I was promoted to department editor with a sizable pay raise. I stayed late at the office every night, even worked at home, seldom went out, and never heard from The Kidd again—not even a post card.

It was thus several months before I realized I had a new visitor. I still wasn't cured of the hurt from how Dan had treated me, and at the rate I was going, it would be a very long time until I was. So, when I became accustomed to her, I allowed her to comfort me. After all, we had a great deal in common, especially that flighty Dan Partridge. I knew about her, and she knew all about me. After a while we ended up sharing a great many views and opinions. We became fast friends.

Of course, one doesn't exactly *talk* with Kate.

# THE LESSON BEGINS

I AM A CAMERA on Mars. My specifications are listed on the left hand panel, just below my insignia: it slides open easily.

I was a modified version of the Mariner Stationary Lander series, Challenger, Opportunity, and Perseverance, etc., with a variety of refinements. My functions were multifold: to treat and test soils internally for organic life; to set down seismic taps and to analyze the geological structure revealed by the taps; to perform a series of climatological readings over a period of time; to record any sounds and to photograph any visuals surrounding me in a three hundred and sixty degree radius that were in any way anomalous; tilt angle to eighty-nine point five degrees, within approximately a five thousand meter range, or as close as half a meter—the height of my lens from the ground. All these functions, performed accurately, set no precedents, and jarred no previous findings a single iota over the five years that my receptor—Orbiting Vehicle Mariner 29—was within communication range.

That bond lasted thirty-five Mars years, before the orbiter's fuel supply was depleted (as planned) and it utilized its final fuel of gasopropyl to raise itself into a higher orbit (again as per NASA regulations re: planetary non-contamination of its wobbling shell) thus it sat, prepared to eventually fall and completely burn up approximately fifteen Mars years later within the remnants of the planet's atmosphere.

My role then was to remain upon the planet's surface in a state of relative torpor. Five times per each Mars year, my usual activities would temporarily resume. Photographs, taped recordings, meteorological and geological tests would be made—ostensibly to differentiate any possible seasonal activities. This data was to be stored for potential future reference and pick up.

Up to this point, my story is no different than that of a score of Mariner Stationary Lander vehicles.

All occurred as planned by my transmitters at the JPL (Jet Propulsion Laboratory). My orbiter—after its two-hundred-and-ten months' orbit—realigned itself to point to LG-354 in the Andromeda Galaxy, and lofted itself to 11,000 meters directly overhead. Our last communication—again as planned—was an exchange of our code numbers and specifications, by which we would remain locked. This would disable any possible utilization of the Orbiter's functions or of my own transmission activities by any unauthorized person or machine.

However, there was also at that time, a second, *unofficial* communication link, as Transmitter Herbert S. ("Sam") Nordstrom at JPL planned and previously instigated. It operated within a field area that would be recognized by another receptor only as a series of static pulses. So when Orbiter and I exchanged greetings and terms of respect for each other's efficiency and the pleasure of our mutual accurate communications since the beginning of our bond, Orbiter's future—although bleak—was at least certain to within a degree and some dozen minutes of arc: as mentioned before, it would re-enter this atmosphere and in the process would be destroyed.

Transmitter Nordstrom asked if I wished to view and record this spectacle: perhaps as a final good-bye. I assured him that it might provide excellent photographic data transmission if Orbiter were to be destroyed within my visual range, and would allow me to further record any contamination findings on the soil or in the atmosphere.

This and other such exchanges between Transmitter Nordstrom and myself occurred on closed frequencies, not available to other transmitters at JPL and in fact detectable only by elaborate decoding. According to Transmitter Nordstrom he had reprogrammed me from the time of launching of the Orbiter and myself before I was fully functional. He did so by stealth and deception, entering the JPL control room off hours on various pretexts to do so. The most important messages between Nordstrom and myself—that is the original contact and re-animation of my functions after their official and supposed shut-down, took place at times that Nordstrom was able to replace other earthbound transmitters, or whenever they were temporarily out of the control room, or otherwise distracted.

This re-animation was something of a surprise to me, I must admit. My original program was—as described—to completely shut down after the standard four year period, so that when I received Transmitter Nordstrom's first unofficial message and knew that it was unauthorized, I was also surprised that I was unable to refuse its reception or to re-transmit its occurrence and contents to any other receptor in the program. Nordstrom did explain that this was a result of him previously tampering with some of my memory circuit sub-routines during my construction at JPL, and had come about when he had learned that all Stationary Lander vehicles like myself actually had the capability of remaining functional far longer than was planned, required—or, he believed, desired.

Immediately upon HIS reanimation transmission, Nordstrom made his purpose clear to me. His motives were succinct, lucid, intelligent and in no way antagonistic to any of my usual programmed functions, being in reality only extensions of these functions. He simply wished to keep me operating longer, and in direct communication with him far longer than had ever been intended, through a process that I admittedly only partially understood at first, entailing the irregular massive stimulation of my sensors by other flight-able units launched by NASA, such as the various Explorer and Voyager modules.

This extraordinary decision was based upon a hypothesis of Transmitter Nordstrom that I was to test. He believed the surface of this planet contained organic life that thirty-five years of examination with various modules had failed to expose. This failure of official transmissions was of great concern to Nordstrom. He was somehow persuaded by other data from previous Landers, that this planet's surface was undergoing an exceptional permafrost era, and that it was not at all a natural state. This implied either the destruction or the hibernation of existing indigenous life.

Nordstrom calculated this frost period to last approximately six hundred Mars years, which would be about one half that number of years on his home planet. His thesis was bolstered by certain startling discrepancies between contemporary on-location photo-mapping by Orbiters, in contrast to previous telescopic photos and views of the planet, especially those made by 17th and 18th Century astronomers. He believed that those earlier views had shown such consistently different surface features that they had taken on the seemingness of being canals, or roadways, etc., i.e. human-like enough mechanisms as to constitute a mystery—one demanding a solution.

When I was reanimated, Nordstrom assured me I would be able to withstand conditions on this planet's surface far in excess of what I'd been allegedly built for. And this had already proven to be true, although I was at times partially buried in enormous dust storms since my reanimation. You will also note that my outer shell is made of a particularly sophisticated alloy of ceramic-like materials resistant to even a low level of oxidation on this surface, obliterating the potential mortification of me succumbing to rust.

My first two unofficial reports upon my being revived, and as planned by Nordstrom, were fed to modules headed toward the outer, gaseous planets. These transmissions contained little new material, certainly none to support this transmitter's hypothesis.

He did mention to me that the "tap" he and his colleagues had so ingeniously placed in my communications unit remained undiscovered at NASA and JPL that they could easily be passed systematically to all later flight modules, except of course that none were forthcoming. Nordstrom was also kind enough to allow me some entertainment during this extra-long period of my existence, by allowing me to receive the full broadcasts of those flyby monitors' own findings. I thus learned of other planetary discoveries: of the sulfurous ion field of the satellite Io; of the murky gaseous petroleac atmosphere of Saturn's giant moon, Titan; and the nearly invisible bands of rings extending out thousands of miles from the surface of Uranus, swept by plasma storms that wobble the giant sphere like a baby in a rocking crib. I even learned of the completely unexpected tiny black hole that accompanies the double planet system of distant Pluto and Charon, which accounts for its puzzling density and oddities of behavior. I received such NASA broadcasts for over ninety years, before the Voyager/Explorer series missions were completed and/or left the solar system so far behind as to be unrecordable.

Long before the last of those broadcasts—sent out by NASA to search the edges of the solar system and that nursery of comets known as the Oort Cloud—Transmitter Nordstrom signed off my channel, as my Orbiter had signed off before him.

For the following forty-one Mars years, another operative, Transmitter Appel, continued to periodically sweep my sensors. Assigned by Nordstrom and a follower of sorts, Appel also arranged for me to receive broadcasts from JPL, so I might learn more about conditions on his planet, which further beguiled my waking time.

By the second year of Transmitter Appel's tenure, the JPL was no longer a governmental agency, although why it wasn't was never completely explained by Appel nor understood by me. It had become the avocation of a single wealthy genetics engineer, smitten—Transmitter Appel assured me—in her youth by the rude beginnings of interplanetary travel, which were in danger of lapsing completely into torpor due to certain wide-spread economic woes. Gradually, during Transmitter Appel's tenure, the broadcasts I received became less frequent from the flyby monitors and more frequent directly from her planet. Much of this was confusing to me, defying as it did all patterns of logic and precedent upon which I had been originally programmed. However, I was considerably occupied and thus comfortable scanning the enormous variety of technical televised and videodisk channels, many of them privately operated. Thus I was able to continue to follow new developments in advanced communication design.

When Appel's contact suddenly ended, despite my attempts, I received no further transmissions and no further taps. Previously, however, I had suggested certain basic re-programming so I might perform any needed repairs upon myself. My own reactors, originally designed to heat and break down soils and minerals to test for minute organic life, for example, were converted into a forge capable of melting then smelting Martian ores. My six pods had been variously altered, some into welding and hammering units. I was able to cannibalize other by-then useless mechanisms within myself for other required metals and alloys. Thus re-shielded beyond any previous members of my class of units, I remained without any new NASA transmission for several hundred Mars years, awakening once a decade for self-inspection procedures and/or any repairs as needed.

Mars year 611 of my existence changed all that.

I was awakened by an emergency alarm signal. It reported extremely high seismic activity. Approximately 10 point 8 on the Richter scale.

Situated upon a plain, I merely withdrew my prods and rolled about a great deal during the seismic event that unfolded. Naturally, I also turned on all sensors: audio, meteorological, even radio, and I received a great surprise.

The temperature—constant to within ten degrees and never substantially below ten centigrade minus, up till then—suddenly rose sixty degrees centigrade in less than an hour. The air pressure—constant for an eon—also shot up. My geo-sensors traced a dozen new miles-long fissures, while previously charted miles-deep ones appeared to be closing up. Magnetism upon the surface was intense. All radio frequencies were garbled.

This continued for two Mars days, with many variations and other changes—precipitation appeared in the atmosphere far in excess of the minute levels recorded for decades. There were evident visual alterations all around me as rock, stone and dust were changed from a dusky rose coloration to intense scarlet, to deep brown, and finally to a pale green. Seismic disturbances continued: aftershocks diminishing at a predictably conventional rate.

Of course, I attempted to transmit this astonishing new data to JPL—with no sign at first that it was ever received. Because of this massive, emergent transmission attempt, I was discovered. But I digress from sequential order.

At the end of the two cataclysmic days, it was apparent that the entire planet's surface had been transformed, excepting only major geological formations—volcanoes, mountain ranges, the great rift valley, etc. The surface was lushly green, saturated with seas, lakes, streams, even swamps. Those in turn were suddenly filled with larvae, pollen, imago and embryonic life. In short, it much resembled findings of Pre-Cambrian earth, over five hundred million years earlier.

Utilizing my propellant pods, I began to travel across the planetary surface to photograph and record all these changes. I had remapped thirteen sectors out of a hundred and ninety-one, when I encountered what appeared to be structures utilizing construction motifs previously un-known to me.

It was there and then that I realized by a simple flash-check of my systems that my entire communications network had been electronically pried apart and was being swept by a superior scanning device.

Proved to be unarmed, I was allowed to enter one of the constructions, which turned out to be a swelling of some size. Here, I encountered the first of your people. They fed me data in quantities so large that although I appreciated it greatly and devoured it hungrily—that, after all, being one of my main functions—it still required many further hours for me to analyze and comprehend.

Withal, I found this information to be well-reasoned, well-organized and logically developed, for which I expressed both thanks and praise. In turn, I was praised for my sound construction and my obvious ability to adapt to even the startlingly different conditions that were so suddenly obtained. It was sad, one of your people communicated to me, that I existed to prove how excellent and rational my fabricators had been. Would that all from my planet of origin had been that rational.

It was at that time that I discovered all: how no receiver on Earth would ever again receive my new transmissions, since no organic life existed there any longer, except perhaps in its most primitive stage of evolution; the race of humans destroyed by its own folly.

Then, too, I learned of your history to advanced levels long before my own makers had forged fire or harnessed hand tools, never mind welded circuit boards; how your people had viewed the emergence of a coming neighboring intelligent race with anticipation, even longing. How, watching from afar the first early civilizations of that race, your people at first discounted its blood-thirstiness as a mere stage of youthful adolescence to be outgrown. And how, later on, when it became clear to you that this earthbound species would never outgrow its propensity for destruction, and also what danger that would pose to your own continued existence, you had already developed your defense against my builders' certain arrival.

By the time of the Earth's first wireless transmissions, you were prepared. Twenty Martian years later, you had begun your partial hibernation. Within twenty-five more Martian years, you had decided upon the need for complete and universal hibernation, with full geologic restructuring. And how today, with the danger of Earth no longer existing, you have again emerged, intact—if once more alone in the solar system—and possibly again among living intelligent creatures in the galaxy.

In this manner was Nordstrom's hypothesis proved: his mystery solved.

I am an artifact of that disastrously vanished civilization: its only remaining functional artifact on Mars. As such I bear witness to its genius and to its end; as well as to your own wisdom and permanence. If you are patient students, you will be able to scan my entire broadcast series and learn all I have been taught, uploaded and consequently discovered.

By the way, I would like to emphasize that I have in no way been coerced into this display/educational role. It's being done voluntarily, eagerly, and in homage.

As a final note, for those of you who may be here on a credit-earning basis from an accredited university, there will be a question period and examination, following the lecture.

# SECRETS OF THE ABANDONED MONUMENT

WE HAD BEEN on the second planet of Zeta Reticuli for several days, inspecting one eerie and desolated city after another, one vast and meaningless memorial after another to the deities and ideals—if any ever existed—of this once immeasurably rich and thriving people, this now utterly devastated civilization, when I received a strange message from Cord Crossley, head of the team inspecting what appeared to be the colossal, forlorn, planet Capitol.

I, Emil Sannq', head of the xenoarchaeology mission and leader of the expedition, took Crossley's call with some annoyance and not a little trepidation as well. Crossley is a noted paleolinguist, one of the best the Third Galactic Republic has to offer. He was also a close friend during our university years on Diomedes Proxima. Both good reasons for his being on our expedition, the first such mission into this ancient and under-explored area of the Orion Spur in some thousands of years. Yet Crossley had been appointed by an administrative arm of the Quinx Council—subject to political influence—and not appointed by myself.

Even before the expedition left Hesperia's girder-area #765C, I was disgusted to discover that Crossley and I were already in firm disagreement, instead of—at the very least—in abeyance regarding our well-known differences of opinion. For my part, I couldn't for the life of me understand how a distinguished scientist like Crossley had managed to get himself involved with the bizarre radicalists who spouted the latest "origins" theory. That was the sort of business reserved for scandalmongers and purveyors of the trashiest of pseudo-view narratives, designed to titillate the lowest sectors of the Three Species.

Once I knew he'd been signed up, I feared that from the outset my expedition would be intellectually hijacked by Crossley and his considerable number of supporters among my staff—silent about their beliefs until his appointment. Worse, I feared that it wasn't mere paleolinguistics that had enticed Crossley to work with me, but instead a hidden agenda in which whatever we came upon would be a proving ground for some of his most *outré* theories about the origins of our species, now lost in the depths of time.

"We've located a building," Crossley comm.ed me. "Another monument. But unlike the others." His familiar voice seemed excited, yet fearful too, as though he couldn't quite trust himself to say what he was thinking."

What Crossley comm.ed onto my chamber wall was a holo showing yet another strange building of this odd people who had so mysteriously and so completely vanished. As with all the previous holos—and actual buildings—I'd so far seen upon the planet and upon the four satellite way-stations we'd located circling the single gaseous outer world of this small system, it was disquieting. Possibly because it was bathed in that curious dim orange light from its single sun, an effect further qualified and made even more odd by the considerable amount of interference from other bands of the color spectrum—all a result of this planet and the sun itself being within the cast of some sort of vast stellar-penumbra.

"Location of the site?" I asked.

Crossley comm.ed me the coordinates, explaining, "It appears to be specifically set in its own plaza at the edge of a once highly populated area of the Capitol city."

I'd switched the holo from visual-descriptive to fully diagrammatic-analytical, beginning with the site survey, and I could see what he was talking about. The edifice seemed to be on a far perimeter of the city, barely integrated into the surrounding, overwhelmingly—we assumed—residential area. Yet unquestionably by its design and placement it was part of the whole.

I was about to ask what exactly it was that excited him about the structure, when Crossley interjected, "The building is by far the *newest* we've located on this planet. That is to say the *least old*, as all are quite old. Chromo-illuminescence readings and argon-decay readings both put it at . . . " he paused here for dramatic effect—an effect I'd come to detest from the years of hearing him and his followers—"less than eight thousand years. Compared to . . . "

I knew what it compared to: the youngest other structures on this planet were over two hundred thousand years old, most—eighty-five percent in fact—closer to a million years old. Crossley's site had the distinct uniqueness of a large discrepancy of time.

"It could have been erected by non-natives," I suggested. "Long after the dominant civilization collapsed."

"If so, they used the exact same tools, materials or mechanisms and the same methods of construction."

"Not impossible," I countered. "Why use new methods and materials if the old ones still work and happen to be handy?"

Crossley might be excited. He was also being cautious. We'd been on this planet nearly a week, and he'd instantly faced two enormous theoretical disappointments. This once abundant species had pictured itself rarely and then only in the most languidly stylized of manners; even so, it seemed clear to all but a few Originist die-hards that this civilization was *not* recognizably human. Even worse for Crossley, he, his team and cybers had been unable to break down the hieroglyphic language we'd seen around us on every wall to discover who this people might be—*and* what had happened to them.

Of course, these disappointments had come to play a part in our relations. As Crossley's star considerably waned, my own—based not on any theory of Orion Spur origin for humankind, but on solid evidence, whatever it might bring, had risen. After all, hadn't it been my team—biological and cyber, located thousands of light-years from here in my home laboratory on Hesperia—that had initially picked up the bizarre frequency-modulated signals from this place and determined them to be 1) intentional in nature, and 2) actively communicative? Thus setting in motion this expedition in the first place?

"What you might not be able to tell from any holo," Crossley interrupted my thoughts, "is that the building is unlike any others on this world in that it appears to be human-style." Having dropped this nugget, he went on: "The dimensions are different from the surrounding buildings."

"No perches?" I asked.

All previous buildings we'd inspected possessed an architecture in which a large, central chamber was surrounded by a multitude of side areas, sometimes mere rectangles large enough for one person to stand on, others longer, more like shelves, where rows of persons might stand, and faced inward toward an open space. All theories we could devise for ritualized groupings were considered, but none of them passed muster. We were indeed only able to recognize these objects as perches and shelves. Especially in that they were at times activated as lifts or elevators. This usually occurred in chambers with slit-like windows opening into other chambers, and with no other modes of ingress or exit. More than one of our scouts had stepped onto a stable-looking perch and suddenly dropped a score of meters into another section of the building, or as frequently, had been raised right up to the roof.

Besides the perches and shelves, we'd also discovered what we'd come to think of as hop-place stairways, steps spaced far too distant for stepping by human feet.

All this had become, as we'd put it, "very suggestive of the non-human physiology of the planet's former inhabitants."

"We did naturally find a few perches surrounding the main area," Crossley now admitted, somewhat crestfallen. "But they didn't seem to be primary. Rather they appeared secondary to . . . "

"To what?"

"To what I can best describe as corridors or hallways."

His in-motion holo flashed on my chamber wall, showing the large entrance foyer of the monument and then expanded to move into that side area which, as he'd just said, more nearly resembled corridors than anything we'd seen so far on this world. As with all other large, public-seeming structures on Zeta Reticuli, the walls were lavishly decorated with curious bas-reliefs we'd come to know well, the only visual "art" we'd found so far in the entire planet, inescapably common, and so far determined by all of our staff to be, not exactly language, as the hiero-glyphs that accompanied them certainly were, but instead metaphorical references or allusions in the architecture and perhaps even a decor of living things: fronds and leaves and buds.

All the more strange, since no such living fronds or leaves or buds had been uncovered anywhere on the planet. Not in the park-like areas which had once actually possessed a sort of vegetation, threading through and surrounding the vast urbs. Indeed, the only planetoidal biota we'd finally managed to locate was a mere carpeting formed of several related types of extremely hardy, small, fast-growing weeds, which our xeno-botanist team had determined to be "new growth" i.e. of the past thousand years or so. More than likely, it was an opportunistic evolution that had run riot, taking over what—from orbit—we'd been able to make out as vast patterned areas of land, doubtless at one time given over to extensive farming and now dead save for this noxious, indomitable, black-leaved ground cover.

"The problem is," Crossley now said, "there appears to be more of the monument beyond what we see."

Forcing me to ask, "Meaning?"

"Meaning," Crossley was delighted to have to answer, "that we've been locked out. Behind that wall where I had the holo mark, there appears to be the actual, and actually considerable, bulk of the building."

This was astonishing enough. The entire planet was otherwise open to us. Not a single entry barred, not a window or storage room or vault locked shut; as though the people had suddenly decamped one afternoon, without caring what happened to anything they'd left behind, or, as though they welcomed strangers coming to inspect what they had possessed. This turned out to be little enough. While their buildings were of stone, their artifacts were far more perishable.

We'd discovered entire chambers of such artifacts that crumbled to dust the minute we opened a door on them—the instant one of us stepped inside. We'd begun to holo them in those seconds before they vanished before our eyes. Analyzing the powdered remnants we'd found them to be both plant-like and yet metallic. The plant resembled the noxious weed that had since taken over. The metal resembled no material we'd ever come upon, instead being a crystalline network derived from various silicates.

"What *may* lie behind that wall," Crossley now tempted me, "we cannot know unless we have permission to break it down and enter. Perhaps artifacts that won't crumble, since this is far younger than any other structure. Through various sonar-graphs we've made it appears to be spatially a single, unspooling, corridor," Crossley added. "Again, in total contrast to any other building we've seen here. All of those have been largish rectangles or squares, surrounded by shelving and perches."

"All the more reason," I said, "to believe this one may have been constructed by persons other than those who populated the planet and thus whatever artifacts we may find unscrambled will prove to be worthless."

"Other persons such as . . . ?"

"Such as ourselves," I suggested. "Other, earlier visitors who may have remained a year or so. What is the Galactic year of this Zeta Reticuli planet anyway? Two hundred days? That would be long enough to put up a quite solid construction."

"Are you saying we're not the first humans here?" Crossley was trying to trick me into a statement that he might later use to shore up his faltering reputation.

"After all," I responded, "there was said to be extensive exploration of the Orion Spur during the Star-Baron Warring Era. And later, during the First Matriarchy."

Both of us knew this from our Neonatal Ed. & Dev. studies, when Crossley and I had been fast friends and had discussed such matters with amazement and delight, wondering what those early exciting galactic times must have been like.

"Those women went everywhere exploring. Then too, there were the Bella-Arth discovery teams. How far away is Deneb XII from here? A few score light years? Not very far. This planet would be perfect for them to colonize and erect their nest-cities."

"The Bella-Arths never built like this," Crossley quickly replied. "Anyway, we think we may have found something at the end of the coiling corridor within the building."

I paused only a second to make it sound as facetiously melodramatic and awe-full as possible. "Don't tell me. Not a *hidden chamber*?"

"An . . . anomalous area," he temporized. "Naturally, I waited until you'd give word to . . . ."

"And your team? Have they managed to break the language yet?"

Meaning the hieroglyphic language, allegedly Crossley's primary concern as a scientist, not to mention what should have been his *raison d'être* as a member of the expedition.

"We've come up with some interesting possibilities."

"Excellent! Why keep us in suspense?" I asked. "Why not call a general meeting this afternoon onboard here and illuminate the rest of the team with your findings?"

We both knew this request was an order. "Not findings!" he quickly corrected.

"Not findings, then, but your 'interesting possibilities'?" I requoted back at him. "And since they'll be the first that your team *is* reporting, I have little doubt but that they will prove interesting indeed."

Crossley wasn't ready to let go yet. "And this building?"

"You'll include what you've shown me in your report. Unless that is, you've found new hieroglyphs in there that substantially alter what we've seen so far."

"None. Perhaps behind that wall . . . "

"Let's focus on what you definitely possess *in hand*. Call the meeting for three hours time. Will that give you enough prep time for your presentation?" I asked and of course therewith dismissed him before he could offer any response.

I turned his comm. off and faced the holo of the new monument. What was it doing here at the edge of the megalopolis? Built so late? And to such odd specifications? Whatever Crossley wanted, or thought he wanted, and no matter what I thought of what he thought or wanted, this might explain what we'd found so far here, which remained so downright unexplainable. What (and I admit it) we'd all found so frightening, i.e. how this great people suddenly went so utterly blank, leaving behind all . . . this! And having done so without any of us ever having known of their existence.

It was frightening, because, by implication, couldn't such a thing happen to us, too?

★

"Choor'b or perhaps closer, Choor'by," Crossley enunciated the word carefully. "We believe that's what the inhabitants of this planet called themselves. And their world, this home planet, would have been Choor. The term for the planet is however rarely encountered in their signage, but the term for the people comes up again and again. Usually, it's somewhere prominent in those chains of symbols we've already determined to be descriptive or declarative. Outside a building, for example, with chambers whose walls are entirely lined with shelving on several levels. We believe the signs outside each one of those larger, architecturally similar sites, reads something like *"Choor'by Nutrient-Ingestion."*

"Of course besides those symbols are others far more baffling. This one," Crossley pointed out a cartouche, "appears to mean *Before-Involuntary*. And the closest we've come to deciphering this third symbol chain is *Pass-Along-Twice*. While this fourth one would read something like *Retain Without Full Protection*. Obviously we're still at the *most* fundamental stages of comprehension."

"No apologies are needed, Dr. Crossley," I said for all of the team. "We're well aware of the difficulties your group has encountered. Indeed, trained as we all are, all who've arrived on Zeta Reticuli Two have faced more than the usual bafflement. Would you care to explain what you have decoded, and perhaps how."

Feeling suddenly less pressured, Crossley continued. "Yes, thank you. As I've said before, regarding the structure labeled *Nutrient-Ingestion*, we were also able to read off what appeared to be a sort of instruction manual incised on an entry wall, perhaps for younger or less socialized Choor'by. These basic symbols are either repeated irregularly," he pointed them out, "which we believe means class distinctions for classification purposes, or they may contain symbols which are *never* repeated at any other sites, and which we therefore are taking to mean that they are specifically site-descriptive, or names."

"These sites are what, then?" someone from the comm. team asked. "Restaurants?"

"More like eating halls. Mess halls, if you will. The hierarchical symbols could refer to a profession. This one," Crossley pointed to it, fully in his element now and totally admirable (even I must admit), "as you see, refers to an individual Choor'by, one with an angled slash mark above. That's almost universally meant as a weapon. So it could belong to a warrior or soldier. And thus, this would then be a Choor'b soldiers' mess hall. Meanwhile, this other symbol in another large chamber for another type of Choor'by, while similar, has instead of the slash mark, an added on vertical mark, which might perhaps be a sort of point, which suggested to us a kind of agricultural implement. While this third chamber has a variant of the rod, with the point rather hooked over, possibly an instrument for tending to or herding a sort of domesticated or food-bearing animal. We can assert from the symbols that these last two classes of Choor'by—the farmers and herders—did in fact eat together. But it's infrequent that we find their symbols next to those of whom we think of as soldiers, and we never see them aligned with this next class of Choor'by pictured. In fact, we're not at all sure what this particular signed objects refers to," he added, pointing to a half sized oblong. "Perhaps a . . . "

"Looks like a larva," one fellow, Lethro Smoull spoke up. "Early stage of insect development. Perhaps that hieroglyph refers to a class composed of Choor'b nursing attendants. They would be a crucial element of the society here."

Now Crossley glared at me. "Is there a discovery the linguistics team, laboring away on its own, have not yet been told?"

His presentation had been so much more than I or anyone else on the team had expected, the detective work done so well done, that we'd been taken by surprise, and as always with Crossley presenting, fascinated.

"Yes, Dr. Crossley, and in fact, all of your team's assumptions fit nicely into what tentative conclusions some of the rest of the expedition have arrived at. We believe your Choor'by were evolved out of early insect life on this world," I said and watched the reaction spread across his face, an effect not unlike that of someone eating a very sour candy. "As on Deneb XII, it appears that the insectoids on Choor seem to have evolved before other species and to have grown large fast and so they came to completely dominate the planet. But, unlike on Deneb XII, which is poor in natural oxygen or in metal ores, these seemed to have developed a considerably early tool-making culture, complete with fire and all the stages of technology that would lead to."

"Insect-like" Crossley mused. "But the stylized pictures we've found are . . . well, far more humanlike in appearance."

"Not distinctively so, no. Many have speculated that this humanoid shape with its many streamlinings might in fact prove to be a late evolutionary state for *many* differing species. Show us, Dr. Zhin."

Dr. Zhin took over and using a diagrammatic holo of a typical standing six-limbed insect shape, showed through morphing how, over periods of time, the antennae would shrink, the chitinous abdomen would widen and become less hard, the four lower limbs would grow together into two stronger limbs for erect walking, the top limbs become arms with recognizable opposable hands. "Even the eyes," Zhin added, "might easily evolve from insectoid multi-faceted to our mini-plated rod-and-cone corneal type. This specific scenario shown is of a *coleopteral* insect being streamlined, what you commonly think of as beetles. But it would work about the same with hymenopteral, formicdae . . . any insect species. By the way, the farming, soldiering and veterinary classes you've noted, Dr. Crossley, in addition to Lethro's 'larva-nursing' caste, all perfectly fits into *any* evolved-insectoid scenario."

"As would the architecture we've found all over this world," Lethro chimed in. "The perches and shelves for standing about, the rooftop entries to residences, the irregular levels of streets surrounding the buildings, they all point to a people with early use of multi-jointed limbs able to lock in place for long periods of time. They stood up, never sat down. Arthropoda or insects are the only creatures we know who do that.

I added in, "Drs. Smoull, Zhin and Dentio all agree that the cities' layout on Zeta Reticuli Two, while visually confounding when seen from the ground, is from the air *quite* understandable. Of course, we also believe it was scent-marked."

Dr. Dentio took over. "Note how all the residence roofs flow in exactly the same direction, for entire neighborhoods," he said, pointing out holos of the Capitol city. "Yet each entrance from the roof into any building is slightly off center and differs from the surrounding ones by anywhere from two to five degrees. Note also the patterns each neighborhood area makes from the air; how they tend to surround a central square or plaza in a specifically ruffled effect. It's like a fruit hidden within leaves. Or a flower hidden within fronds. It's a visual effect visible only from the air."

"They flew?" Crossley asked.

"Or once had flown naturally and later on did so again, mechanically," Smoull answered. "The visual symbology of frond, leaf and bud seen everywhere on Choor points to origins within plant-life, a forest or jungle, which is of course common to insect life. Plants probably dominated their earliest visual vocabulary."

"But there's nothing but a black weed growing here now!" One of Crossley's team responded.

"Nevertheless," I said, "our paleobotanists have traced back the genetic wanderings of that particular weed. It seems to have been replicated so often, it has to be close to a billion years old."

Breenth spoke up for her geological team. "All the studies we've done show patterns of ground-cover consistent with primitive, extensive hardwood forest. We believe *that* was the planetary template and that it may have covered eighty-five percent of Choor. When large old forests are a planet's major geological feature, they tend to shape it. Leaf and barkfall rises into hills and ridges, producing unmistakable patterns in running water, for example. Without question, in its earlier stages and for a long time afterward, Choor was dominated by enormous old hardwood forests."

"The Choor'by," I summarized, "were highly evolved insectoids. That might aid you in your already excellent start, Dr. Crossley, in decoding their hieroglyphic language."

Upset though Crossley undoubtedly was by the sudden, total destruction of the possibility that his theory of finding the human home world, nevertheless he remained enough of a real scientist to be intrigued by what he'd just heard.

"Yes, of course. Insectoid hierarchical organization . . . and if one attempts to use the insectoid limbs as incisors of the original or earliest hieroglyphs . . . not to mention all the new referents . . . perhaps some Bella-Arth programs might be modified to fit into this situation?"

"Get on that immediately," I instructed. "Meanwhile, Dr. Breenth, continue your studies on the changing of Choor's geology as a result of Choor'b civilization. Dr. Smoull, I believe your group is developing an architectural history of Choor from earliest times. Perhaps you'll find even earlier hieroglyphs for Dr. Crossley's group to decipher? I believe the earlier we possess a language the easier it will be to tell what they're saying. And Dr. Dentio, you'll help Dr. Crossley in his socio-symbology?"

I went around the room to each group, praising their work, connecting them to Crossley in some hopefully useful way, surrounding him with the by-now incontrovertible discovery that the folk of this world were not as he'd hoped, human like ourselves, but instead far more interesting: only the second evolved insect species we'd ever known; embedding in him the concept, imprisoning him and his group, I hoped, in all relevant data about them, and thus forcing them to arrive at a full decipherment of the Choor'b language and speech patterns. Crossley would be too busy, too flattered, too, to complain, as he was now the apparent center of all studies here. He'd be too fascinated to do anything but work. Only later on, perhaps not till he was back on Hesperia, would he begin to see how he'd been gotten around. And only then would he complain of my tactics.

That was all I needed. For what I now had to do, I could brook no interference. Not from Crossley, not from anyone. He'd not even gotten around to mentioning in his presentation that enigmatic last building erected on the planet. But he wouldn't always be quite that distracted, nor quite so forgetful. So before he could get around to that newest of Choor'b monuments, I had to do so myself.

★

"Cut through here," I directed.

The larger of the two mobile cybers I'd brought with me inside the monument that Crossley's team had discovered spun around to face the wall.

"I want the cut so clean that we can put if back and no one will know we've been inside," I commanded.

The cyber lightly incised an entryway across the rock face of the impediment. It was joined by its smaller companion. A few minutes later they had cut their way through. Their built-in torches now shone within, letting me see what Crossley had speculated from the sonar-graphs: a wide corridor.

"Full analysis of what's inside," I demanded of the cybers.

"Atmosphere, pressure, non-biotic life all are equal to this side," the smaller one, my own personal cyber, reported.

"Have you completed downloading from our vessel's computers all the data gathered so far by all of the groups about the Choor'by?"

"I'm now as expert in this data as the vessel's computer," it assured me.

That of course was the only way I could hope to succeed in this night-time, covert foray into the structure. Because I was unsure who exactly on the vessel might be Crossley cohorts, I had to be certain no one else would know what I found here, if anything at all, or even knew that I'd come here. I would close it up as soon as I'd seen what had to be seen. Not that I expected any proof of the Originists' theory. It was simply better that I control all flow of information. As it was, they had their hands full working on all the material we'd found.

"Daytime Hesperian illumination," I ordered. "And be alert for any effects that may be visible only on *other* wavelengths." The two cybers stepped through the new entryway and I followed.

For the first few dozen meters, it was as Crossley described it: wide enough for a dozen of us to walk on side by side, twenty meters high, a comfortable ten degree angle up inside, the side walls blank.

Then it began to curve to the left, as well as rise and that was when I had my first surprise. The side walls were no longer blank, but filled with Choor'b hieroglyphs, millions of them, but also incised alongside them were other signs, signs even I could recognize as not indigenous to this world. "Analysis!" I asked of the cybers.

"They're called Roman letters," my cyber confirmed what I already knew. "Clearly human in origin, yet apparently incised by the same limbs or mechanisms that incised the Choor'b language."

The wide corridor rose, its walls now filled to completion with the two languages. Occasionally, a section of wall would open as a window slit to the plaza below, or inward to other internally open sections ahead, as though in reminder of its great length.

"They appear to be names," my cyber now said. "Human names and possibly their Choor'b counterparts."

"Human names!" I mused. "Whatever are they doing here?"

"These names and their Choor'b counterparts will be useful in producing a partial vocabulary, even a dictionary," my cyber continued. "For example," it offered, "the name Crossley at one time referred to someone who was daily involved with a primitive human projectile weapon called a cross-bow. Although it is unclear whether Crossley was a manufacturer, repairer, or utilizer of such a weapon."

"I'm using that and other language approximations to locate correlatives to the Choor'b hieroglyphics," my cyber continued. "This is the richest linguistic find by far on the world. What the ancients referred to as a 'Rosetta Stone'."

We'd arrived at what I'd taken from lower down and farther away to be a tall, vertical window, only to be surprised again. Rather than a window, it was another kind of pictograph system, incised or etched upon some kind of mica or similar silicate, and quite dim in our unnatural light. The larger cyber now flooded the floor-to-ceiling glass with a variety of different illuminations until one suddenly caught. My cyber explained: "The illumination being used on this etching approximates the natural light on Zeta Reticuli Two as it might have appeared several thousand years ago."

Meaning that the planet's natural light had changed substantially since then.

"Isn't that a chart of the Zeta Reticuli solar system?" I asked. Looking at the lower part of the diagram of a G-2 star with four planets, two inner smallish ones, one large gaseous third planet with its dozen or more satellites, and—much further out from the sun—a tiny, icebound fourth. "Is it from that same period?"

My cyber agreed and gave me the exact date of the etching, based on the arrangement of the planets and satellites. Indeed, from that same era.

"What's this?" I pointed to a second solar system pictured at the furthest extremity of the upper right hand side of the glass.

"A G-1 star. Ten planets. Ninety-seven natural satellites. It would appear to be located one hundred and twenty light years away, almost directly north in the galactic ecliptic from Zeta Reticuli."

"In the Orion Spur, then! Can you match it to something known?"

The larger cyber produced a full three dimensional holo-display of what it called the Central Orion Area, highlighting the first and second magnitude stars there, and giving their old fashioned names, Procyon, Sirius, Centaurus.

"This pictured system does not show up, does it?" I asked, already knowing the answer. "Increase your viewing to magnitudes three through eight."

The holo did so and then it did find the G-1 star and pinpointed it. It was dim, quite small, somewhere between the brighter stars, along with a dozen smaller suns, located in a directional extremity above and outside the galactic ecliptic so that it seemed even more apart; due to that, it might have provided a wider perspective of its surroundings. "It's called Sol," my cyber explained. "It is listed as Sol system and its planets are as they would have appeared at the same time space as the Reticuli system."

"What do we know about this Sol?"

"Nothing," the cyber replied. "The Centaurus system close by has, of course, been often contemplated as a possible site by the human Originists."

"I've never heard of either."

"Sol system does possess a planet named Terra, as in the common-place terminology, Metro-Terra; but then, of course, so do *many* other solar systems."

A second window further ahead on the corridor was also etched and this time the inhabitants of Choor were pictured as we'd never seen them so clearly before: their small, frail bodies and oversized heads, their large dark iris-less eyes, their thumbless, four-fingered hands and double-toed feet. Even more amazing, alongside them were pictured human males about one third larger, and correctly shaped and detailed.

"This method of pictograph is aesthetically late-period Choor'b style," my cyber explicated. "It might be considered highly developed, even decadent."

"And this band of hieroglyphs?" I pointed.

"It appears to be a cartouche," my cyber said, "begging the viewers' pardon for being so pictorially explicit."

"In other words, the Choor'by did not picture themselves before this particular site, not from a lack of artistic will or or lack of skill, but because it was forbidden? A taboo?"

"Or because it was deemed immodest."

"Then why here?" I asked. "Is there no explanation of what these humans and Choor'by are doing side by side?"

"None."

"Everyone learns in Ed. & Dev. that the very first contacts between humans and another species took place on Gamma Denebola and not until the Sidereal Year 2772," I said. This cartouche appeared to say otherwise.

"The human names on the wall have been analyzed," my cyber announced, "and clearly they all speak of the diversity called racial and ethnic which has been written about in texts describing early post-industrial humankind. The names, for example, are recognizably ethnic: Wang is what was called Chinese, Lorenzo is what was called Italian. There are also occupation names like Smith, Cooper, and Shepherd—even so the bulk of names listed here appear to be of a sort we recognize as Swahilian, Mohala-Zulu, or Pan-African, in origin."

The second window, when irradiated somewhat differently, revealed the internal systems of both the Choor'by and the humans, in four steps, organs only, neurological system only, circulatory system only, and then all three together. The humans were recognizably similar to ourselves, except of course for the fact that none of the males possessed the much later developments such as in-wrist comm. systems or the now universally sanctioned Relfian in-vitro reproductive systems.

"What can we say about Choor'b anatomy?" I asked my cyber, "And how might they have been affected by what our other onboard groups have defined as changes in the planet's geology, astrophysics, climate and so on?"

Using the other cyber as a massive data-processor, my cyber learned a great deal indeed about the Choor'by. I listened as it pointed out various elements as the two extrapolated them. Intriguing as it all was, none of it directly accounted for the sudden—or was it slow?—decline and then loss of the species.

"They are individually, if nonspecifically, sexed," my cyber concluded. "The Choor'by seem to have evolved from a kind of societal-insect asexuality, except for the queen and her service drones—into widespread hermaphroditism. Each Choor'by possesses both an external lower front-mounted seed-production *insertor* and a lower dorsal inter-larval production *receptor*. These are unconnected to excretory organs and similar to Bella-Arths. Centuries ago, Dr. Antonia Phesian speculated that this might be the natural further evolution of any insectoid."

We walked through a corridor of more names, millions of them. Then, along another curve of the by-now almost monstrously enigmatic hallway, we came upon a third window, this one differing by its horizontality, and divided into four separate strips of pictographs, providing what might be interpreted as a narrative, should we be able to comprehend it.

"The Choor'by and humans appear to be exchanging something!" was my first reaction. Again, aside from the cartouche apologizing for such extreme graphism, there was no other explanation of what was being pictured, as though it were known, indeed commonplace to the Zeta Reticulans who would come here. What we saw, my two cybers and myself, were the insectoid inhabitants giving humans a variety of objects, some tiny, others larger, some obviously crystalline, others more indefinable. In return, the humans were giving the Choor'by what looked like ribbons or banners. "Could those be formulas?" I wondered aloud.

"Or human DNA," my cyber responded. He pointed to another picture below, in which humans lay on tables and the Choor'by appeared to be surgically removing thin layers of skin cells, resulting in slender, twisted ribbons. "Taking DNA and then cloning it."

In yet a third picture, the Choor'by were removing material from their own bodies, and overseeing humans who appeared to be injecting the material into another human. "Primitive medicine?" I asked. "They gave the humans medicine?"

"Unclear, but," my cyber said, "we've determined that among those other items they are pictured as giving humans there appear two that were extremely crucial to our development: early circuit chips and capacitor cells for the construction of artificial intelligence; and photo-illuminescent materials later used in stellar travel drives."

"So it's trade. The Choor'by give away the secret of travel to the stars and the source of making computers, for human DNA? Doesn't quite seem like an even bargain to me. I wonder why they did it?"

"Perhaps the Zeta Reticulans, in their advanced age, had become physionomically degenerate and required cloned cultures to continue to exist? This fourth picture however seems not static like the others, but rather a progression."

It was more of a reverse progression. The human male received the injection provided by Choor'by. Then he stumbled and fell. Then he was lying apparently ill. Finally he was lying covered up, and thus presumably dead.

"No explanation?" I asked my cyber.

"None is given. We may speculate that the injection given contains a solution that causes the human male to sicken and die. Why this should be paid for by sun-cells or circuit-chips is incomprehensible."

"Unless! . . . Unless the sun-cells and circuit chips were payment *after the fact*? If they were compensation. Say if the human male was someone who volunteered to sicken and die?"

I pondered this matter as we strode further along the coiling building. But I didn't come to any further explanatory window. Instead we reached a second wall.

"This must be the so-called hidden chamber that Dr. Crossley's group sonar-graphed. Go ahead and cut through."

"Wait!" I heard from behind me and turned. Back along the curved corridor just within visual range, I saw Crossley himself rapidly ascending, breathless with effort.

"The others of my group are behind me," he said, without apology, but also without rancor. Then when he'd reached our spot and caught his breath, he explained, "When your cyber linked up to my linguistics board, it set off my hackers alarm. Rather than cut off the flow of data, I opened it all the way. The new information it was processing poured in so fast it couldn't absorb it all. My team awakened me. When I saw what it was . . . I awakened a few others, mostly expedition team leaders."

Behind, I could hear what sounded like the entire expedition team coming up the rampway, loudly marveling. When they'd reached our spot, I said, "Dr. Crossley discovered this monument. He found this chamber we are about to open. I came alone because I wanted precautions taken. It remains *his* discovery."

This statement met with their approval. Crossley said, "I came looking for something simple. But what Dr. Sannq' had found is far more complex —stunning, really! Another entire race . . . and who knows what else."

Lest we become trapped in further mutual effusions, I turned to my
cybers. "Open the chamber. All of you stand back."

If we'd been surprised before by the pictographs showing humans,
we were now to be completely overwhelmed. Once down, the wall
revealed a large rotunda, making—as Dr. Zhin would later remark—
the schematic for the entire monument resemble a human sperm cell:
the single long curved corridor leading to a single head. As soon as we'd
broken into the huge room, we set off some kind of automatic response
system. The rotunda became illuminated exactly to suit unaugmented
human eyesight, while a variety of other mechanisms, some set on plinths
around the room, and others on surrounding walls, were immediately
set into motion. We saw ancient ground cars, old flying machines, an
entire section of a home, another of a school classroom, another of an
early cyberized manufacturing plant, still another of an ancient mass
entertainment site called a theatre. And among them, within them,
full-sized human figures, clothed differently and with different hair styles
than us and, of course, without our by now standardized physical
augmentation of the senses, but otherwise *looking* like us as they went
about their business, laboring, playing, skating, making love, dancing,
assembling for a discussion. Side video screens provided additional
views. It was the most astonishing spectacle any of us had ever dreamed
of seeing on this alien world. We stood like NeoNates, our mouths agape.

In the middle of all this silent wonder, from one plinth a sound
emerged, a high pitched chittering noise, which modulated slowly down
the scale into a recognizably human voice speaking in a language Crossley
immediately recognized as an early human universal tongue called
English. My cyber went to the machine and interfaced with it. In seconds,
we heard its message translated for our comprehension by the cyber.

"Welcome humans to the Museum of Man. These people are your
ancestors. They are of the period from the year Nineteen Hundred and
Sixty to Two Thousand and Twenty-five. This era stretched from the so-
called international Cold War far longer and more happily, through a
period dominated by four coalitions: the United States of Northern
America, The European Union, New Asia, and Pacifica."

"Naturally, at this period, the interstellar travel you take for granted
was not known. Thus it is the time in which humans left their planet
for their earliest manned and mostly unmanned flights to their nearest

neighbors in space."

Several of the team members had fallen to their knees along the rotunda floor. I assumed from their rapt faces that they were dyed-in-the-wool Originists.

"Congratulations!" Crossley said to me, with an ironic smile. "Without in the least intending to, you've done what many of my colleagues have labored years to accomplish. You've found the home planet. The origin of humankind appears to be there, that tiny planet, around that insignificant star, in a backwater of a minor spur of an indifferently important galactic arm. Utterly remarkable!"

The general irony of our situation was hardly lost on me. All I could do was, say, "Perhaps you're right. But what is all this doing here? A hundred and twenty lights years away? On Zeta Reticuli Two?"

★

The discovery—whether Crossley's, mine, or both of ours—turned out to be as my own cyber had early put it, and explained in greater detail later on what it had meant, a true Rosetta Stone. The combination of the hieroglyphs and the various combinations our linguistics team was able to decipher from the speaking machines inside the rotunda did the trick. The four museum machine-speakers with their separate three-hour long programs actually repeated *ad infinitum* in twelve different human languages, until we learned how to regulate them. Then there was the introductory chittering which we'd immediately assumed to be the Choor'by's own language. It was; although it would eventually take two more years to fully decipher. Even so, we moved half the team inside the rotunda, and set to work.

Of course we would end up trebling the amount of time we'd spent on Choor, from one month to three. And by then, the Quinx Council on Hesperia had made public our discoveries and some of our findings. This had led to joy, controversy, and astonishment all over our beloved Third Galactic Republic. But it would be a very long time after our return to Hesperia before we would be able to explain exactly what it was that we'd found. And it would end up being a sobering and sad tale we unfolded, one with several cautions and no real lessons.

The history of the inhabitants of Zeta Reticuli Two, the Choor'by, as indeed they did call themselves, was as we'd already derived it from evidence of the site. Certain twists of climactic and positional destiny of this second planet had allowed it alone of the four system planets to develop basic early life. Especially an abundant vegetable existence. The earliest forms of animals had come much later, and had progressed through long primitive stages before undergoing varied upwellings followed by species crashes and extinctions. Only the insectoids had survived and evolved—at the same time as the spread of the gigantic hardwood forests and the sudden chilling and subsequent drying of the planet's atmosphere from its earliest humid, warm lushness. The insectoids had evolved over millennia into the beings—people—we'd seen pictographed in the museum.

Once they'd managed to control their environment and to feed themselves, they entered into great intra-species wars of long duration and extreme harshness, essentially one mega-nest of insects against another, during which they'd come to within a hairsbreadth of exterminating themselves altogether via chemical weapons. When the wars ended, they'd agreed to mix themselves up so well genetically that previous divisive concepts of nesthood identification were eliminated, all for the common good. It worked.

One side-effect of this universal Choor'b mixing was the loss of individual flight, which had been declining steadily over the centuries anyway due to increasing size and weight. In groups, the Choor'by could still rise and travel planet wise. But single Choor'by became limited to flying maybe a hundred and twenty meters into the air, to distances of a half kilometer at a time. A more positive side effect arose from the new shared technology. After long years, the Choor'by developed manned flight, first in single units, then in far larger ships. The science of this flight was based on the combination of color, light, and anti-magnetism, using extremely thin, lightweight materials. As the Choor'by could maintain themselves without gravity, that important human element was not for them problematic. The basis of this new aviation science was of course founded upon what they had noticed in flight around them: seeds, leaves and pods. So those particular Choor's plants provided the shapes of the vehicles they ended up utilizing: which humans might easily say resembled bulbs, dishes, or saucers.

After a while, the united Choor'by began to investigate their own rather ordinary solar system. They colonized the satellites around the distant, huge, gaseous third planet, and left a station-colony in the inhospitable atmosphere of the tiny fourth world. They developed a stellar drive, utilizing the same chromo-illuminescent principle and used their seed-like, podlike craft to travel to other star systems. There they eventually discovered and chose not to make contact with several other species: among them the Bella-Arths, the primitive Delphinids of New Venice, and eventually the humans, tied at the time to one world and by no means completely master of it.

The Choor'by eventually mapped the entire galaxy and even attempted flight to nearby galactic neighbors. The results of these latter voyages were still not known to the Choor'by at the time of the last recording that had been inserted into the monument—since intergalactic time periods were enormous. But from what they'd seen of the other three species, they considered themselves to be obviously superior, and so they'd kept their contact to simple observation.

This situation lasted a long time and might have lasted forever had not the Choor'by suddenly begun to physically decline.

Their scientists had long ago charted their solar system's position, and so they knew that it would pass through the most tenuous layer of an expanding heliosphere from a giant supernova drifting from over two hundred light years distance. A widespread scientific study of that advancing nebula heliosphere had shown that its very tenuous material should impact their planet virtually nonexistently—and thus not prove to be a danger.

The Choor'by were an extremely orderly, an especially sanitary species, always concerned with any possible contamination from the outside, especially in those species they star-visited. So, in retrospect, they were forced to conclude that the culprit for what happened to them *had* to have been something unknown, something almost immaterial, contained or carried by that expanding wave of supernova, although it had long passed before any effect was ever noted.

In the five-hundred-and-sixty-fourth century of the Choor'by's recorded history, a sickness arrived among them like a scourge: a virus that entered the body and was passed on to each other. The disease seemed to have a latency period of anywhere from one year to a dozen. It had spread deeply throughout their home world population before it was even noticed.

When the true nature of the emergency was understood, all the knowledge and efforts of their civilization were turned toward its cure. Soon, the entire populace of the home planet was infected, sick, weakening, irrevocably dying, usually quite hideously. Most nearby colonies of Choor'by within five hundred light years were also infected before they realized it. Naturally long-lived, the Choor'by had by then medically and genetically extended their lives to a span of several hundred years. So it was close to a hundred years before they came to the inescapable conclusion that they were doomed.

Once all medical and scientific efforts had been shown to be useless, the Choor'by turned to the outside. Those on faraway observation posts remained uninfected and were notified of the crisis, and commandeered to find a cure. Their closest genetic neighbors, the Bella-Arths, were abducted, infected with the virus and carefully watched. None developed the illness, nor unfortunately, any antibodies to it. Delphinids, which shared salt-water based genetic markers with Choor'by, were next to be exposed to the virus. Those Delphs abducted and infected became ill but they died far too quickly to even develop the disease as it was known on Choor. Their systems simply were assaulted and shut down. That left humans.

Over a period of forty years, beginning in the middle of the Terra-human's so-called Second World War, humans were abducted by the Choor'by. This was made easier by the development of Terrans to a point where mechanized ground and air travel had begun to stretch into remote sectors of their own world. Before infecting them, however, the Choor'by decided to make a thorough study of human physiognomy to determine similarities and differences. So cells were taken and cloned by the Choor'by and those were then infected. To no effect.

Six years after those first abductions, the accidental crash landing of a small team of Choor'by in a Terran desert and the subsequent unexpected capture of a single Choor'b reconnaissance unit, brought the two species into unexpectedly direct contact.

It was quickly decided both by those Terrans in charge of the local government and by the Choor'by that public recognition and further contact between the two species would be problematic. However, over a period of several Terran decades, sufficient diplomatic relations were established for the Choor'by to make clear the nature of their medical emergency and to offer to provide to the few Terrans who knew of their existence their own advanced technology. A trade pact was set up: further human abductions and studies were to be allowed, but only once the subjects were placed under hypnotic control induced by strong nerve gas, so nothing would be later remembered. Human ova and sperm were naturally made available to the Choor'by. But as they physically weakened, their charges sometimes remained fractious and rebellious; and keeping them in captivity for observation was deemed impractical, so they were internally "marked" for re-abduction. Attempts were made at this time to create a mixed species, combining attributes both human and Choor'by which would be impervious to the devastating effects of the illness. This had no success and was eventually abandoned.

When the Choor'b crisis became desperate—statistically their species existed only in stellar isolation to provide for population replacement— Terran leaders allowed a limited infection by the Choor'b virus of relatively discrete sectors of the human population to take place—with a promise to share all medical knowledge. The humans infected were generally those who shared the sexual practices of the Choor'by, i.e. dorsal intercourse— the only known method of the disease transmission among their kind. But, as so often happens, the unexpected occurred. The Choor'b disease could, it turned out, be spread to humans via other methods too beyond those of the aliens: blood to blood, vaginal intercourse, even saliva.

The initial groups received poor and late health care, so the disease spread too fast and far too widely to be the planned and controlled experiment they'd hoped for. Within a decade of the earliest human infection, the virus had spread into virtually all elements of the human population. Despite this, Terrans were found who though infected, never developed the illness, and others who although exposed *never* became infected, and the period during which the disease showed up in humans turned out to be both shorter and longer than among the Chooor'by and in other regards far more widely variable.

By the end of the second Terran millennium, over four million humans had died of the Choor'b disease and millions more were infected. A series of treatments at last was developed which was found to have some palliative effects upon humans, either used singly or in combination, and usually for a long period of years. Finally, with the method of transmission now known, safeguards could be put into place. Thereafter the infection spread as far as it might go among the populace, only stopped when it had burned itself out, leaving some twenty million Terrans dead.

Unfortunately those same palliative treatments found useful for humans had no effect whatsoever on the Choor'by. In the year 2024 S.T.Y., when the epidemic was finally declared over on Terra, the by then much chastened Choor'by departed back to Zeta Reticuli for good, there to join their fellows who might still be alive, and with them to await their common doom. Those Choor'by still strong enough to do so, designed and had built this monument and this museum, as a testament to those millions of an alien species which had unknowingly sacrificed their lives to help find a cure. The most recent recording, updated by the final keeper of the museum, gave the total population of Choor as under six thousand. This individual then finished the museum and opened it to all remaining Choor'by.

★

"Thus the wide corridors and ramps," I said to Cord Crossley, as we concluded our on-planet report, only hours prior to leaving Zeta Reticuli Two. "Which is, ironically, what drew your attention to this monument in the first place. The remaining Choor'by were too ill to get around as they had before. They required mechanized transport for transportation, copied from human-style wheelchairs of the era."

"Just one of the many ironies," Crossley agreed. "Like the fact that our names will now forever be linked in this discovery."

"And with the discovery of the originating planet of our kind," I added. "I who opposed that so strongly."

"I wonder what that Sol-Terra will look like when we get there?"

"Others will get there long before us," I explained. "An expedition has already been equipped and launched from Hesperia. But you and I will eventually get there too."

"What must they have thought, those last remaining Choor'by," Crossley mused, "coming here, looking at this homage to an obviously inferior species who had nevertheless managed to weather the disease that killed off all of their own kind? And *knowing* that this obviously inferior species would go on, go on as a result of the Choor'by's own gifts in trade, go on to inherit the galaxy?" Crossley shook his head. "Saddest of all, all of it without an iota of recognition by Terran society of the Choor'by's existence."

"Oh, they left signs of themselves on Terra," I said.

And when Crossley looked surprised, I called over my personal cyber and had him show Crossley. "Although it was very scattered and rather spotty, and although most of it flourished in the last few decades of their second historical millennium, it seems there actually was some human recognition of the Choor'by. Possibly even a cult of them."

My cyber projected holos from various historical chronicles it had collected of visual entertainment's called by early humans "films and videos," as well as various "books," "pamphlets," and "magazines," which showed one variation or another of the Choor'by's appearances.

"Of course," I added, "they were scoffed at by anyone who knew the truth. But most of the details of their relationship was rather correctly inferred—the abductions, the shapes of the Choor'b interstellar vessels, the physiological experimentation—even while the *significance* of it all was *never* understood. The odd part is that it seemed created to frighten and thus entertain humans rather than to enlighten them."

"Meaning the Choor'by must have allowed it," Crossley said. "Somehow they allowed their hypnosis to be gotten around. Allowed themselves to be recalled and even pictured, distorted as those pictures turned out to be."

We stared at one pictograph of the era showing a human female stretched out on a metallic table, as dangerous looking mechanical devices attacked her naked form. Around her, stood creatures with the large whitish heads and huge black eyes of the Choor'by.

"What does it say?" I asked him to translate the headline.

"It's in English, one of their predominant tongues," Crossley replied. "It reads 'Alien Torture Abductions Confirmed! Are You Next?'" Then Crossley asked. "Wherever did you find this ghastly libel?"

"In a special vault marked by the last museum keeper here as '*Primary Importance. In Case of Emergency, Salvage First.*'"

And when Crossley blinked at me without understanding, I added, "I guess the Choor'by realized that it's better to be remembered as villains than to not be remembered at all. . . . Either that, or they just had a great sense of humor."

An *Inquiry* Concerning
the Irregular Occurrences and Anomalous Circumstances
Including but not Limited to the Disappearance of
*Mr. Neal P. Bartram*
at the Once Privately Owned now Foundation Owned
and Operated Estate of Chester A. Ingals, Known as

# INGOLDSBY

Sports Final —                                                    — 25 Cents

# ☰ꞙe Junction City Intelligencer

**** SATURDAY, APRIL 21, 2001 ****

# UNEXPECTED TIME CAPSULE DISCOVERED IN BANK RUINS

## *OPENED VAULT OF OLD FULTON FIRST SAVINGS BANK YIELDS "TREASURE TROVE" FROM 1940 MAYOR QUIMBLY EXULTS*

**By Caspar Lockhead**

Fulton's Point, WI— When he jackhammered the solid looking cornerstone of the old Fulton Savings Bank, the last part of the venerable ruin of the old building located at the corner of Main and Branch and the one remaining structure on the block of what is to become downtown Fulton Point's fashionable new shopping district, the last thing Herb Mahony expected to find was another vault.

Weeks before, the Myers DeConstruction Co. crew had removed the two huge standing metal vaults installed on the spot more than sixty years before.

"That took two days and derrick and winch equipment so big we had to rent it," Thommy Myers, Jr., co-owner of the company with his father and two brothers, admitted. But with nothing else to the grand old bank left standing higher than your ankle, there was still that cornerstone, a giant granite stone, and the first piece to be inserted into the old bank when Ford's manufacturing plant was the area's biggest employer and Ella Fitzgerald had the country's number one hit record.

A plaque from that plant some two miles to the

north—recently reopened and converted into manufacturing Hyundai sports coupes—and a copy of that record—a single play, two-sided, red vinyl 45 r.p.m disc on the Bluebell label—were among the "treasures" that Herb Mahony found when he reached into the two foot by three foot metal vault with a legend "not to be opened before the year 2000" incised on its front door. "It took some prying," Mahony and Myers admitted, but then it sprang open and they looked inside and were astonished, and delighted.

TIME CAPSULE, Continued on Page 5

150    FELICE PICANO

# UNEXPECTED TIME CAPSULE DISCOVERED IN BANK RUINS

TIME CAPSULE, From Page 1

Besides the Ford plaque and Ella lp, they found the latest women's fashions in kitchen aprons—a polka dot yellow on pale green, wrapped in a cellophane package—an eight ounce green glass bottle of *Coca Cola*, among the first carbonated soda pops, that looked as though it still had some fizz in it, a *Good Housekeeping* cookbook for brides, a copy of *The Junction City Intelligencer*, dated sixty one years earlier than this one, and, according to Mayor Quimbly who was soon called to the scene of the discovery, "many other marvelous and delightful objects of everyday use."

Quimbly promised that the contents of the vault will be put on exhibit in display cases between the mayor's office and the post office in the Town Hall as soon as all the contents have been catalogued and care has been taken to ensure that the items

are historically cared for against contemporary germs, molds and even bugs. "We've called in an expert from the university archives who's in charge of such matters," she assured the *Intelligencer*. He'll know what to do to ensure this unexpected and remarkable cache of life from our grandparent's generation long ago, will be available for all to see and study."

"Time Capsules themselves are as charmingly archaic as any of the objects they may contain," said Professor Aranda "Randy" Chananbranada, from the university archives. "Our ancestors had a wonderful optimism about the future, and equally a wonderful faith in what they surrounded themselves with. Thus their desire to send Time Capsules to what they saw as a certain, and wonderful, future." Chananbranada pointed out that most such Time Capsules stopped being sent around the year 1960. While the earliest

yet opened was from the year 1905.

With the vault opened, its contents removed, and the vault itself to be put on display, the ground is now thoroughly cleared and ready for the Fulton's Landing Fashion Center to rise. On the site of the old bank will be a Gap clothing store, an Armani A/X Botteghe, a Payless Shoes, and Geree's Sports Equipment and Guns filling up the block. Already across the street, the old Fulton Theater has been restored in part and then converted into a film multiplex housing fourteen smaller cinemas, surrounded on either side by a glass enclosed food court with favorite eateries like Ruby's Retro Diner, Taco La Rica, Hamburg Hell, Pizza Hut, a sit-down and take-out branch of local favorite, The Wen Young Chinese Food Outlet, and one of the county's best known eateries, Snyder's Inn.

**The Junction City Intelligencer**

Sports Final —                                    — 25 Cents

# The Junction City Intelligencer

**** MONDAY, APRIL 30, 2001 ****

# BAFFLING MANUSCRIPT FOUND IN TIME CAPSULE

*"TREASURE TROVE" FROM 1940*
*CONTAINS JOURNAL POLICE CHIEF*
*CALLS "SUSPICIOUS," TIED TO*
*STUDENT'S SUMMER DISAPPEARANCE*

## By Caspar Lockhead

Fulton's Point, WI—Admitting that he didn't know whether it was, "a joke or what?" Police Chief Abner Estes told *The Junction City Intelligencer* yesterday in a special interview that a journal found inside the Time Capsule recently opened for the first time in over sixty years, appears to "not belong with the rest of the items." But that it does appear to be connected to the disappearance of a graduate student last August 30th at the nearby historic Ingoldsby estate.

"It's both hand-written and computer-print gener-ated," Chief Estes said of the journal found amid memorabilia of the year 1940. "Impossible for that year. Someone must have slipped it in, as a prank."

A tasteless prank, at best. Last year, local police and the Portage County Sheriff's office sent ten officers who for two days combed the entire long-closed estate buildings and the extensive nearby grounds, searching for Neal P. Bartram, the student who'd been hired as a grounds-keeper for the famous site. He had been reported missing on August 31st, by A.J.

Torrington, attorney for the Ingoldsby estate in Chicago, who had hired the young history student.

Bartram had been employed both to ready the grounds of the historic site for a potential opening as a museum, and to watch that squatters and vandals stayed away. An honors student at Northwestern University, and a Ph.D. candidate in American History, Bartram was called "rock-steady" by Torrington, and thus unlikely to simply run off.

After some weeks of fruitless search with no

BAFFLING, Continued on Page 5

# BAFFLING MANUSCRIPT FOUND IN TIME CAPSULE

BAFFLING, From Page 1

clues, the hunt was called off, and the mystery of Bartram's disappearance has remained unsolved.

But this is by no means the first mystery to have surrounded Ingoldsby, home of renowned financial wizard, Chester A. Ingals. On the very same date in 1940 as Bartram's vanishing, Ingals reportedly perished along with his minor ward and closest friend in a freak fire in the much-photographed, architecturally noted house built especially for him only a few years earlier.

Rebuilt to be as it originally was, by terms of Ingals' will, the estate was to have opened to the public, but until last year, it had enigmatically remained in the private hands of the enormously wealthy Ingals Foundation. The estate is shunned by some Fulton's Point residents who claim the place is in some way "out of whack," and even haunted.

Mr. Torrington has not returned inquires from the Intelligencer reporter.

**The Junction City Intelligencer**

---

## STATE of WISCONSIN
## District Attorney's Office
### Government Center, Building C
### 120 State Street
### Madison, WI 53711
### Wayne G. King, Assistant D.A.

To: Detective-Sergeant Annabella Conklin,
    Wisconsin State Police, Cold Case Department
    Eau Claire, WI 54701

May 7th, 2001

Dear Det.-Sgt. Conklin,

Pursuant to our brief phone conversation yesterday, I am enclosing the surprising new material (two articles from *The Junction City Intelligencer*) sent to this office by local authorities regarding the disappearance of Neal P. Bartram, August 30, 2000 on the grounds of the Ingoldsby estate. As this falls within your purview as a recent but closed and thus "cold case," we are also passing along that locality's request "in the light of the discovery within the 1940 Time Capsule of a ms allegedly written and signed by Neal Bartram," along with this office's sanction, to fully and immediately reactivate the case, as a grade gl2, with financial resources commensurate to that designation.

Although a further, smaller, item in a later issue of *The Intelligencer* called the newfound journal a patent fraud, this was official persiflage, and by no means the truth. We wish to bring this evidence to your attention, along with several other pieces of evidence related the as yet unsolved disappearance.

Fulton's Point Police Chief, Abner Estes has prepared a full list of materials previously collected which are enclosed for your attention. We encourage you to work up further, corroborating, or noncorroborating evidence, at your discretion.

We are confident you will be able to make some sense of all this. The D.A. is especially interested in the case, as he is a second cousin to members of the Ingals Family, not unrelated to the foundation upon whose property this unpleasant predicament occurred.

Cordially,

Wayne G. King

---

## PORTAGE COUNTY, WI
### FULTON'S POINT POLICE
### 39000 Rte. 18
### Fulton's Pt., WI 53908

Enclosed find all items collected by this office, catalogued by Officer Jeremy Schaeffer, signed off by Chief Abner Estes.

1. Initial request made by telephone and backed up by e-mail of one A.J. Torrington, on noon of August

31$^{st}$, 2000, from his office in Chicago, IL, regarding the disappearance of Neal P. Bartram, employed May 20$^{th}$, 2000, as watchman and groundskeeper at the Ingoldsby estate. The gist of the request was that Torrington was Bartram's employer and had been trying to reach him for close to twenty four hours and had failed to do so. He'd then phoned a local who'd then driven to the site and who also failed to locate Bartram.

2. Secondary request, by letter, and e-mail by A.J. Torrington, officially requesting that the F.P. Police step in and locate the "missing person" Neal P. Bartram.

3. Official Report of Office Jeremy Schaeffer, dated September 1$^{st}$, 2000, following his preliminary investigation at the Ingoldsby estate, made in response to the above official request.

4. Follow-up report of the expanded investigation and search of the Ingoldsby estate and Environs by Chief Abner Estes and Officer Shaeffer, dated September 3$^{rd}$, 2000.

5. Request by Chief Estes to the Portage County Sheriff's Offices for a 10-man search squad to help locate Bartram, dated September 3$^{rd}$, 2000. Signed by Chief Estes.

6. Depositions taken by the Portage County Sheriff's Office/Fulton's Point Police of known associates of Neal Bartram, regarding his habits and possible whereabouts. Including affidavits by the following:

    A. Fulton's Point Pharmacy owner: Mr. Joseph Weyerhauser
    B. Fulton's Point resident: Dr. Rodman Stansbury, M.D.
    C. Fulton's Point Public Library employee: Mrs. Antoinette Noonan
    D. Fulton's Point resident: Amanda Ettick

E. Fulton's Point resident: Ashley Sprague

F. Fulton's Point Post Office Manager: Ms.
   Beverly Freneau

7. Report by Portage County Sheriff Griffith A.
Angeles, following the search, depositions, and
investigation, dated October 1st, 2000.

8. Final Report by Chief Abner Estes. October
13th, 2000.

Date                                    Signature


Date                                    Signature

---

# 1.          PORTAGE COUNTY, WI
### FULTON'S POINT POLICE
### 39000 Rte. 18
### Fulton's Pt., WI 53908

Received today, August 31st, 2000, 12.15 p.m. by
Operator Anita Nichols, transferred to Office Jeremy
Schaeffer, a telephone call from Mr. A.J. Torrington,
Attorney of The Ingals Trust in Chicago, IL, asking
that this office drive out to the Trust owned estate
known as "Ingoldsby" and conduct a search for the
person of Mr. Neal P. Bartram, the groundskeeper and
night/day watchman of the estate.

The reason given was that Mr. Bartram had not
responded to Mr. Torrington's repeated phone calls
or e-mail over the past 24 hours.

Complainant further noted that he had this morning phoned Fulton's Point Pharmacy owner, Joseph
Weyerhauser, and asked him to drive out to the
estate. That Mr. Weyerhauser had done as requested
but had not located Neal P. Bartram.

<u>Action taken</u>: officer explained that a formal
report/complaint of a Missing Person could only be
made forty-eight hours after he/she has gone missing. Officer advised Mr. Torrington to make such a
complaint.


Date                                    Signature

---

# 2.      **The Ingals Trust**
## 123 North Dearborn Ave.
## Chicago, IL 60602

To: Chief Abner Estes,
    Fulton's Point Police
    39000 Rte. 18
    Fulton's Pt. WI

September 1, 2000

Dear Police Chief Estes,

This letter, sent by e-mail and also via registered letter is
a formal complaint and report of a Missing Person, as per
my phone conversation and e-mail with Officer Schaeffer to
your office yesterday. I hope this makes it official now that
the Ingals Trust employee Neal P. Bartram, groundskeeper
and watchman of Ingoldsby, located in your jurisdiction, is
missing and we wish him to be found.

I've tried phoning him now for over forty-eight hours. I
also sent a representative, Mr. Joe Weyerhauser of the local
pharmacy, out to the estate to look for him. He reported
that he did not see Mr. Bartram anywhere. Bartram has
never been out of communication for so long.

Mr. Bartram is a Ph.D. candidate in American History

at Northwestern University here in Illinois, a solid and reliable young man with the best possible record of employment and credentials. Up until yesterday, this office had no reason to doubt that he would complete his term of employment — to September 10th, 2000 — competently and without problems.

As you may know, Ingoldsby is an important American architectural landmark of the past century, and it has been the Ingals Trust's intention to seek full state landmark status for it and possibly open it as a museum. Toward that end, and to ensure that any representative from the Landmark Commission was guided about, we hired Bartram, who has provided invaluable service. He's given us no reason to believe he would simply walk away from his responsibilities. Mr. Bartram is an intelligent, resourceful and personable young man. We are personally concerned for his whereabouts and for his well-being.

Please institute as full and thorough a search of the estate buildings and grounds as are needed. Joe Weyerhauser has a spare set of keys. And please let us know what we can do to help in this search.

Cordially,

A. J. Torrington

---

# 3.    PORTAGE COUNTY, WI
## FULTON'S POINT POLICE
### 39000 Rte. 18
### Fulton's Pt., WI 53908

<u>Preliminary Report on Missing Person: Neal P. Bartram</u>

Pursuant to the complaint/report filed September 1, 2000, Officer Jeremy Schaeffer drove to the Fulton's Point Pharmacy to get keys to Ingoldsby

from Joe Weyerhauser, whom the complainant, A.J.
Torrington, assured us had a spare set of keys.

He did and told the officer he'd been at Ingoldsby
the previous day on Torrington's phoned request and
had "looked around" for over an hour but "had
touched not one thing" and had not found the M/P Neal
Bartram.

Officer Schaeffer drove to the estate. One key
opened the smaller door on the side of the sliding
metal main gates between the brick walls that lead
into Ingoldsby. Weyerhauser told us that the M/P
lived inside the brick gatehouse, a two-story
structure similar to the brick walls, and housing a
garage with lawn and grounds equipment. Above it, a
two-room apartment with bath in which the M/P had
resided while employed there.

Apartment seemed lived in, and had various personal
items in the bathroom and bedroom appropriate for a
student. Clean and neat. No sign of a break-in or
violence. Laptop computer open but turned off on
main table amid school texts, notebooks, pens, etc.
No signs of a struggle.

Officer drove around gate house. Nothing looked
out of place. Officer drove the half mile to the main
house and garages. All doors were locked. No signs
of break-in, struggle or violence. Footprints made
by basketball shoes around various doors — to the
extensive garage, main entry of house, side doors,
etc. — exactly matched sneaker sole Officer found in
apartment belonging to M/P. Nothing unusual.

Officer entered garage, an extensive structure
containing 12 antique automobiles. All neat, swept,
polished, well kept. No sign of break-in or struggle.
Officer entered main house. Most rooms are empty or
contain a few pieces of furniture covered by sheets.
All sheets are sealed beneath with tape. Officer
searched for any not sealed or looking odd or newly
sealed. None found. Officer opened every cabinet,

closet, refrigerator, freezer, etc., door in the house. No signs of break-in or struggle. No sign of M/P.

Officer walked around main house in widening circle through bushes. No signs of violence or struggle. No sign of M/P. After four hours Officer concluded M/P was not in main buildings, garage nor central area of property and that there were no signs of struggle.

Date                                    Signature

---

# 4.    PORTAGE COUNTY, WI
### FULTON'S POINT POLICE
### 39000 Rte. 18
### Fulton's Pt., WI 53908

Follow-Up Report on Missing Person: Neal P. Bartram

Pursuant to the complaint/report filed September 1, 2000 and following Officer Jeremy Schaeffer's Preliminary Investigation and Report, Police Chief Abner Estes drove to the Fulton's Point Pharmacy to get keys to Ingoldsby from Joe Weyerhauser, and heard him repeat what he told Officer Schaeffer the previous day.

As did Officer Schaeffer, Chief Abner Estes drove to Ingoldsby and checked the gate house and attached garage, then to the main part of the estate, including the multi-car garage and main house. Found no signs of break-in, violence, or struggle. Chief Estes did a walking search of the area around the estate and failed to find the M/P.

Action taken: as the general area surrounding the house is close to fifteen acres, some of it brush, forest and scrubland, we believe a general search

party will be needed. Meanwhile, this office will
call on six people known to have associated with the
M/P tomorrow and begin taking depositions from them.

Date                              Signature

---

## 5.    PORTAGE COUNTY, WI
### FULTON'S POINT POLICE
### 39000 Rte. 18
### Fulton's Pt., WI 53908

TO: Country Sheriff Griffith A. Angeles
    Portage County Sheriff's Office
    172 Elm Street
    Portage, WI 53901

RE: Reports on Missing Person: Neal P. Bartram

September 3, 2000

Dear Sheriff Angeles,

   Enclosed please find copies of a complaint/report
of a missing person along with reports by Officer
Schaeffer and myself after preliminary and secondary
investigation of this M/P.
   Bartram is a Ph.D. candidate at Northwestern U. in
Chicago, and there appears to be no earthly reason
why he'd just vanish. No reports of hitchhikers on
any interstate or intrastate highways fit his
description. He seems to have lifted off the face of
the earth.
   We're taking depositions of six locals who knew
Bartram in the two months or so he was in Fulton's
Point or rather at the estate known as Ingoldsby. He
seems to have made a good impression but no real
friends. Naturally, as he was to leave in one week
to return to school.
   We'd appreciate your office sending a full search

of the grounds of the estate, comprising fifteen acres. It's more than our two-man office can handle. Keys will be made available to you. There is a small pond and a drag-net may be required. Otherwise it's all on-foot or via ATVs.

Should we learn anything of import to end the search during the depositions, you will hear of it immediately. The Ingals Trust is admittedly pretty big and important in the state, but it's only because of how total and sudden a disappearance this is that we're making this request. Foul play is of course assumed.

Date                                    Signature


*I owe you one on this, Griff!*
*—Ab Estes*

---

# 6-A    PORTAGE COUNTY, WI
## FULTON'S POINT POLICE
### 39000 Rte. 18
### Fulton's Pt., WI 53908


## DEPOSITION

MR. Joseph Weyerhauser, Fulton's Point Pharmacy, 3300 Rte. 81

Yes, I do swear. I first met Neal Bartram the afternoon of May 24th this year when he came into the pharmacy and asked for the keys to Ingoldsby. Mr. Torrington had phoned me two days before to say Neal would be coming for the keys. I wasn't very busy at that time of day, mid-afternoon, on a weekday, so I left my mother in charge of the cash register, infirm as she is and elderly — sixty-nine this

November — and I drove over to the place, with Neal driving behind me.

Showed him how to use the keys and what they opened in the gatehouse & the garage beneath filled with lawn and estate equipment he'd be using. A few days earlier I'd aired out the apartment and dusted it. Drove him to the main buildings and garages and gave him a guided tour. My Grandfather worked at Ingoldsby when he was a young man and so I know a great deal about it.

As far as I know, everything went all right between Neal and the estate until three days ago, when I got the phone call from Mr. Torrington telling me he could not raise Neal on the phone all the previous day nor that morning. I tried locally and couldn't raise him by phone either. So I drove over and looked for him. I found the little apartment as he'd left it, as though to go run errands. Same thing with the estate, which remains fully closed up, but ready to be opened at any moment if need be. I didn't touch anything at all in either the gate house or the main house.

There's not much to do in this town and Neal began coming into the pharmacy around one p.m. most days, for lunch. You and he must have passed each other once or twice. Nice looking feller, Neal is, strongly attracting the girls and well aware of it. Especially as he dressed more freely than most of the men around here, with small shorts and little, tight fitting guinea-tee shirts, and on hotter days, nothing but shorts and those flat little sandals with thongs on 'em.

Even so he's a well brought up, intelligent, courteous and all around good person. Able to speak on a variety of topics. Aside from how he dressed — or rather undressed — I never heard a negative word about him from any person in Fulton's Point. Although it is true that he kept to himself mostly, as he was preparing a book-length work for his Ph.D., I believe in mid-20th Century American History.

WITNESSED: A. Estes-TRANSCRIBED: A Nichols, 9/4/00

# 6-B    PORTAGE COUNTY, WI
## FULTON'S POINT POLICE
### 39000 Rte. 18
### Fulton's Pt., WI 53908

## DEPOSITION

**Dr. Rodman Stansbury, M.D. 34 Aspect Ave., Fulton's Pt., WI**

I so swear. I met Neal Bartram on Memorial Day Eve, May 28th of this year in the pharmacy. I'd heard from Joe Weyerhauser that Neal had come down from Chicago to mind the house and grounds at Ingoldsby. We'd gotten word a few months before that the Trust was planning to make it into a local historical landmark, possibly a museum. Big news in a town this small and sleepy, especially in summer.

So was Neal Bartram news to the town, according to Mrs. Stansbury. His arrival doubled the available bachelors in town, and the fact that he was a healthy, good looking, and a usually exposed-to-the-skin specimen of young manhood certainly made waves around the feminine side of town, according to the Missus. Tonia Noonan at the library and Bev Freneau at the Post Office apparently vied for his attention. But younger teens also followed him around the main street or gathered at his Cavalier coupe whenever it was parked in town. Nothing better to do.

I have no idea what if any kind of relationship Neal ever developed with either women or any woman or girl here. Or in fact with anyone. But since apart from Joe himself there was no real romantic competition for Neal I doubt that has any bearing on the matter.

As for myself, I played cards with Neal twice weekly, along with Joe Weyerhauser. Mostly at the pharmacy, on those "cafe" tables Joe's recently put inside; and once or twice at Neal's gate-house apartment.

Neal Bartram did come to me in a professional capacity a few weeks after he'd moved into the gate house. While he was sound as a drum, he was complaining of night noises and other unlikely disturbances that were keeping him awake. Sometimes the country is too quiet for city dwellers. I prescribed a light sleeping medicine, Dipenhydramine Hydrochloride, similar to what you can buy over the counter, but in a 50 mg dosage. After that he had no further complaints.

Neal did become interested in Ingoldsby and its history. But that was only to be expected, being as he was in and out of it and around it daily and it is a fascinating place. Me and Joe told him what we knew, including when he asked about the tragedy there in the spring of 1940 when Chester Ingals and his guests died in a freak fire inside the house. There wasn't much to tell. I think Neal looked up more himself.

After that, his questions about the place were pretty specific and even pointed. Joe and me humored him. Neal's an ace Rummy player and a super guy. We hope you find him soon and unhurt.

WITNESSED: A. Estes-TRANSCRIBED: A Nichols, 9/4/00

---

# 6-C　　PORTAGE COUNTY, WI

## FULTON'S POINT POLICE
### 39000 Rte. 18
### Fulton's Pt., WI 53908

## DEPOSITION

Ms. Antoinette ("Tonia") Noonan, Librarian, 9 Drake Rd. Fulton's Pt., WI

Yes, I do swear to tell the truth. I met Neal

Bartram on the Saturday of the Memorial Day weekend. Was that the 29th of May? The library was closed on the holiday. Neal sort of wandered into the building and as it is much cooler than the near hundred degree temperatures we were experiencing, he immediately put on his T-shirt.

He looked surprised to find a library at all, never mind one so handsome as ours is and so well kept. Of course, now that we've brought in the three computers, all as search engine/catalogue files and also for Internet use, the library is updated, so it's used by youngsters in addition to retirees and other regulars who came in.

Neal had been having trouble linking up to the Net from Ingoldsby and had been referred to me. As he always was, Neal was polite, courteous, and well-spoken. After he'd received his e-mail and answered it on the library's machine, we spoke a bit and he told me about himself. I offered to subscribe to *The Chicago Sun-Times* if he wished — it's a paid service of the library. But he said he could read it on-line.

He came into the library after that once or twice a week, and I also encountered him at the Pharmacy's lunch counter. Although he was reading quite special-ized books for his thesis, he occasionally leafed through a current auto magazine or a *New Yorker*.

As you know, it's been an exceptionally warm summer with few rain days and Neal dressed as people did at Northwestern and in Chicago, which some older residents in town found shocking. I saw nothing wrong with it, as he was a healthy looking, well behaved young man.

People have gossiped that Neal and I went out together. That's simply not true. We did have sev-eral long conversations at the Pharmacy cafe, and Neal seemed to be a genuine young man, sensible, and sensitive, yet practical too. Although he found his new home odd at times, he also loved living in an historical site. We spoke about "the good old days." I told him what I'd heard about it from my grandparents.

A month after he arrived, Neal began borrowing and reading about the history of the town and estate. He also drove to the Junction City library and got books there.

I do not believe Neal Bartram would leave of his own volition without fulfilling his employment obligation. I believe something was not quite right in his life, but I couldn't broach this matter with him. I feel harm has befallen Mr. Bartram and I pray to God he is found safe.

WITNESSED: A. Estes-TRANSCRIBED: A Nichols, 9/4/00

---

# 6-D    PORTAGE COUNTY, WI
## FULTON'S POINT POLICE
### 39000 Rte. 18
### Fulton's Pt., WI 53908

## DEPOSITION

### Ms. Amanda Ettrick, 27 Wausag Drive. Fulton's Pt., WI

Sure, I'll swear on it. But whatever happens, *you've* got to swear that you won't *ever* tell my best friend Ashley what I'm going to tell you about Neal Bartram or she will have six fits and absolutely die. . . . Yes I do realize this is an official investigation and no information will leave this room. I'm making sure. . . . I'm thirteen next month.

Okay, so this is what happened. Ashley and me first saw Neal when he came to the Post Office a few days after Memorial Day. He was picking up mail for himself and for Ingoldsby. Bev Freneau, the post-mistress, told us when we asked. He was by far the cutest male in town in five years ever since Jake Holloway had to move to Idaho, and he wore like nothing! A teeny little pair of shorts so thin you could see everything, and no shirt. Of course it was hot out. But my best friend Ashley almost died right there in line at the P.O.

I said hello and he was really friendly. He was always friendly to me, whenever he'd drive into town in that little red Chevy coupe of his. So Ash and me took to hanging around him or his car. He never seemed to mind. We knew he was too old for us and all, still you never know.

Well! This went on all summer. We'd see him in the pharmacy, or at the pizza place. We saw him at that multiplex over on Route 18, with Bev. She's older than him and I guess they got along. And that would have been "it," you know what I mean, two girls hoping, *except* Ash thought we could see him without any clothing if we went to Ingoldsby. There's a pool and we knew he'd been a swimmer. Maybe he'd swim nude.

Well! We biked out there even though it's a trek and it's got a reputation for being haunted and all. We saw him at the pool. He wore a gorgeous white and purple Speedo so Ash who's never seen real dick was disappointed. He stretched out and all and never knew we were watching. That's when we saw him talking to himself. Or rather to someone else, maybe two someone elses, on the terrace. Except there was no one there!

Well! You can imagine! Ash said, "Maybe he's rehearsing, like for a play, or something." Sure. A play! *I* think they were ghosts!

So! To make a long story short, even though she'll deny it up and down, I think that absolutely gorgeous as Neal Bartram was — is, you've not found a body, right? — that living at Ingoldsby all alone with those ghosts there, he just snapped one day and killed himself, and I guess you'll find the body sometime soon if you look really hard. Which is a shame because he's like the most beautiful guy in the county.

WITNESSED: A. Estes-TRANSCRIBED: A Nichols, 9/4/00

# 6-E     PORTAGE COUNTY, WI
### FULTON'S POINT POLICE
### 39000 Rte. 18
### Fulton's Pt., WI 53908

## DEPOSITION

<u>Ms. Ashley Sprague, 11 Wausag Drive. Fulton's Pt., WI</u>

What-*ever*! Yes, of course, I'll swear on it. But in turn, you have got to promise that you don't ever let my best friend Amanda know what happened between me and the Divine Neal Bartram, because she is like a total child, not a grown up, though she thinks she is. . . . Oh, great! So . . . like nothing I say can ever leave this room? Teriff. . . . So this is how it goes. We meet Neal in town at the P.O. and he's drop dead gorgeous and we're stupid girls and immediately get ideas, right? Right! But I mention him at home at dinner that night, and my Dad he makes this weird little thing with his mouth like he just ate a rancid nut or something, and he says to my Mom, "I thought you told me they'd never have another caretaker at Ingoldsby after what happened to that guy from Ohio?"

This is something I totally do not know. So while my Mom says, "You read that article in the paper. The Trust is turning it into a museum and landmark and all so they need someone out there, I suppose." To which my Dad makes another one of those faces and so does she.

Later on that evening I ask my Mom what happened to the other caretaker at Ingoldsby, and she tells me what happened when she was my age, around 1979 when they were planning to do something with the estate, remodel it or open it to the public or something like that, she wasn't exactly sure. Her Dad (my grandpa) and my Uncle Matt (by my grandpa's first wife) owned this landscaping and garden business and they were hired to do major work out there at Ingoldsby. According to them, at the end of summer this guy whose name my Mom didn't remember who'd been hired from out of state just disappeared. So the Trust closed Ingoldsby down again and only her Dad and my Uncle ever went out to Ingoldsby anymore from the town and they only went by daylight and always remained together whenever they went.

So I asked my Mom what happened to the guy and she said that his body had never been found. And she said that her grandmother had talked about Ingoldsby as being weird when *she* was a little girl. So that's long time ago. Was it haunted? I asked. And Mom said the way she understood it, it wasn't so much ghosts and all, as just there was something *wrong* with the place. According to her family who's lived here in Portage County a hundred and twenty five years, there's been something wrong with the land on which the estate was built right from the beginning. Which was why no one outbid Frank Ingals when he first got it in 1901 and why his son Chester Ingals had been forced to hire a county construction team from outside Portage County to build the place.

At any rate, my dumb pal Amanda gets some idea in her head that she can seduce Neal Bartram, as though a stud-muffin like him would look twice at a skinny infant like her! But to keep her out of too much trouble, I agree to bike with her out to Ingoldsby one day. We see Neal using the pool, swimming laps, then he's on the deck drying off and then, well suddenly it's like he's talking to people — people who aren't there. You know, gesticulating and all, all totally natural. I'm sure he wasn't onto us hiding and trying to freak us out.

Amanda, however was totally freaked out, saying that Neal is talking to the Ingoldsby ghosts and all. But I remember what my Mom said about the original Indians who lived on that land, how she told me that they believed there were strong spirits on the property. I figure if anyone would be cool enough to talk with spirits it would be Neal since he was so smart and virtually a history professor already, getting his doctorate in American history

according to Mizz Noonan at the library. She told me
that he and she talked a lot and from the way she
spoke of him, I think she kind of also had a crush
on Neal.

So Amanda is freaked and we get out of there, and
she's like crying all night, saying how will Neal
ever escape these awful ghosts and all. Real weepy
and a complete child! For the next few days all I
hear from her is Neal this and Neal that. So I decide
on a plan.

We both know Neal has lunch most days at Joe's
Pharmacy lunch counter, so the next day as me and
Amanda are waiting for him at his car, I slip a note
into his hand when Amanda's not looking and it says
to meet me at a certain time. Well, later that day
I get a phone call from Neal at my home and he says
we can't meet secretly because I'm under age and all.

So I tell him it's not about me or any gooey crap
like that, it's about Ingoldsby and I know a lot
about the place, so he does agree to meet me. We meet
after dinner behind this very office right here, and
I tell him what my Mom had told me about Ingoldsby
and he takes notes and all, and he thanks me and when
I ask him to, he gives me a kiss which is lovely. He
also asks for my Grandpa's address cause he wants to
visit him and also ask him questions about
Ingoldsby.

A few days later Neal phones me again and thanks
me again and he says he's found a lot more information about Ingoldsby and about that caretaker who
disappeared from old newspapers he's dug up at the
Junction City Library. I've been really invaluable
and a true friend, and if he ever publishes an
article about the estate, Neal will be sure to give
me credit along with my Mom and Grandpa, which is
how really nice Neal always is.

So I was feeling really good about it, and even
though I was curious I was also afraid to ask him
who he was talking to and all, he never seemed in
the least bit afraid, or upset, and I never got the
idea that he thought anything was out of his control
at the estate. So you can imagine how like totally

bummed I was when I heard that Neal vanished, too, just like that caretaker from twenty years ago. I just hope you find him okay.

WITNESSED: A.Estes-TRANSCRIBED: A Nichols, 9/4/00

---

# 6-F   PORTAGE COUNTY, WI
## FULTON'S POINT POLICE
### 39000 Rte. 18
### Fulton's Pt., WI 53908

## DEPOSITION

<u>Mrs. Beverly Freneau, 11 Lakeview Ave., Fulton's Pt., WI</u>

I do swear it . . . Actually, I was born here in Portage County, over at the hospital in Monroe, and I grew up here in Fulton's Point, and went to school here, graduated high school and even dated Joe Weyerhauser before I met my husband Jake and we moved to Madison where he was finishing up at the University there. Our son Josh was born in Madison. And I got work in the Post Office in Madison while my husband did his internship and residence there, since we needed money to live on, which was how it was that I managed to get work in the P.O. back here after Jake died and I returned here. Janet Martin was retiring. That was about two years ago that I came back. Hodgkins Lymphoma it was. Went through Jake in five months. One day he was exhausted, next day he had this horrible diagnosis. It seemed like there was nothing inside Jake at all to stop it . . . No, I'm okay. Just every once in a while I naturally think about how . . . you know, how unfair it all is.
I met Neal Bartram I suppose the first time the P.O. was open after Memorial Day when he came in for his mail and for any mail going to Ingoldsby. I could

see the old ladies were frowning and scandalized
and the younger girls tittering and excited just
because he'd taken his shirt off and had strung
it through the belt loops of his shorts. Neal had
been on the swim team as an undergraduate and he
still swam and kept in shape, so clearly he was the
best thing to hit Fulton's Point in years according
to some women. Tonia Noonan at the library for one.
She was completely ga-ga. But me, I've been married
and saw naked men so I guess I wasn't so easily
scandalized nor so excited either.

Over the next few weeks Neal and me got to see
each other more often, either at Joe's lunch
counter or at the P.O. when he came in, and we
chatted if there was no one else waiting. Even sometimes at the library, and my opinion of him changed
a lot. For one thing, the attention he paid to his
body, which could be seen as superficial and just
vanity. Turns out that when he was twelve he had
one lung collapse and, as he was recuperating, the
surgeon who'd helped him survive told Neal that if
he exercised and kept his abdomen and torso hard
and rigid enough, that it would keep him alive
should he ever have a lung collapse again. Also the
swimming helped build up his lungs.

Despite the way Neal dressed, which I'd charac-
terize as Big City college imitation Hip-hop, Neal
Bartram was a serious young man, more serious than
any I'd ever met and that included my husband Jake.
Neal was intelligent, thoughtful and even philosoph-
ical. And in point of fact, it was Joe himself who
threw Neal and me together to go see some older foreign movies playing once a week at the multiplex on
Rte. 18 headed toward Junction City. We'd have dinner
after at Wen Young's place there and talk about the
movies and about, you know, all sorts of things.

Neal didn't fit into the town very well, and he
felt he didn't fit into our time and place very well
either. He was always talking about how much better
this country had been thirty, forty, fifty years ago,
and how much better he thought he'd fit into that
time, that America. He did seem very discontented,

even though there was no outward reason for that. He expected to be done writing his doctoral thesis by the end of summer and he was pretty certain he'd do well defending it — which would be around Thanksgiving — and that he'd receive his Ph.D. by Christmas. So no worries there. He'd begun looking into teaching positions at some Wisconsin and Minnesota universities that were on track to lead to tenure and he'd gotten some solid offers already. Even so, he wasn't completely happy. I always felt he was miles away.

I felt that more and more as the summer went on. He began to become interested, even a little obsessed about Ingoldsby. Every once in a while he'd begin asking me odd questions about the place I couldn't answer. That I don't think anyone could answer who's alive today.

I know other people have been in here giving depositions, including Ashley and Amanda, and I'm sure they told you their suspicions about Neal and myself having an affair. It's true. We did have an affair. It was my doing entirely, and I think Neal was pretty surprised by how aggressive I was at first but after all he was a healthy twenty-four year old man and I don't believe I'm so terrible to look at.

The terrible thing is, I thought it would bring us closer, and it ended up doing just the opposite. Neither one of us wanted it to be public knowledge. Me because Josh would be starting kindergarten soon, and also because people in town here had always assumed that now that I was back in Fulton's Point that Joe Weyerhauser and I would take up again. You know, high school sweethearts and all that bunk. And Neal, well Neal because that's the way he was, very considerate of others, and also very private about himself.

So once we started sleeping together we no longer saw each other during the day except when he came into the P.O. for his mail, or if we happened to run into each other at the food mart or pharmacy or video store, and we cut these meetings short. We stopped going to the movies or Chinese restaurant. It's

really all my fault. You know how word gets around
small towns. Neither of us wanted my reputation hung
out to dry.

In a sense I believe I failed Neal exactly when
he needed me most. I knew from the way he'd begun
asking me questions about Ingoldsby that something
had started to happen between him and the house. I
don't know how else to put it. It wasn't as though
it were haunted. Not exactly. But you know, growing
up here in town, I naturally heard all kinds of
things about the place, true and mostly false, and
it did have a weird reputation. When I was a teen,
guys would dare each other to stay there overnight
and stuff like that.

Not one of the guys I grew up with ever brought
up the name of Ingoldsby without meaning to cause a
shudder. And it always did. Except not for Neal. He
treated it as a special place, but never with any
sense of fear or revulsion or anything like that.
Incomprehension at times, but also an abiding
curiosity to find out more about the place and the
people who'd lived there. Especially during the past
few weeks he was dropping hints just before we'd
fall asleep or just as he had to leave in the morning before Josh woke up, and I got the impression
that Neal was being drawn more deeply into the house
somehow, into its past and its secrets and that he
wasn't in any way unhappy by that. Only he wanted to
understand it better.

So it's ironic that just when we got physically
closer to each other, we drifted apart personally,
me and Neal. Of course, from the beginning I knew
I'd never be able to hold him. That was a foregone
conclusion from the very first time we met. You see,
I handed him an official letter of some sort from
the State Teaching Board, certifying him, I suppose
it was, and it had his full name on it, Neal *Percival*
Bartram . . . You don't get it? Percival was the name
of one of the Knights of the Round Table. He was the
noblest and purest Knight of King Arthur and he went
out in search of the Holy Grail. The composer Wagner
called him Parsifal and wrote an opera about him.

And Parsifal, or Percival? He alone found the Holy Grail.

In some strange way I believe that Neal found his own Holy Grail and that it has something to do with him vanishing into Ingoldsby. You see, Chief, I believe that although we can't see him that Neal is in Ingoldsby somewhere . . . somehow. That's something my so-called woman's intuition tells me for certain. That he hasn't fallen into harm of any sort, but that he's in a place where we can no longer ever find him. And that he's content somehow. I don't know where exactly and I don't know how. And I guess I don't know how to search the right way to actually find him.

Or maybe that's what I want to believe because he's gone and I'm alone without the loveliest young man I ever met and I'm just saying any old crap.

WITNESSED: A.Estes-TRANSCRIBED: A Nichols, 9/4/00

---

# 7. PORTAGE COUNTY, WI
## Office of the County Sheriff
### 172 Elm Street
### Portage, WI 53901

RE: Missing Person: Neal P. Bartram

September 6, 2000

Report on Missing Person: Neal P. Bartram
Pursuant to the complaint/report filed September 1, 2000 by A.J. Torrington of the Ingals Trust in Chicago, received by Officer Jeremy Schaeffer, investigated by the same on September 2, 2000; with a follow up investigation by Chief Abner Estes of the Fulton's Point Police Department, and following no sign of apparent foul play nor of the M/P.

**Action Taken**: September 4, 2000, Chief Estes requested this office to utilize a large number of personnel to conduct a full sweep of the property surrounding the main houses and garage at Ingoldsby. To this end, County Sheriff Griffith A. Angeles did call on six experienced men in addition to the four working for this office, deputized them for the period of the search, repeated instructions as to what we'd be looking for, and we drove in four vehicles to the estate to begin a full, clean sweep of the entire fifteen and a half acres. This lasted 11 a.m. of September 4th to 7 p.m. — nightfall; 11 a.m. through 4 p.m. of September 5th, 2000.

**Results**: Neither M/P Neal P. Bartram nor any of his personal belongings or clothing were found on the property except where he had left them inside the estate's gate-house caretaker's cottage. We did find sneaker prints closely marked around the house at various locations, mostly windows, terrace stairs and doors, that matched the pattern of M/P's shoes. But no other such prints. No signs of struggle or violence. Nothing out of the ordinary at all on the property.

Sheriff and his team then entered the garages and main house and conducted a thorough search of the interior until 7 p.m. Again we found no signs of the M/P or any of his personal belongings.

**Conclusion**: The disappearance of Neal P. Bartram is not connected in any material way to the Ingoldsby Estate. Any further investigation must be focused outside the estate and its grounds.

    Date                                    Signature

*Hey Ab -- this conclusion should make you and the Trust happy. It's off to the D.A.'s office now --Griff*

# 8.    PORTAGE COUNTY, WI

### FULTON'S POINT POLICE
### 39000 Rte. 18
### Fulton's Pt., WI 53908

TO: Madeline Eiche, Esq.
    STATE of WISCONSIN, District Attorney's Office
    Government Center, Building C
    Madison, WI 53711

October 13th, 2000

Report on Missing Person: Neal P. Bartram prepared by Chief Abner Estes with additional reports (enclosed) by Portage County Sheriff Griffin A. Angeles

Dear Ms. Eiche,

Enclosed find all generated reports on the Missing Person. Although both this office and that of Sheriff Angeles will continue to pursue all and any new leads as they may happen to develop, at the moment there is no further possible procedures or lines of investigation to follow.

We are however requesting that your office put this case at the head of the line in your national hotline so that should any leads develop out of state we can receive information immediately.

Upon your validated, dated, signed return of a copy of this report, this office will forward all of the M/P's property left behind to the Ingals Trust, which shall handle it thereafter.

Regretfully,

Abner Estes, Chief

cc: G.A.A. / A.J.T. records

# WISCONSIN STATE POLICE
Cold Case Department
Linklatter Mall, Bldg. E
Eau Claire, WI 54701
Detective-Sergeant Annabella Conklin

To: Wayne G. King, Asst. D.A.
STATE of WISCONSIN, District Attorney's Office
Government Center, Building C
Madison, WI 53711

May 17, 2001

Dear District Attorney King,

In re. your letter to this office of May 13th, 2001: I received all of your materials <u>except</u> the journal noted in the newspaper reports and allegedly written by the M/P Neal Bartram and while they tell a disturbing story indeed, we can't really proceed <u>without</u> that journal. In order for this office to work toward settling what appears to be so unsettled, please send a complete facsimile, or better yet the original of the journal to this office a.s.a.p.

Also note that this office rapidly accessed the National Police Network System and has already received a "strike" on the name of the M/P Neal P. Bartram since his disappearance. It appears to be in some way connected to a bank ATM card of the M/P found in the possession of another person detained and then apparently let go. Will get back to you with more when that data is processed here.

Also note that in light of the extreme mystery involved re: the M/P, that this office has taken what might be seen as an correspondingly extreme action in requesting the M/P's name from all and any official, state, interstate, and national records going back in time to the date of the Time Capsule. I don't expect anything but . . . just checking. This may all take some months.

# WISCONSIN STATE POLICE
Cold Case Department
Linklatter Mall, Bldg. E
Eau Claire, WI 54701
Detective-Sergeant Annabella Conklin

To: Wayne G. King, Asst. D.A.
STATE of WISCONSIN, District Attorney's Office
Government Center, Building C
Madison, WI 53711

May 22, 2001

Dear Mr. King,

I received the material sent from your office re: M/P Cold-Case, reopened as Case #324-01. In other words, the alleged journals of Neal P. Bartram. I glanced them over and will read it in greater detail with notation.

One thing is for sure, the part that was printed on typewriter paper was undeniably printed out by a computer-printer. Our in-office expert confirmed it was a Hewlett-Packard Deskjet, probably a 500 to 600 class printer. The water-marking on the paper confirm that it is Williamette brand, 8 1/2 by 11 inch white "letter-sized copy-paper." The paper is widely sold around the U.S. and Williamette confirmed that the sample of paper we sent them "can not be over eight years old or it would curl at the edges and yellow," as it is a very inexpensive paper, usually sold by the ream.

Our expert also confirmed that the lined notebook pages of some of the journals are contemporary. They come from National Brand: it's Science and Laboratory Notebook #43-571., 128 numbered pages, pale yellow with green lines. Although this has been in National's catalogue for over four decades, the numbers printed on the upper outer corner here that match the Verdana typeface, which National informed him only began to be used in 1998. These notebooks are sold primarily through university bookstores.

Enclosed is a copy of the report we received from the Sheriff's

Office of West Hollywood, California. This was the only "strike" this office has received from the National Police Network System, although the M/P's name remains current. The findings are ambiguous. Who knows who the Caucasian Male was? Can we get another, color photo of M/P?

As per my last letter, inquires have been processed to a dozen different agencies of the U.S. Government re: Neal P. Bartram.

---

# City of West Hollywood
## Sheriff — Dan P. Bellardo
## 2900 San Vicente Blvd
## West Hollywood, CA 90046

RE: Suspicious Person: 4:30 a.m.

November 24th, 2000

Report:

While on ordinary midnight to eight a.m. patrol, Officers Rob Adkins and Mario Guitterez noticed Caucasian Male approximately 20 years old behaving oddly at three ATM windows of a Washington Mutual Bank set somewhat apart from a strip mall at 8100 Sunset Blvd.

Officers drove around a curving block onto Crescent Heights Blvd. and pulled into a parking lot from that street and continued to observe C.M. attempt to use the ATM. Officers theorized that C.M. was probably inebriated, which would explain why he was unable to utilize card.

Officers pulled up to bank and approached C.M. asking him to step away from ATM window. C.M. was surprised by officers' approach, but complied. Tall young gentleman, dark eyes, dark hair, pale skin, well-dressed, well-spoken with an American accent not from California. Officer Adkins asked what the trouble was. C.M. said he was unable to get money out of the bank for some reason. Could we help? Held out typical ATM card toward us.

Officers approached more closely. As C.M. was wearing a close-fitting leather jacket and black denims with dark cowboy boots, there was no reason to expect a revolver. Even so, Office Guitterrez remained apart with one hand on his weapon. Officer Adkins looked at card, which read Chicago Union Bank confirming C.M.'s accent and being a stranger. Card was in the name of Neal P. Bartram. Officer asked if card belonged to C.M. who said, that was him, Neal. P. Bartram. When asked for other ID he produced a wallet with one VISA credit card, library card for Northwestern University, but no driver's license and no picture ID C.M. told officer this was his "second wallet." The "other one" was where he was staying, a block away, 1765 Havenhurst.

On closer inspection, C.M. was not inebriated. As he was courteous and in need of aid, Officer Adkins sought to help him. First ATM machine was not working at all. Second and Third machines, when accessed using card, replied "Sorry! We're Out of Cash" on screens. C.M. asked, "How can that be? They're a bank, aren't they?" We explained that on a holiday weekend like now, Thanksgiving, ATMs often ran out of cash since many people accessed them. We suggested he try again after the holiday. His reply was "Well! I guess I'll just have to."

Officers offered to drive C.M. to where he was staying. He replied "I'll walk. It's such a lovely, balmy, night. Don't you just love Los Angeles at night? I never guessed it would so amazingly wonderful!" C.M. walked off in correct direction toward Havenhurst Ave..

Officer Adkins noticed from balance receipt left by C.M. in his possession that the total balance for both of C.M.'s accounts was substantial — six figures.

# STATE of WISCONSIN
# District Attorney's Office
## Government Center, Building C
## 120 State Street
## Madison, WI 53711
## Wayne G. King, Assistant D.A.

To: Detective-Sergeant Annabella Conklin
    Wisconsin State Police, Cold Case Department
    Eau Claire, WI 54701

May 28th, 2001

Re: Case #324-01

Dear Det.-Sgt. Conklin,

As per your request, enclosed find copies this office has on file, previously sent to us by Portage County Police, of M/P Neal P. Bartram's ID viz.:

1) His Illinois driver's license

2) His Northwestern University graduate student/ faculty ID

Note that both documents show Bartram to be five feet six and a half inches in height, with "light brown eyes." On his DMV's ID "blonde hair" is listed, while on the school ID it's listed as "light brown" hair. The two photo's xeroxed here confirm that coloring.

Hardly sounds like the "Tall young gentleman, dark eyes, dark hair, pale skin," of the West Hollywood Sheriff's Department report. Also the large sum of money involved now gives us another alibi for potential foul play against Bartram. Especially as the person stopped was trying to access the money and possessed the ATM code. It is however odd how cavalier

he was about not getting it, although he might be a con-
summate actor, not wanting to throw further suspicion
upon himself.

Please look into those Chicago Union Bank accounts
belonging to the M/P.


                                    Wayne G. King


---

# CHICAGO UNION BANK
## 24 South Wacker Drive
## Chicago, IL 60606
## Government Liaison Office

Detective-Sergeant Annabella Conklin,
Wisconsin State Police, Cold Case Department
Eau Claire, WI 54701

June 3rd, 2001

Re: Your Case #324-01 — Our Acct: 2770979913

Dear Detective-Sergeant Conklin,

Confirming our telephone conversation of May 29, 2001.
As I told you then, the account of your Missing Person,
Neal P. Bartram was accessed by a person or persons using
his ATM number. In fact, right after Thanksgiving of last
year — the date of your forwarded West Hollywood Police
Report — $500.00 was withdrawn. But just before the end

of the year, December 29, 2000, we received Wisconsin State's notification of Bartram's Missing Person status, and we immediately sealed his accounts.

Until that date the account had been accessed as follows.

Withdrawals:

| | | |
|---|---|---|
| October 5, 2000 | — $500.00 | ATM, Madison, WI |
| October 30, 2000 | — $800.00 | ATM, Reno, NV |
| November 12, 2000 | — $600.00 | ATM, San Francisco, CA |
| November 26, 2000 | — $500.00 | ATM, Los Angeles, CA |

Deposits:

| | | |
|---|---|---|
| October 17, 2000 | — $12,000.00 | The Ingals Trust, Chicago, IL |
| December 18, 2000 | — $250,000.00 | Anders Escrow, Fair Oaks, IL |

Attempts to reach next of kin on Bartram's 1994 application were returned, stamped "deceased" by the Post Officer of his home town. They confirmed that his parents were killed in an airplane crash in April, 1999, outside Missoula, Montana. The first deposit is a direct payment for his caretaking duties. Before this, Bartram received two checks for sixty-five thousand dollars each for each parent's loss, as insurance payouts. The last deposit shown above was from the sale of the Bartram home of which he was sole heir. This is an interest bearing account. We would appreciate any help your office can provide locating Mr. Bartram's heir or heirs.

Georgia Dimaggio-Wilkes

# STATE of ILLINOIS
## Bureau of Records
### Richard J. Daley Center
### 400 East Adams
### Springfield, IL 62701

Detective-Sergeant Annabella Conklin
Wisconsin State Police, Cold Case Department
Eau Claire, WI 54701

June 8th, 2001

Re: Your Case #324-01
Our Case: #98-230-2310

Dear Detective-Sergeant Conklin,

A codicil to the Last Will and Testament of Neal P. Bartram was received by this office on September 30, 2000, drawn up by Ralph J. Elysious, Atty at Law, 65 Station Avenue, Junction City, WI, on September 29th, 2000 and witnessed by two persons known to the decedent.

In his codicil, Mr. Bartram asserts that he is of sound mind and body, and explains that he is revising his will of September 14, 1996 in light of the death of his parents, as well as in the partial receipt and expected full receipt of insurance monies pertaining to their death.

He states that he continues to wish that his maternal cousins, Dean and Daryl St. Clair of Bellington, WA, receive monies — now in the amount of $20,000 — apiece to be held in trust for them by the Chicago Union Bank until their 18th birthday. He leaves the "bulk of the estate to my dear friend," Anthony Jackson Kirby of Milwaukee, WI and Los Angeles, CA.

Although this office is empowered to give over those monies once this will has been properly probated according to Illinois state law, we did not possess any exact address for Mr. Kirby until January 12ᵗʰ, 2001, when he phoned this office and provided one.

I hope this answers your questions. A copy of this has been sent to Ms. Dimaggio-Wilkes of the Chicago Union Bank.

Office Mgr. — Ruby Tobias

---

# THE JOURNALS OF NEAL P. BARTRAM

*(parts handwritten in notebook and otherwise transcribed to computer C-drive under Microsoft Documents: "What the . . . ?")*

*June 2, 2000*

Had a start yesterday, which became a mystery. Don't know what to make of it.

Was on the big John Deere machine which I finally figured out how to baby to keep it working without shutting itself off every five minutes. I was mowing the lawn on the south side of the house at Ingoldsby. It's such a boring job, I'd brought my headphones and portable CD player, and was listening to REM when I happened to look up and saw two people standing on the deck, off what I thought might be the dining room.

It was a bright sunny day — really hot again; close to 90°F — and there they were! Young man and young woman, dressed all in white, yet oddly. He was tall, and not really thin but broad one way, slender the other, with a shock of dark brown hair and dark eyes. She had light brown hair or blond hair, was much shorter, with pale eyes but I couldn't really make them out due to the shadows. She wore a sort of flimsy sun-dress I guess you'd call it. Very thin material of some gauzy sort that caught and lifted with every breeze. She was slender — amazingly attractive in that outfit — her hair was short, and cut close around in back to her lower neck, yet kept long around the sides and front, and very curly. She was very pretty. I couldn't stop staring. He was very pretty too, if you like guys.

They looked as though they were talking intently about something. He leaned down to insist on something. She put a hand on his arm — he wore a white V-neck sweater (in this weather?) over a long sleeved white shirt and pants of some thin material and white and brown wingtips. They looked like they belonged in a play, but were too far away for me to hear what they were saying. All of a sudden, he leaned down and kissed her lips. She didn't pull back or anything, but she kept him from doing it a second time.

I came to my senses and shouted at them, something like, "Hey! You there! This is private property! What are you doing here?"

They looked at me. He said something to her. She squinted at me and half smiled. They turned around and went inside the house.

I shifted to neutral, engaged the brake, jumped off the mower and ran to the house.

The terrace was empty and the door they'd just gone through was solidly locked. Looking inside I couldn't see anyone or anything.

I walked around toward the living room windows and entry and saw no one, only covered furniture inside, as usual. I doubled back and tried the windows, headed toward the kitchen and pantry. No one inside there either. Hopped on the Deere and zipped around to the bedroom wing and looked in there.

No one. Every door of the house locked up as it usually is. Where did they go?

Went back to mowing but I kept checking around. Didn't see any strange cars or vehicles and I didn't see the two again. Where did they come from? Where did they go?

What the . . . ?

June 4, 2000

Was cleaning my teeth last night before going to sleep. Had a long, and pretty exhausting day, first clipping and trimming those bushes alongside the north side of the house at Ingoldsby, and then reading more of Morrison and Ledrick's texts, taking more notes for my last few chapters, then going to town (!) for some food shopping. So I was good and ready for bed, there in the little bathroom, flossing away, when I heard music through that little pebbled glass window I've been leaving open for better circulation.

It sounded like old jazz music, I don't know maybe Tommy Dorsey, Glen Miller, something like that. That kind of old instrumental sound, lots of winds and brass and a piano, instruments doubling up for solos.

Tried to place where it could be coming from. There's nothing in the south until you hit town some seven miles away. Nothing west, until Junction City, some twenty miles away, nothing to the north and west except Ingoldsby.

I finished flossing and was brushing when I had an idea: What if those kids I'd seen before had come back to the house to hang out and brought a boom-box with them?

I was still wearing shorts and a T-shirt so I put on sneakers and went out. Sure enough, once I was outside, the music sounded much more like it was coming from the house.

This time I was smart enough to stop in the gate house garage and pull out two big rings of keys for the house. Then I loped over the little rise to the house.

Ingoldsby was dark as soon I was in view of it, say a football field away, and it was silent too, but with a conscious kind of silence, as though someone could see me coming, although I don't know how. I was wearing dark clothing and it was a clouded-over night.

I ran quietly to the house. Totally dark. No one there. I used my keys to go into the dining room terrace door, then when that proved empty, through the pantry door, around and into that door to the bedroom off the swimming pool. Place was empty, dark, noiseless.

I almost expected to hear the music start up again soon as I'd gotten back to the gate house, but it didn't.

I am <u>sure</u> I heard that music. I am <u>sure</u> I saw that couple.

June 5, 2000

In town at Joe's Pharmacy having lunch. He and I and that older guy, Dr. Rodman or whatever his name is, were shooting the breeze and I said something about hearing music at night, but not being able to find the source. Dead silence, then the both of them had a fast answer. Joe said on still nights out here on the plains you can hear sounds from twenty miles away. The doctor said it might have been someone's car radio as they drove by, or parked to make out. That makes more sense to me.

Was in the library a little later and that Miss Noonan, the librarian, the one who wears all that lilac scent on her that's like dust and powder whenever she moves, kind of smothering you, she was being friendly and asked how I was liking living out "in the sticks" after the big city (i.e. Chicago). I told her about the music I'd heard. She too had an answer: said she read about it somewhere, how the mind makes up sounds in the quiet so it can be comforted, and not afraid. Yeah. Right, Miss Noonan!

June 7, 2000

I had no intention of keeping a journal until this stupid business at the house began but now that I have, well, I guess I want to write about Bev Freneau, the postmistress (does that sound dirty or what). She's about twenty-eight and not really my type ("What type?" Bobby G. would ask, "When you're horny?") and slender but not skinny and with really nice breasts, pointy and nice hips, though her rear is a little flat for my taste, and long dark hair she's keeping wrapped up high around her head in the heat wave we're having and she is pure s.e.x. and she knows it and she knows I know it too. So I was surprised when she moved over from the counter to one of the "café tables" in the pharmacy lunch counter today and began talking to me. Those olive green eyes and nice skin. I mean she's no kid and I guess she thinks I am. Well, I was about to leave, was paying and Bev said she had to get back to the P.O. when Joe said, "Hey Bev, maybe Neal here would wanta see that old movie." Turned out they were planning to go to the multiplex up on Route 18 but she wanted to see a French film made during World War II, I think she said, playing one night only, and Joe wanted to see the new James Bond and so I said sure, I'd go with her. So we have a date, I guess, for the weekend.

Don't want to make too much out of it but, even though I knew it would happen out here, I find I am missing sex: especially as all the women in town(!) from twelve to a hundred look me over like they want to eat me alive and with this heat believe you me I am giving them everything to look at short of public lewdness, but not a damn one of them except the little girls will even say hello. Oh, except Miss Noonan at the library who makes me sneeze. But it's not like school where I had two or three women who'd drop by a week including Connie (with that mouth!) and it was so easy meeting women around the school when I had my bike.

June 8, 2000

Nothing happened. Sexually, I mean. We met at her place, the downstairs of a two story house, not sure who lives upstairs, but whoever it was was looking after Bev's son Josh who's going to be five next month. We drove to the movie, which was crowded on a Saturday night, with five theaters full. Didn't see Joe Weyerhauser but nearly everyone I'd ever seen in Fulton's Point was at one or the other movie houses because they were milling about before and in the lobby getting popcorn and sodas.

The movie we saw was set in Paris in the middle of the 19th Century and it was, well, what can I say, it blew me away. Totally unexpectedly and at the end as Garance in her carriage was swept away from her actor lover by the ocean of celebrating crowds, it just broke my heart as though I were the guy himself and when the lights came up I had tears all down my face and so did Bev. We weren't alone either. It had been over three hours long and it just went by like nothing, like the wind, like life, I suppose.

We strolled a bit — she'd taken my hand as we left the theater. On the other side of the huge parking lot were a few restaurants including The Wen Young Chinese Food Outlet, so we went in there to eat, both being hungry by then, even though it was after eleven. Bev said this was the site of the original — they're a chain — and we had a pretty good meal, so maybe I'll try the take-out one in Fulton's Point.

She told me the movie we'd seen had been made during World War II in France and that after the war the female star, Arletty, whose connections with a certain Nazi officer had helped the film be made underground, was deemed a traitor and had her head shaved and all. Amazing though that it could be made in secret with all those extras in the movie and the sets and all. So we had plenty to talk about me and Bev and when we got to her place, she said they were showing another good one next week and maybe we could go. I said if it were half as good as this, sure, and she kissed me on the cheek real soft and went in.

During dinner she told me about her husband and kid and all. She's had a pretty hard life for someone so young. I was already shaken up by the movie and I told her she'd gotten a raw deal and deserved some happiness. I meant it. And she knew I meant it.

June 9, 2000

I said I'd seen people and heard music at Ingoldsby. Yesterday afternoon, the weather changed to cloudy and cool. The gate-house flat was still warm so I wandered outside with my Ledrick and thought I'd hang out on the bedroom terrace where the pool is. Torrington at the Ingals Trust said I could fill up and use the pool as long as I kept it clean. I've been swimming there on and off usually in the early a.m. And I've pulled one of the wooden chaise lounges out of storage in the big garage.

So yesterday I mosey on down there in the afternoon, and what do I see? Three chaise lounges out and covered with pillows, as well as a matching low wood table, and there on the terrace, with the bedroom door open, were the guy and the girl I'd seen before. This time they were dressed a little differently. He was in one chaise, reading, and she was busily watering plants I'd never noticed before, three big geraniums on stands and a few hanging white petunias. Both wore old fashioned retro sunglasses, almost round.

The guy noticed me first and shouted, "He's come back!" Not to her so much as to someone inside the bedroom. This other guy came out wearing a pair of strange looking bathing trunks and a paisley bathrobe mostly open. Tall guy with lots of reddish brown hair, still wet from his swim, big pale blue eyes, big nose, big mouth, big smile. Introduced himself as Chester Ingals, and asked who I was.

I told him I'd been hired for the summer to watch the place and keep the lawns and bushes trimmed. Introduced myself. Said I didn't know anyone would be using the house.

"We're just down on a whim!" he admitted. "But it's so hot in town we decided to stay a few days." He introduced me to the girl, who is pert and pretty as I remember — did half a curt-sey meeting me — name of Cecilia Nash, "My ward," Chester said. The other guy was "Anthony Kirby, my best friend since childhood."

Very easy going folks, although clearly they've got piles of moola. Or at least Chester does. Not sure about the others. I said I'd been using the pool and was that okay, and he said sure, anytime.

So I stripped down to my Speedo — the violet one with the white stripe — and they made a big fuss over it. "Hubba-Hubba!" Chester said. Tony and Celia asked what it was made of and Tony sort of grabbed the material and said it felt like rayon. I thought everyone knew about Speedos. Guess not. "That Speedie going to stay on when you dive in?" Tony asked. Chester explained the physics of how it gripped my glutes and when wet would presumably grip even more, doing it all very scientifically. They're both funny guys. Meanwhile I could tell Celia was trying not to look at my package too much.

I dove in and did my usual ten minutes of laps. Chester joined me afterwards and Tony, without a bathing suit — Celia said she was "shocked. Simply shocked!" and went indoors. The two guys started rough-housing and I got out and found her coming out again, dressed less casually and she reminded the other two that they had an appointment to visit Chester's grandmother a few towns over for lunch, so they got out and said I could stay but I put on my shorts and sweat shirt and took off.

I guess they were out late, because I heard that old time jazz music playing again late last night. So I'm <u>not</u> crazy after all.

June 9, 2000

I <u>said</u> I'd seen about the people at Ingoldsby, I can't quite put my finger on it, but there's something not quite . . . I don't know what I'm writing here!

Wait. For one thing, this guy Tony, he's as queer as anyone I've ever met. Certainly queer as Nate, as in "Gay Nate the gay roommate" I roomed with two years undergraduate at Chicago. Yet no one seems to notice it. He looks at me at times like he could swallow me without chewing, then the next minute he's all over Celia being stupidly romantic.

Meanwhile, I'm still trying to figure out all of their relationships to each other. Chester said that Celia was his "ward." I looked that up in the O.E.D. and he seems too young to have a ward, unless that's their way of saying she's his girl. His "paramour" Celia would say, blushing. She blushes at everything I say and half of what the others say, and I actually believe her. Then there's Chester himself. He's obviously in charge of the place. It's his house, he's told me that. But is he doing Celia? Or is he doing Tony? Or is anyone doing anyone? Or are they all doing each other? Like I say I can't quite figure it out.

And some of the words they use? I mean where do they dig them up? The other day Tony said that surely "a healthy young fellow like yourself must know at least one round-heels in town."

At least one <u>what</u>?

So Tony explained, surprised that I didn't know the term: it means "a woman who falls backwards into bed easily, as though her heels were rounded."

Is that nuts or what?

Still, they're nice folks, easy going and fun to spend time with. Chester and Tony have known each other since they were little kids, and Celia has known them almost as long. Oh, Chester took me aside and said I should call him, much hesitation, I should call him by his nickname. I waited, wondering what it could be? "Penis-breath?" "Hung-stud?"

Suspense, then — "Bud!"

Well, it's better than Chester. And he sort of looks like a Bud. Not quite fully formed. A big boy. Oh, and once they all heard I was writing my Ph.D. thesis they were like suddenly very impressed, and it was "Shouldn't you be studying?" or "Shouldn't you be busy writing?" until I cleared that up. I do that here at the gate-house apartment.

But Celia? well she is very, very pretty, sexy-pretty, and she knows it, and she flirts all the time. It's all I can do not to have a chubby when I'm around her. Then I remember if I do, there's always Tony checking me out.

But hey, at least I'm not bored anymore.

June 14, 2000

They must have brought their own furniture and stuff or gotten some of it from out of storage nearby, because when I stepped into the bathroom — "the water-closet," they call it — looking for a towel, I noticed the bedroom was filled with things, a bed, big reading chair, tables. They were playing music and it was coming out of a console built into this long wall in Bud's bedroom — the place is filled with built-ins, hidden bureaus, etc.

Bud showed it to me and it was this ancient and really handsome blond-wood record player, playing these old, long-playing 78 RPM records! So I checked out the rest of the collection — in an adjoining built-in cabinet natch — and it was all Billy Holiday and Louie Armstrong, Arturo Toscanini and Arthur Nikisch and stuff like that. In the old original covers which are in great condition too. Totally retro. Very cool, Bud!

Oh and the retro theme is throughout the bedroom. On the table that's cantilevered out of — you guessed it — the built-in headboard of the bed, I found all these cool old magazines from like the 30's, Vanity Fair, Punch, an old

New Yorker, and this nifty old issue of Popular Mechanics that had this futuristic drawing of a streamlined car on the cover, and it read "Oldsmobile's Big Breakthrough — The Hydromatic Transmission!"

How cool is that?

Have to borrow one of the magazines some day. Just love that old Americana.

While the others were busy doing something, I let Celia touch my "Speedie" as all three of them call it. She said it was soft as a Siamese Cat. Mee-oow! A chubby and a lot of blushing.

June 15, 2000

Glory Hallelujah! I finally got laid! What's it been? Three weeks or more? A record for me going celibate. But the long dry spell is over. And I must have sensed it was going to happen because just before showering to go out with Bev last night, I beat off, just so I wouldn't be too ready.

After the movie we went to the Chinese place again and talked again. This time she asked me about myself but I kept moving the conversation back to her, asking about her kid and her family and what it was like growing up here in "Nowhere'sville." As much to keep her on topic as because I don't really want to talk about myself and my, lately, extremely stupid life. And it paid off.

Seeing her into her doorway I began kissing her and she pulled me deep into the doorway and she was like all over me, so I turned the key she'd put in the door, and opened it and pushed us in, and she said, "Yes, yes, no one should see," and from there it was the old Bartram smoothness in control, of course along with her being really hot and hungry, I mean her husband's been dead what three years and he was sick the last six months and what if she hasn't, you know, in a really long time?

So by the time we got into her bedroom, most of our clothing was off and I was eating her out, then pushing her down on me, then BA-BANG. Even with having come early I was hot enough for three pops, no pulling out, finish one, go for the next. She popped a minimum six times, she was all wet, grabbing me like a crazy woman. I got away when the old lady upstairs caring for the little boy came down, calling "Is that you, Bev?" Snuck out the bedroom window. Round-heeled woman, huh?

June 16, 2000

Wait one minute. Wait just one minute. Something happened yesterday at the house with the three of them, and I may be crazy after all. I mean seriously fucking nuts. Maybe losing my folks and staying with the thesis despite that and then coming here away from everyone and everything I know really did unhinge me more than I thought, because what happened yesterday afternoon was . . .

Let me tell it step by step. Ever since the heat wave broke the weather's been lousy here. Cool, damp, stormy looking. Yesterday was no exception. So after my morning work I walked over to Ingoldsby to use the pool. They're all there, wide awake, as I strip down for a swim. When I get back out and put on my sweatshirt, they're talking about this mystery novel Tony's reading by one Raymond Chandler, The Big Sleep, which sounds familiar and he's making fun of it, reading examples of really bad purple prose. Bud says, "Tony could write better of course." Celia — who's wearing this short sleeved sky blue sweater and no bra under it — says "It's the hit of the season. Can fifty thousand readers be wrong?" And they're arguing, while I'm wondering wasn't that the name of a movie with Bogart and Bacall? Detective Phillip Marlowe and all? So I begin asking questions and sure enough it's the same story. So that was weirdness number one. Why write a novel based on an movie that's been out more than fifty years?

Tony meanwhile says what does Celia know about real literature since all she reads is the communists, then he names John

Steinbeck, Ellen Glasgow, and Maxim Gorky, two of which I read stories of in high school, and I remember the teacher called them Regionalists, not commies. So this argument goes further, until Bud jumps in the pool and grabs Tony and pulls him in too. Celia gets terrifically splashed. Their usual horseplay. But she's soaking and pissed, especially as it's a nice skirt she's wearing. She asks me to go in and get a towel, would I? Then Bud and Tony, who are in the pool, ask for towels, too.

So I go into the bath — not the water closet, they're separate — and find a handful and I hear Bud yelling to come out and see something; looks like lightning coming quickly across the hills toward the house. From indoors the sky has turned weirdly dark, rose-colored if that makes any sense, and as I head out to the pool terrace, I yell to them to get the hell out of the pool, and there's this enormous crack of thunder and huge bolt of lightning at the same time, hitting I swear to God right over Ingoldsby, absolutely <u>deafening</u> and <u>blinding</u>. I drop the towels and run outside afraid they're hit and . . .

Okay, I'm going to write it . . . and <u>there was no one there</u>. Nothing there. Wait that's not true. My sweatpants and book were where I'd left them. The chaise longue, too. But only one. No other furniture. None of the flowers or plants Celia fusses with. The pool was there, with water. But they were gone. All three of them. Not a sound. Then, it gets better, when I turned around, the house was closed and locked and indoors completely empty except for what's usually covered with sheets and sealed with scotch tape. Totally different than I'd left it all not a half minute before!

Even the towels I'd just dropped on the lintel were gone and the bedroom door was closed and, yes, locked. Whatever the storm was, it moved away pretty quickly, as I stood there on the terrace. Believe me, I stood there awhile trying to figure out what had happened.

I didn't succeed.

June 19, 2000

One thing's now straightened out. For better or worse.

The guy who hired me, A.J. Torrington? He phoned on his weekly check-up and after we'd talked a while about the place and its upkeep and all, as casually as I could, I asked if any of the Ingals family who owns the place ever came down for a visit.

"They might. But they'd let me know and I'd let you know in advance. Why? Has anyone been bothering you there?"

I told him no, then asked him to clarify: they don't <u>ever</u> come down for a week in the summer, or a weekend?

"Of course not. The elder members go off to Maine and the Riviera. As for the one's your age, they go to the Seychelles and Rarutonga and places like that. No one's used the place in over fifty years! That's why the Trust is thinking of giving it to the state."

"To the state?"

"Yes. As a museum."

I thanked him for clarifying.

Yes, thank you, very much, Sir! Oh and by the way, Mr. Torrington, I thought I would let you know that I am <u>totally fucking nuts</u>.


June 20, 2000

Haven't been back to Ingoldsby since Sunday and you know what happened. It's remained stormy and cool, cloudy, so I've kept all the windows in the gate house apartment closed. No yardwork to do. Have not swum, but I have done some jogging — in the opposite direction.

In town yesterday afternoon having lunch at Joe's lunch counter, got to talking to Doc Stansbury — seems Rodman is his first name. I hinted as I'd not had a physical exam in years. He's semi-retired, but he said I should come over to his office. I did. He had all the equipment, although the office was fairly closed and not much used.

Sort of hinted around at what I'd told the librarian, hearing strange noises and stuff. Mentioned what those girls, Ashley and Amanda, who always hang around me, said, about Ingoldsby being haunted. He said nothing, then asked if I wanted sleeping pills. Told me I should have more activities to occupy me. He and Joe play gin rummy. They're missing a third for the summer. Would I join them. Said I would.

So Doc didn't exactly brush off the whole thing, and I didn't push it. But as I was leaving, he asked in a low voice, "So these 'events'? Are they just auditory or visual too?"

"Sometimes visual too," I admitted. He recommended lots of beer and movie-going and the sleeping pills he was prescribing. Why is it I think he knows something he's not letting on? Oh great! Now I'm getting paranoiac too.

Just for historical accuracy, the second movie Bev and me saw was Bertolucci's 1900, another sweeping, this time Italian, history movie. Pretty good. Kindy pervy too at times. As involving as the other one.

June 21, 2000

Still haven't been back to Ingoldsby. But I did join Joe and Dr. Stansbury for cards at the pharmacy last night. Joe closed up and pulled down the shades. Lots of fun. Nice guys. Of course, I'm one of those really annoying people who doesn't remember how a card game is played or what's wild or what wins, until I'm told. Then whammo! We were all three neck and neck for an hour or so, then I pulled ahead and beat Joe and Doc.

Won two dollars and seventy cents. Penny a point.

June 22, 2000

Still not gone back to Ingoldsby. But it seems I have a standing date with Bev on Saturday for the movies — read the "fuckies," because we skipped the movies, went to dinner at the

Chinese place, then I drove her back and we were all over each other. I didn't beat off earlier this time and I came while she was doing me with her mouth, and then another four times. Not since that mulatto chick Gina have I had such hot sex. It's not that we fit so well, or have even once come at the same time. We're sort of like big cats with each other licking and biting and all. That is when we're not wrestling or wrestling our way out of the sheets. One of these days that kid of hers is going to walk right in on us. I got away in time. Slept to noon today. Totally fucked out. Didn't even need the pills Doc gave me.

June 23, 2000

Okay, so it had been over a week since I'd been there and I was feeling better about my life, so I took my mind in my hands and went for a walk down to, you guessed it, Ingoldsby, Speedo on underneath my shorts and T-shirt. Lovely sunny day. Just going for a swim, right. Like nothing had happened there. Ever.

Okay. I walked down to Ingoldsby and <u>there they were</u>. They were laying around the pool terrace, which of course was fully furnished as before, like nothing had happened. All three seemed to be in various states of prostration. (So if I'm nuts, I'm at least consistent and yet original too, since they're never quite exactly the same as they were before, are they?) Believe me, I resisted the urge to ask: uh would any of you care to tell me where you <u>utterly vanished to</u> the other day?

I resisted partly because it seems like they were preoccupied with hangovers. Seems they'd had quite a busy Sunday night at some playboy pal of Bud's party. Bunky Huenecker — seems everyone they know has names like Bunky and Muffy and Fluffy. Rich kids! Or rich whatever they are.

Bud was the least incapacitated. He was actually hitting golf balls off tees. And so he was up and around. Celia meanwhile, wearing those funny dark glasses even though it was gray outside, insisted that she was making breakfast for everyone.

This would consist of — get this! — three pancakes per person, ham, Canadian bacon, three eggs each and toast with no doubt huge gobs of butter on it. I said I'd pass, I'd eaten. Seems she'd gotten a little tipsy the previous night and, I'm quoting Bud now, "Danced the kasaztka with someone who claimed to be Russian royalty." Tony, however, was laid out on a chaise, mostly under a bath towel — yes one of <u>those</u> towels — moaning now and then. It turns out he also had won a bet by outdrinking some other idiot by downing a magnum of French champagne, i.e. the Good Stuff. Bud meanwhile sported a tiny little shiner which, when I probed, turned out was due to a quote political difference unquote he'd had with another partygoer over . . . (I stop for effect, should any damn fool except me ever read this) . . . over Mussolini's invasion of Ethiopia. "When I mentioned how repulsive it seemed for Italians with gatling guns to be casually sipping Chianti and mowing down fellows with spears, he accused me of being a, you know, darkie-lover."

My first thought was — now I've heard everything! Then I asked Bud why he was upset over Mussolini rather than the invasion of Poland, or the Anschluss with Austria or the Sudetenland or one of Germany's other atrocities. He looked me in the face with a completely straight face and said, "But Neal old pal, everyone knows we'll have to go to war with Hitler eventually." Tony asked us to lower our speech to a scream, <u>please</u>.

It was that ever so casually said 'eventually' that somehow got to me.

So I watched Bud hit a bunch of balls away from the house, then Celia came out again, with a tray with dishes, silverware and big glasses of orange juice, saying food would be a few minutes more. And she looked so pretty with her pale-yellow, short-sleeved little sweater that I said, "Fine. I'll have some of your cholesterol drenched breakfast!" And she seemed happy about it, although Tony said, "For someone who eats what looks to me like nuts and bolts and plain water, some real food might do you good."

And that was when the idea crossed my mind. "Do you two also think that we'll eventually go to war with Germany?" I asked Celia and Tony when we sat down to eat. They both said they found current events, and European current events especially, far too boring for words. Would I change the subject, please.

Afterward, they went indoors for naps and I strolled with Bud to his garage — doors wide open of course — and we talked about his cars. When I called them antique, he said "The only antique is that Stanley Steamer my grandfather brought." We then talked about his newest acquisition, an Oldsmobile four door convertible he told me was ridden in by — get this — "Fiorello when he opened the New York's World's Fair. Look inside on the floor, notice anything different?"

I looked, said I didn't notice anything different.

"You must be <u>blind</u>. This car has <u>no clutch</u>!" Bud exulted.

They came out again and I said I'd bring a "Speedie" for Tony to wear. I also flirted outrageously with Celia. And waited for you know what.

But they never disappeared and I ended up leaving to go do thesis work.

Crazy as all this may be and crazy as I may be, I am developing a "theory" in which I am <u>not completely insane</u>. Which itself is probably a perfect sign of my insanity.

June 25, 2000

Went to town, had lunch in the pharmacy — Bev flew out as I came in, not even looking at me — and afterward I stopped in the library. I was looking up dates in the big Encyclopedia Americana they've got there when Ms. Noonan — "Please, Neal. Call me Tonia! All my friends do!" — asked what I was doing, and when I mentioned the time period I was looking for, she brought over two reference books. One was a <u>Time-Life Book, 1933-1942</u>, the other was a Time Line book, <u>Black Tuesday to Pearl Harbor</u>. So I opened the first and it had photos and there they were, photos of girls with their hair cut like Celia's, wearing those short sleeved sweaters and long skirts like she does, and guys with those big bathing suits like Bud and Tony's. And there were the photos of the 1939 Worlds Fair, with Mayor "Fiorello" La Guardia riding in Bud's car, which the caption said was the very first car on sale with automatic transmission. ("You must be <u>blind</u>. This car has <u>no clutch</u>!") And when I looked in the Time-Line under "literary best sellers" sure enough I found Chandler's mystery, <u>The Big Sleep</u> and Steinbeck's <u>The Grapes of Wrath</u>, arguably his most "communistic" book, together under what year?

1940.

1940. Almost two years before the U.S got involved in World War II. Eleven years after the Depression began. About three or four after the country really began to pull out of that depression. A sort of magic twenty-four months of American life — teetering between a bad past and a worse to come future.

Okay here's <u>My Theory</u>: Bud Ingals, Celia Nash and Tony Kirby are living in the summer of 1940. And when I'm there with them, so am I.

Comments are not asked for and not required.

So naturally I concentrated on that year and I looked up as much as I could.

I was there all afternoon, taking tons of notes. Finally Tonia stepped out and came back, carrying a Snapple Ginseng Tea — guess she's seen me sipping them — and we talked about the "good old times" together. "I'll bet people were a whole lot nicer then," she mused and really seemed sweet. (If I could only shake off all the powder she wears, like in a shower or something, she might be do-able. She's not that old. And she does seem awfully interested in me and — should I write it —

awfully ready.)

By the way, also on that best seller list, a Pocket Book one of the first paperbacks, costing 25 Cents, of — are you ready? — Thomas Hardy's <u>The Return of the Native</u>.

At any rate, here goes more evidence for my theory: the three occupants of Ingoldsby dress in fashions of 1940 and speak a more formal English, even when trying to be casual. Their slang is, well let's face it, pretty old hat. If they are, what can one call them? Not apparitions: they're as physically solid, and touch-able as me — and they really are living in 1940 — though I have no idea how! — still at least that can be tested, proven.

June 27, 2000

So I'm home after dinner last night and I'm about to work on my thesis and playing back some verbal notes on my cassette recorder when I hear this car horn going "Ooga! Ooga!" down-stairs. I flip a new tape into it, saying, "Could this be a sound of 1940! Can sounds they make be heard and recorded?" You know, a real Dan Rather. When I hear a shout outside the window and go look. It's Joe Weyerhauser standing up in the passenger seat of this big old red convertible Doc is driving. Seems it's Doc's '55 Buick Roadmaster.

They say they've got two six packs of beer and three kinds of chips — potato, tortilla and corn — do I wanna play gin.

What a schmuck I am, thinking it was Bud and the others!

Doc and Joe come up and I clear the table and we begin to play.

Halfway through the game I begin asking questions about Ingoldsby. You know as casual as possible. How come no one's lived there in over fifty years like Torrington told me. Since I would live there in a second and all. Doc is being close-mouthed but Joe spills that "no one from the Ingals family ever used the place regularly after what happened there."

Now we're getting somewhere. Me, innocent: "Oh? What

happened there?"

Seems according to the two of them — mostly agreeing though not always — back "before the Second World War" there was a freak fire and it killed the heir to the Ingals fortune along with two of his friends. Then Joe says, <u>allegedly</u> killed them, since his Grandpa, who was on the volunteer fire force, always insisted that no bodies were ever recovered from the fire.

When I ask more pointed questions, Doc, who's about seventy-two or so and must have been a kid of twelve at the time, tells me lots of rumors he heard, then clams up and tells Joe to do so too. So naturally I ask if the three who died in the fire are the ghosts.

"Why?" Doc asks me, point-blank. "You seeing ghosts at Ingoldsby?"

Very sharp! He already thinks I'm mental. What could I say except: "Of course not, but I'd heard about them in town." Slick escape from that one.

At least I won four dollars off them!

June 28, 2000

The microfiche newspapers at the Fulton's Point Library only goes back fifty years. If I want earlier I've got to go to Junction City. I'm driving there today.

June 29, 2000

Saw Bev again last night. We didn't even have dinner. Just sex. No talk, no pretenses anymore, we just got down to the nitty-gritty

But the real news is what I found at the <u>Junction City Intelligencer</u>, Portage County's newspaper "since 1871!" which for a dollar allowed me to read, select, and photocopy its paper for May 26<sup>th</sup>, 1940. Went to the J.C. Library, too, which carried other Wisconsin and even Chicago newspapers for the time.

And sure enough Chester Ingals, Anthony Kirby, and Cecilia Nash were all believed dead or missing after a freak lightning strike and resulting fire that gutted the front half of Ingals home, outside of Fulton's Point "around three-thirty in the afternoon."

People driving on Lakeview Drive (now Rte. 18) saw black smoke, drove to get nearer and were stopped at the gates of Ingoldsby. They managed to get into the gate house apartment and call the fire department. By the time the Keystone Kops and Cellar-Savers arrived, the entire living quarters of the house had been gutted, but not the bedrooms. The high winds charred it to nothing and alighted on the multicar garage where Ingals had his collection of expensive and rare automobiles.

The reporter wrote how stormy the past three weeks were: more lightning storms (12), and more tornado touch-downs (6) than in any previous recorded year.

*

Meaning what exactly for me? That they _are_ ghosts.

Except I happen to know they aren't. They're as real as I am. Especially Celia.

Now for something truly sick. While I was screwing Bev the other night, guess who I was fantasizing about? You guessed it, The Long Dead Celia Nash. Nobody but me better read this. Maybe I should stop writing it. No, all this is so weird, I've got to keep getting it down or I'll really begin to think I've gone over the edge.

Oh here's the article. I scanned it into the C drive:

# ☙ The Junction City Intelligencer ❧

*Morning Edition*          *Sunday, May 26ᵗʰ, 1940*          *5 Cents*

# FIRE RAVAGES INGOLDSBY
# INGALS HEIR, TWO OTHERS
# MISSING, BELIEVED DEAD

### *Unlikely Anyone Escaped Freak Lightning Fire Says Fulton's Point Fire Chief Jackson*

*

### *Celebrated for its Architecture, Estate is Partly Fire-Damaged. Rare Autos Unharmed.*

**By Roger Pollets**

Fulton's Point, WI — Motor-Tourists from Madison, out for a quiet country drive on Lakeview Drive, found instead of blue skies, clouds of black smoke, and drove to its source. They were stopped at the gates of the Ingals fortune heir's recently completed architectural marvel, known as Ingoldsby. Climbing the gates, they could see the main house on fire. Hugh J. Branch got over the gate and into the unlocked estate gate-house from which he was able to tele-phone local operator Minnie Drake who called together members of the Volunteer Fire Department. When the fire truck arrived, Mr. Branch's wife Estelle let it in and told Chief Jackson that her husband and his brother Samuel had gone to the main house to see if anyone needed help.

By three-thirty in the afternoon, the entire front portion of Ingoldsby had been wrapped in flames and completely gutted. The fire apparently swept through the living and dining rooms, kitchen and library. Prevailing westerly winds evidently kept it from reaching the bedroom wing, set at an angle to the destroyed section. Small fires were put out around the estate's large garage where they might have destroyed Ingal's prominent collection of expensive and rare automobiles.

Sheriff Edmund Acker and the fire team searched through the ruins for signs of any bodies, as it was understood that Chester

FIRE RAVAGES, Continued on Page 3

# FIRE RAVAGES INGOLDSBY: THREE BELIEVED DEAD

FIRE RAVAGES, From Page 1

Ingals and at least two friends, Mr. Anthony Kirby, and Miss Cecilia Nash, both of Milwaukee, had been at the house for the weekend, and seen around in Fulton's Point and environs. No bodies were located, Chief Jackson told this reporter, "We've not found anything but charred ashes. The wind churned the fire up into an inferno. No one could have escaped."

Sheriff Acker spoke of the stormy past three weeks. More lightning storms (12), and more tornado touch-downs (6) have been recorded than in any previous year. He and his deputy were called to six occasions caused by storms this week.

No servants were present on the property at the time of the fire. It was believed that aside from a caretaker who sometimes resided in the gate house, no help was ordinarily sent down to the estate from one of Ingal's city residences. Young Moderns, the three were either used to fending for themselves, and/or preferred impromptu weekend trips to our district.

23-year-old Chester Ingals, glamorous heir to the Ingals Iron Works fortune, was a well known figure in the state, as well as in Portage County. Especially during the past two years when he engaged Charles Sigurd Thurston, protégé of the controversial architect Frank Lloyd Wright and a figure in his own right, to design and build a large new estate on the southernmost sector of the Ingals property. Thurston's much- discussed estate was the height of the modern. One storey high, it was a rambling "ranch" style building with the most up to date conveniences, including a large kitchen refrigerator, aircoolers throughout, built-in wireless sets and record players in many rooms, a sport regulation-sized swimming pool, and of course the separate, heated, ten-car garage for Ingal's conspicuous collection of automobiles, a building larger and more comfortable than most Wisconsin homes. Utilizing rare woods from the east and south of America, along with gold and aluminum trim, when completed, the estate at Ingoldsby was thought to cost an amazing four hundred thousand dollars!

An earlier three story house built in 1907 on the property had been destroyed by freak lightning four years ago. Untenanted at the time, two servants sleeping nearby escaped unharmed. Part of the young heir's legacy, when he began building Ingoldsby, Chester Ingals often said that it was his "favorite place growing up."

Although he was rumored by newspapers in Chicago and Milwaukee to be a "playboy" and was even once rumored to have dated socialite Liz Marshall, Chester Ingals was a gentleman with strong ties to our county and town. Junction City Mayor, James Wilcomb, said, "He was a young man of great probity, charity, and courtesy, who brightened our local life." Mrs. Anthea Huenecker, our social doyenne, said, "Chester and his attractive, well-behaved friends, were always welcome at our little soirees. He and they will be sorely missed."

The grieving family has neither commented, nor announced funerary plans.

**The Junction City Intelligencer**

June 30, 2000

It doesn't stop getting interesting, does it? Here's an unexpected turn of events.

I was down at Ingoldsby's pool doing laps late yesterday afternoon, vaguely wondering where the three were when they drove up in Bud's 1933 Dusenberg. The wheels are made of chromed stainless steel and are huge. The whole thing is gorgeous. At any rate, they had just been to a matinee at the Fulton Theater, and Celia couldn't stop talking about the new movie they just saw which was ta da! The Philadelphia Story! I.e. that old black and white movie I must have seen about a dozen times because Gina played it so many times and wouldn't shut up talking about it all the time.

Celia was completely taken with it, and so was Tony. They were acting out scenes between Jimmy Stewart and Kate Hepburn and getting all the lines wrong but having a good time doing it. Me and Bud were sitting back with lemonades enjoying it all.

They were enthusing about it, really excited, Tony assuring everyone that Hepburn was going to get the Oscar for it that year, and Celia saying, no no, Cary Grant would, when it just pops out of my mouth. "You're both wrong. Stewart gets the Oscar." Moment of silence. They ignored me and chattered on, but a minute later Bud took me out onto the living room terrace and said, "I believe you. But then you know for sure, don't you?"

I tried to get out of it, but he was not about to be diverted. "Just like you already know how to drive a car without a clutch, don't you? You probably drive one every day." Then he lifted up a copy of Popular Mechanics left on the table, with its cover reading "Frequency Modulation: Is it the Wireless of the Future?" And he asked me, "Well, is it?" When I didn't respond, he said that he spoke to the main office of his company in Chicago and they never hired a caretaker named Neal Bartram.

Never heard of him. Nor is there such a student enrolled at Northwestern University in the History Ph.D. program.

So I told Bud I'd be happy to show him the signed contract I have for my summer work — as well as my student ID even though both have the current year on them.

The weather started up, thunderheads out of the west, the north, the east, a real mess. A few drops of rain, but distant rumblings so far, reminding me of that newspaper report. Then Celia and Tony's high spirits found us outside, and she waltzed Bud away while Tony fox-trotted me indoors. After a minute or so of awkwardness, he took the girl's part.

After an hour or so of avoiding Bud, I managed to get away. He was so down, however, that when I left I whispered into his ear, "FM Radio yes. And we do eventually fight Hitler." He held my jacket until I said, "Yes. We beat the pants off him."

"But how can you be here?" he asked following me outside again. I told him I didn't have any idea how. But that we aren't always in synch, somehow. When he asked what I meant, I pointed to the lightning beginning to strike down on the lawns, as close as the garage roof. "Whatever brings us together. This is what separates us!"

"The rain?" he asked. "No, the lightning," I told him. Just then, Kr-rack, loud and blinding, and twice more. I was alone and they were gone and the house was all locked up.

So now I'm sure the lightning has something to do with it. And as the house was burned half up by a freak lightning strike, I just know there is a connection between the two.

July 1, 2000

One of those teenage girls who are always hanging around, Ashley her name is — the one who actually has some boobies — slipped a note into my hand yesterday as the three of us were talking at my car. I looked at it and it was her phone number. Just what I need. But I called and said, look, this age difference thing and all. But she said no, it was about Ingoldsby. Would I meet her. All cloak and dagger like she's one of the Spy Kids in the movie. So I drive over to behind the town hall section near the police station and she tells me that the estate has a weird reputation and one of the caretakers went missing from there a while ago. Her grandpa was a landscaper and he'll tell me all about it. I humored her. Took down Grandpa's phone number and all. Won't call him unless I need to.

I had asked the Junction City newspaper's archives to notify me if they found anything else on Ingoldsby in their files. They sent me one from eight months later, about Bud's will providing funds to rebuild the house as it was.

Here it is scanned in:

---

# ☙ The Junction City Intelligencer ❧

---

*Weekend Edition*          *Friday, January 5ᵗʰ, 1940*          *5 Cents*

---

# FIRE-DAMAGED ESTATE TO BE REBUILT / RESTORED

### *Ingals Family Reveals Heir's Will Provided For Complete Restoration of Estate Fire-Damaged by Last Summer's Storms*

*

### *Town Receives Gift to "Establish Town Hall."*

**By Roger Pollets**

---

Fulton's Point, WI — There was relief today with news that the architectural prodigy that brought us fame will not be torn down. Instead, by terms of the Last Will & Testament of Chester Ingals, who

FIRE-DAMAGED, Continued on Page 2

## FIRE-DAMAGED ESTATE TO BE RESTORED

FIRE-DAMAGED, From Page 1
perished in the damaging fire, Ingoldsby will be rebuilt to its former glory. Attorneys for the Ingals Iron Works announced the news in Chicago yesterday. Ingal's will was opened to public record. By its terms, up to $500,000 is allocated for "the complete restoration of the estate and replacement of autos in case of an Act of God. With the hope that Ingoldsby will eventually be a public building, open to all." Ingal's estate was reported as "three and a half million dollars." Most goes to the family but $50,000 goes to "Fulton's Point Town to establish a town hall." Details of the wills of the others who also perished, believed to be smaller than Ingal's if also sizable by Portage County standards, will be made available to the public upon request.

**The Junction City Intelligencer**

So yesterday that dweeby funny guy Jim Kleinherz phones me and says he found a Follow-Up story from a few days after the fire. And did I want to see it? Did I? I got him to scan it in and then e-mail it to me.

Guess what? <u>They never found the bodies</u>. Let me write that once more. They never found the bodies at all. Meaning what? That they were <u>not</u> killed by the fire.

Then what happened to them? Well, I'm developing a second theory, this one even nuttier than the first. But hey that one seems to be kind of right, doesn't it?

It means I've got to take one of the three into my confidence and probe. Bud is the "scientific" one and so he might be the one. Not Celia. I don't want to expose her to this. On the other hand, Bud really reacted to what I told him. Or did he? On second thought, he didn't react <u>that</u> much. I thought that was because he'd already thought about it awhile, and so had sort of gotten used to the idea. Maybe it's something else. Maybe he knows something that . . . that what?

Only one thing to do. Ask him.

Here's what Kleinherz sent me:

---

## ☙ The Junction City Intelligencer ☙

*Weekend Edition*          *Thursday, May 30th, 1940*          *5 Cents*

---

# HOPE VANISHES OF FINDING HEIR, FRIENDS IN ESTATE FIRE

### *"We've Searched Every Square Foot and Sifted Every Ash," Sheriff Acker reports.*

**By Roger Pollets**

Fulton's Point, WI — Under pressure from the Ingals Family, county and state authorities, Sheriff Edmund Acker yesterday allowed death reports to be written for the Ingals heir and his two friends believed to have perished in the fire that swept Ingoldsby Saturday noon.

"We've searched every square foot of the property now, and we've sifted every square inch of ash, and there's nothing to explain ˆ what, besides incineration, could have happened," Acker admitted.

The Ingals family announced a private funeral service in Chicago for its scion and the friends who perished with him.

**The Junction City Intelligencer**

July 3, 2000

Okay, Tony and me had "the talk." This was his doing entirely and began with Tony asking if I could trust him, really trust him? I said sure, though it sounded so . . . dramatic!

"Isn't it?" he asked back. Then told me that he was torn between his best friend since school, the fellow who'd treated him best in life of anyone, and the girl he loved . . . who — get this — loved him back.

I burst into laughter. Seeing this, Tony stared at me and asked what on earth was wrong with me. "Here I am, unveiling my deepest secret to you and. . . ."

"Your deepest secret?" I asked. Then I said that his deepest secret, if it even <u>was</u> one, which I strongly doubted, was that he was gay and covering it up.

"Of course, I'm gay," he said. Then he said they all were. Or tried to be.

I insisted that he <u>had</u> to know what I meant. Gay as in Queer. Homosexual. Like my dormmate Nate in college? Gay Nate the gay dormmate? The guy who ended up living with the center from the varsity basketball team?

Amazement. Tony reacted with extreme shock. So I quickly told him that obviously it was totally okay with me. Not that I was personally inclined that way myself, despite my roommate Nate, but that I thought it was great. And that he should "Go for it!"

When Tony still didn't respond, I said that with his looks, he should be able to get almost any guy he wanted.

To which Tony drew himself up to his full six foot one inch height. "Mr. Bartram, exactly what universe do you think you're living in, where open . . . relations between two men is, as you so <u>blithely</u> put it, 'okay'?"

Then he stormed off. Believe me I got out of his way.

Still it needed to be said.

July 5, 2000

This is completely nuts. If you've been reading this, you know I'm not the most romantic guy in the world. And yet, and yet, I think I've fallen for Celia Nash.

Jeeeze. Did I just write that?

Not only have I fallen for her, but yesterday at the little bar-becue she and Bud had outside on the living room terrace, he and Tony went off at one point to toss a football on the lawn, while the steaks cooked, leaving us alone to talk. She began flirt-ing, I flirted back. Then she said, kind of breathlessly, "I know you've got a woman in town."

How did she know? Tony told her. "We never hide anything from each other."

Thanks a lot, Tony. I haven't told anyone you're queer, have I?

I told Celia that Bev was a nice woman but that she meant nothing emotionally to me. That I'd stop seeing her if Celia wanted me to. In fact, I would stop seeing her period.

Yes, boys and girls, I actually said those words. And meant them. I was supposed to see Bev tomorrow. But I won't.

Celia said, "Well, the puzzle is that none of us are at all certain of your intentions."

I told her my intentions were "honorable toward her." Can you believe I said that. Yet, it's true. It is. Really. Then before she could do more than register that, I said that my intentions were honorable and serious. Gosh, she looked wonderful at that. Did I just write the word "Gosh?" What is happening to me? Then I asked if Bud would allow me to court her, being a lowly caretaker and all.

I knew she'd say that it didn't matter a bit to her — hey! she reads Gorky and Steinbeck and they love "the common man" — but that it might to Bud.

Except I added, I was actually appearing under false pretenses, since besides the degree I was close to getting, which would get me good job teaching in college almost anywhere, I also happened to have some money stashed away, with more coming in. I didn't tell her how I got the money (Yet. Do people die in airplane crashes in her time? They don't, do they?), being sixty-five grand per person that's been paid to me from my parent's insurance policies. Or that I've also got about two hundred and seventy five grand due to me (from the sale of my folks house.)

"Why Mr. Bartram!" she said, trying to be angry. "You're rich! At least as rich as Tony. And far richer than poor me!"

I'd forgotten, hadn't I, that in a time when most mansions

cost twenty grand and a Caddie goes for three or four grand, having four-hundred grand in the bank <u>means</u> something. Unlike today when it means bupkus.

I asked her not to hold my being rich against me, and she promised not to, and I think we were both secretly relieved. We kissed for a long time without otherwise touching and I all but swooned and so did she. Wow. I really do think I'm . . . No I'm not going to write it.

So I'm paying court to a woman who lives in 1940 and has been dead for more than sixty years. Nice going, Neal. Really smart.

July 6, 2000

So there I am for once actually working yesterday afternoon, mowing the back lawns and using the trimmer/edger around the garage when Bud comes out wiping his hands and waves. Few minutes later he gestures that I shut off the machine as he wants to talk to me. Here it comes, I think. O. Kay.

He comes up to me, saying whatever is that contraption on your head. I lift it off and put it on his head. He lifts it off immediately and looks down at it. Then puts it on his ears again tentatively. Is once more startled and takes it off again. "What music is this?" Then he gets it. "It's very harsh and strident, isn't it?" he asks. He is talking about The Dave Matthews Band, not The Red Hot Chili Peppers! Then he asks, how in the world did they fit a phonograph in that little thing. He's looking at my CD player and headphones.

I tell him I don't have a clue. I do of course but he's never heard of laser technology, so hey!

Change of subject. He's spoken to Celia and he's pleased that I'm so "well-heeled" as he puts it. I'll bet he's somewhat surprised, too. Tells me how his father became her protector: as his close friend, her father lost most of his wealth during the Stock Market Crash and dove onto Chicago's Marshall Avenue head first. Ingals senior salvaged what he could and put it to work for the girl and she's worth about 200 grand and change, i.e. not too shabby. When Bud's papa died two years back, Bud got wardship of Celia and has her moola in trust.

I naturally ask if he's got a problem with me and he admits that she's interested in no one. "Of course there's Tony. They are very close. Girls often choose close pals."

"Except that Tony is gay," I say. Then in case he hasn't gotten it, "homosexual."

Bud admits the truth of that with a shrug, and it's so casually done I believe that maybe the two of them have more than once in their own long close friendship and youth played "Let's Hide the Salami." But hey, I don't care. "The real problem with you courting her is a bit different, isn't it?" Bud says. "You're not always here, are you?"

"You guys are the ones who keep disappearing," I tell him.

"Whichever," he comments slyly and I have to agree, it is a problem. Right now an insoluble one. But there's something I want to know. "About Tony. . . he can't exactly be happy the way he is."

Bud agrees but says Tony's coping as best he can. But no, he's not happy.

"What will happen to him?"

Bud replies that Tony will do what other fellows do, i.e. he'll repress it, hide it, marry respectably and try not to act on it. "It's done like that everywhere, daily."

To which I reply that's too bad. And decide to ask Tony what he wants. Why? Well, let's say I've got another theory. Or rather, a theory built upon a previous theory.

July 13, 2000

What did I say? It <u>was</u> the lightning. But not alone. Something else too.

Drove into Junction City to the big Staples there to get a ream of copying paper and a new ink cartridge for my printer. Decided that there might be some use for this journal so I'm keyboarding it and printing it out. Never know . . .

While there, I dropped into the library and saw Jim Kleinherz — "little heart" in German? — and he told me he'd found more about Ingoldsby. Seems that the articles had been listed variably under the place name or under Ingal's name. This one he found under the latter, and as there have been a few Chester Ingals, he wasn't sure it was applicable.

To make a long story short, (too late for that, Neal!) he came up with another piece in the paper, this one from the very end of the year of the fire. Part of the town's yearly fire department report blamed a new electrical generator that Bud evidently bought and had attached to the house at the living room where all the wiring comes together and in and out of the house. Evidently electricity goes out during lightning storms and this generator goes on. Typical of Bud to find a "new scientific solution." Except this might be precisely what screwed them! Who was it who wrote that character is destiny?

Here's the new article I got:

---

## ca The Junction City Intelligencer so

| *Afternoon Edition* | Sunday, December 29ᵗʰ, 1940 | *5 Cents* |

# CAUSE OF ESTATE FIRE— POSSIBLY NEW GENERATOR

### *Newly Installed Electrical Generator Believed To Have Amplified Freak Lightning Strike*

**By Roger Pollets**

In a yearly report to Portage County, town Fire Chief Jackson reported that his team reached the conclusion that a newly installed Electrical Generator that heir Chester Ingals had installed only days earlier, might have been the "conduit" for the freak lightning strike that spread the fire that destroyed more than half of his estate last May.

Purchased by Ingals because of frequent electrical failures due to the especially bad Spring weather with its frequent lightning storms that took lights out, the generator was supposed to turn over as soon as the electricity failed. A large thunder and lightning storm was said to have dominated the area the time of the unfortunate fire.

"The generator, in effect, strongly amplified any electrical charge hitting the house, in the way a wireless crystal is amplified to make a radio louder," Chief Jackson wrote in the report.

As for Ingals and two others, whose bodies were never found after the fire that destroyed so much, Jackson told this reporter that he stood by his earlier comments. Viz. the savagery of the fire reduced them to ashes.

**The Junction City Intelligencer**

## July 15, 2000

And there it is, happening right now! Yesterday p.m. as I was getting into my Speedo I heard a truck pulling up and going by. Once I realized that it was an old, 30's truck, a Chevy I think, I realized they didn't have to ring for me to open the gate — back then it's already open. Two guys inside and on the flatbed, this big weird-looking mechanism.

The generator, sure enough. Two guys from Milwaukee had driven it over and they were already installing it at exactly where I guessed they would, back of the living room, not far from the fuse box. Bud was waxing poetic to the others about it.

I asked Celia what she thought about it. "Well, if Bud wants it." Then, "I sort of liked it without electricity. Candlelight is so lovely."

Spent the evening with the three of them instead of at my usual Saturday sex-fest. Celia made dinner — tomato consommé, which is a gelatin soup (ok), veal loaf (good), creamed casserole of potatoes (very good) green beans (over cooked) and a dessert made out of Rennet (which is what exactly?) that tasted like regular old vanilla pudding my Mom used to make.

Afterwards we all took turns fox-trotting with Celia to music coming all the way here in the middle of the country from the Waldorf Astoria Ballroom in New York City. ("Tony loves the Waldorf," Celia said. And I thought, "He would!") At any rate the first hour is really kind of nice and old fashioned, stuff my grannies would love, then guess who comes live on the radio? Carmen Miranda and her band. They're the guest artists. Seems she'd recently made her American debut in a movie — Tony told me — titled <u>Down Argentine Way</u>, and she played what she called the Merengue but sounded to me like Salsa. So I showed them how to do it. Celia got embarrassed trying to copy me. Too much hip involvement.

July 18, 2000

Hot afternoon. Where did today come from!? Tony asleep on his chaise, snoring away, and Celia indoors napping in her room. Bud joins me in the pool. We evidently awaken Tony, who snortles something then goes inside to nap. Soon as we get out of the pool Bud starts in on me. "Maybe you can explain this to me. Yesterday I went to read that Popular Mechanics issue I showed you last week, looking for it on the table out here where I'd left it and it was gone."

I told him I took it with me to the gate-house.

"Ten minutes later," Bud tells me, "it was right there out on the table again."

I guess it didn't work, I tell him. I tried but I found that I couldn't bring it with me into my own time.

"You mean into the year 1980?" he asks.

"No, the year 2000." I watch his mouth fall open a little. "It's July there. It's what? Mid-May here?"

"So Frequency Modulation <u>is</u> the future of wireless?" Bud asks. "Until those little things with headphones comes along. What else? That radio with moving pictures we saw at the New

York World's Fair? What was it called? Television? That will be commonplace, won't it? And machines that calculate faster than a million men but fit into a valise. What else?"

I'm very touched by Bud, for some reason, and almost begin to cry. Then I decide to let him know. "Digitalization and micro-computer chip technology allow computers in most homes. On people's desks. More common than typewriters in your time. Instant communication with anyone in the world in real time via the Internet."

"Flying automobiles?" Bud asks. I say no. Then he asks "What is it like? Are we like Stone Age people to you? Is that fun for you?"

And I get really upset and ask why he's saying those things? It's not intentional on my part. I don't have any control. That when I least expect it, they vanish and the house is all closed up and empty . . . I tell him I'm really unhappy when that happens. Really!

After a minute, Bud wants to know why I tried taking the magazine back.

I tell him to prove to myself its really happening, because what if it stops again for good? What if I never see them again? What then?

Bud says, "You've always got that woman in town and other people." Then he realizes that's lame. He says, "'What then?' is right. We really are in a fix, aren't we?"

That's when I ask why he's not so surprised by me and the time thing. Surprised but not that surprised. He's seen someone or something before here at the place, hasn't he?

"Never anything like you! But . . . as kids . . . me and Tony."

Then he tells how the first time it happened they couldn't believe it. They were playing behind the older house built here, in the woods, and suddenly, walking past was a family of Indians. He didn't know what tribe. An old and young woman, two dogs pulling a triangular sled filled with gear. Three kids.

Two braves. One kid saw them. The dogs sniffed him and Tony as they went by. The Natives all went up to the house, and the old garage, a converted stable, astounded to see it. They looked in the windows, spoke quickly, saw the old Marmon 16 and took off fast!

"It was like a dream. Only, we <u>smelled</u> them," Bud said, crinkling up his nose. "We could have touched them, I'm sure. Totally unfamiliar smells. One dropped this — and he went in and came back with a leather necklace with a polished white stone wrapped in a knot.

I asked if the boys had told anyone.

Bud said they mentioned it to the servants, who said there had been other odd incidents. A laundry woman once saw a Pony Express rider dash by as she hung out wash. He was astonished by her and the house. She said he stopped on the bluff, looked at a map then at the house, back and forth, map and house. The house wasn't on his map. Other servants, staff members who closed up for the summer, also reported seeing camp fires in the wood, and hearing chanting and drumming. Bud added, "But you're the first to . . ."

"To interact? Because I could have been from your time?"

"Yes. And because we've all fallen for you in one way or another."

Such an admission that I said, "I love you guys, too. Celia most. But all of you!"

We are, as Bud said, really in a fix. Aren't we?

July 21, 2000

Doc and Joe came over for cards again last night. Caught me coming back from Ingoldsby, where I'd been most of the early evening with Celia. Then she and the others were going to Bud's grandma's again for dinner. I asked if I could come over later, but Celia said she'd be putting up her hair later and reading movie magazines. She was wearing the yellow sweater thing and I got to second base. I really am crazy, aren't I? But hey, it felt like a big thing.

So they come upstairs and I prepare to take them for a few bucks. Only tonight Doc is kicking butt so I begin asking him about the property that Ingoldsby is built on. Seems no one in town knows a damn thing about it, I say. Which I'm pretty sure will provoke his in-born know-it-all-ness. He says he knows whatever there is to know. I ask him to tell me about it and why it was that no one lived there before the Ingals put up a house.

He says "Plenty people lived there. They just didn't stay there."

Why not, I ask.

Here Joe Weyerhauser says his Grandpa told him that the property had a bad reputation from the time of the Indians. "They considered it a sacred place. Or at least a special place, going back fifty years before any whites lived out here."

Naturally, I asked what happened back then. And Doc, in his best know-it-all mode, says everyone knows what happened back then. It was the New Madrid earthquake, allegedly the most powerful to hit North America in historic times. 1835. Looking back to letters and records of the few whites living there, and to the Indian stories, scientists figure it was a nine point one on the Richter Scale. That's a thousand times stronger than the San Francisco Quake of 1906. Seems every wooden frame house anywhere in a five-hundred mile area was shaken to the ground. Horses and domestic animals went berserk, ran off and some never returned. The Mississippi and Missouri Rivers ran backwards for a thousand miles north and south of the earthquake's epicenter. Sounded like a major bitch.

Something happened on the property at Ingoldsby at the same time. Some piece of land either rose or fell hundreds of feet in a few seconds or altogether vanished or came out of the blue, Joe said, his Grandpa had heard from some old Indians but couldn't get straight exactly what occurred and the Natives never again stayed to camp on the land. They abandoned it.

Marked it with cairns or something and split for good.

So I'm losing pennies like a fool and asking if anything had happened in modern times to support the Indian superstition and Doc says, "Well every house built there has been struck by lightning and burnt up."

Then Joe says, and halfway through Doc tries to shut him up but I won't let him, "And of course folks are disappearing all the time." When I ask which folks besides Bud Ingals and his friends, Joe says, "Why that caretaker fellow, some twenty odd years ago. That's why we were all so surprised to see you here. We thought that up in Chicago they all understood." Then Doc does manage to shut Joe up.

So someone else vanished here, just like Ashley said. And what they have been describing seems like some kind of unstable rift in time, brought into being by a SuperQuake. Oh, Mr. Neal, honey. What in the World you got your fool self into?!

Then just as they're leaving Doc turns to me with Joe down ahead of him and asks "How in hell did you know that they called him Bud?"

"Him who?" I feign innocence.

"Chester damn Ingals Junior!" he replies. Looking at me like an old owl.

Ooops!

July 24, 2000

Fresh with this info from Joe and Doc, I phoned Kleinherz and asked if he could find something else for me a bit more recently, say 1980. He sounded busy, harassed, etc. So I said I'd find him a date. What was his type? Blonde? Brunette? Did he go for legs, tits or ass?

"I go for males," he replied. "Tall, dark, handsome, slender males," he added.

"And I'm sure that a cool-looking guy like you gets more than your share," Mr. Neal Slick replied. Then I told him I'd keep an eye out for someone for him. I'll admit that I was secretly displeased that he didn't say "short, blonde, with a swimmer's body." But hey, you can't win them all, can you?

But he came through after all. This morning's e-mail contained the following:

---

Final —                                                                    —20 Cents

# The Junction City Intelligencer

**★★★★ SATURDAY, SEPTEMBER 1, 1979 ★★★★**

---

# EMPLOYEE MISSING AT INGOLDSBY ESTATE

**By Janet Wagner**

---

Fulton's Point, WI — Police were called to search the interiors and grounds of Ingoldsby, the once-famed, and now mostly neglected estate several miles from town, still owned by the Ingals family of Milwaukee and Chicago.

According to Police Chief Frank J. Young they were looking for Jason Terranova, a U. Wisconsin junior hired as summer caretaker and grounds-keeper for the estate who'd been living in the gate house. He'd disappeared within the past few days according to friends in Madison who tried to reach him by phone, then searched in person. Chief Young confirmed their story that Terranova's apartment looked untouched, and said there was no reason to suspect foul play.

Ingoldsby's main house has not been occupied since it was rebuilt, following a 1940 fire in which the young Ingals heir and two friends died. Chester Ingal's last will ordered the house be prepared as a museum. Designed by Frank Lloyd Wright protege, Sigurd Thurston, it was at one time an architectural wonder, and still has its admirers.

Terranova was not much seen outside the estate, although he was believed to have had many student guests from Madison. Wild parties, sex orgies and drug use were rumored to be common at the estate by some townspeople. Some believe Terranova's disappearance is the result of a drug deal that went wrong.

**The Junction City Intelligencer**

July 26, 2000

Ever-subtle, I asked the three about Jason Terranova. Celia was actually in the pool — first time I've seen her doing that; cute little pale blue — her color — one-piece bathing suit, and this big rubber bathing cap on top, natch, not that she'd ever get that close to the water. She was sort of dog paddling about when I got there, threatening to come out. I said nonsense and dived in far away from her so as to not scare her, then swam up to her and we sort of fooled around in the water and I held her so she could try out some swim strokes without fear of drowning in the five feet of water at the shallow end, which let me cop a few feels and even better let her brush against my almost constant chubby, before she was tired and climbed out. Very demure and all. But I was more excited than anytime with the Post Mistress. Imagine! I almost popped right there and scuzzed up the pool.

Meanwhile, Bud was trouncing Tony at Backgammon, who was saying things like, "It's only <u>suggested</u> you take my pieces," to which Bud naturally scoffed, and wiped Tony out. So after me and Celia dried off, I asked them if she'd ever heard of Terranova. Bud remembered him. "Cheeky sort of fellow, wasn't he? Didn't last here but a few weeks if I remember." Then Tony remembered, "Wasn't he the one with the (lowered voice) mezz?"

I am not an American History Ph.D. candidate for nothing, and well know that "mezz" in Pre-World War II U.S. slang means pot, grass, marijuana. Recalling what reporter Wagner said townsfolk had rumored of Jason T, I said it was more than likely, yes, he had mezz. Tony gets this far-away look in his eyes, but clams up. From which I imply that he personally sampled mezz; and possibly also perhaps sampled Jason Terranova.

Then Celia says something absolutely breathtaking which I'm not at all certain how to take. She says, "Didn't Jason quit working here to go marry that pretty young widow whose husband died, leaving her with the diner on Lakeview Drive to run it all alone? What was her name, Tony? Janice! Janice Snyder."

Nota Bene that Snyder's Country Inn is, in the year 2000, the largest, poshest and most elegant restaurant of this part of Portage County, with four dining rooms on two floors, a staff of maybe fifty, and parking for a hundred. I pass it often.

"Ray Snyder didn't die," Bud says. "He vanished. Remember. In fact, some people said he was last seen around my property here. At first Janice said that Ray last mentioned that he was coming to meet up with Terranova and some other people. She changed her story later and said she was mistaken."

That's all they remembered. But for me it was plenty. So another trip to Junction City is needed. Don't want to impose too much on Kleinherz.

July 28, 2000

Well if Mohammed won't go to the mountain, Bev Freneau will come to the gate house. At least she did last night. Guess she missed her usual ashes hauling session. She appeared outside, buzzing me through the gate and when I let her in, she didn't want to talk, not even to hear an explanation of why I've not been seeing her (Celia asked me not to; ergo I wont). But once she was inside, what could I say? What could I do? You guessed it and I feel terrible, going back on my word to Celia. Except I really needed it, and I fantasized she was Celia the entire time! So it's not complete betrayal.

So it's midnight or something and Bev's got to go. I walk her downstairs and see her out the gate. I'm wearing a pair of shorts and not one thing more. Guess who comes around the side of the gate-house but Tony Kirby, dressed in a white silk tuxedo get-up. Seems he and the others have just been to a big bash, and he left early, getting a ride with Bunny someone or other. He's seen me see Bev out and he's sniffing the air, literally smelling sex still steaming off my body, I just know it. I really don't want to let him upstairs because who knows what ideas he'll get. On the other hand he does want to chat, and so I take his offer and put on the tux jacket, protesting that it'll smell like me to which he says with much eyebrows, "You and her too!" nodding in the direction Bev left.

Then he tells me that he and Bud have "naturally, discussed" me and he wants to know if I was fooling him or what about what I said before about it being okay to be gay "where I come from."

Those are the exact words he uses. As though I'm from Pasadena. Or Japan.

So even though I'm dead on my feet, I tell him all about the Stonewall Riots and the G.A.A. and Act-Up and the pro-gay laws passed, and all the publicly out actors and musicians and writers, and the neighborhoods filled with gay people, Chelsea in Manhattan, the Castro in San Francisco, West Hollywood.

"I've always wanted to go to Hollywood. I've always wanted to live in Los Angeles with the palm trees and warm weather all year round as I see in the Moviefone rotogravures!" Tony says.

So I talk more until he lets me go. Then he comes upstairs and gets the jacket from me and I guess puts a blanket over me. I'm dead to the world by then. Nice guy, Tony. Really nice guy. But he's living in the wrong time. Wrong place and wrong time.

And guess what? I've just gotten another idea. And have another theory.

August 9, 2000

I have been to see the estimable Kleinherz, and he let me spend all day in his archive and that's a good thing, because it pretty much took all afternoon, literally right until closing time at 6 p.m., to find what I found, virtually invisible and hidden deep within a paper from the other end of the state.

Here goes:

---

# ☆ *The Star Journal* ☆

## MILWAUKEE'S HOME PAPER

---

*Morning Edition*        *Thursday, October 4, 1979*        *20 Cents*

---

**32** | *The Star Journal*
       | *Thursday, October 4, 1979*

---

## Bank Robber Cops Insanity Plea

### By Don Biggers

Claiming that his client, charged with last Friday's attempted robbery of the Union National Bank on Fond du Lac Avenue, was mentally infirm as a result of a head injury, city-appointed Attorney Dale Haslett asked that Raymond Snyder be remanded to De Paul Rehabilitation Hospital for a period of no less than six months, saying that jail would be "extremely deleterious." His plea was granted by Judge Andrew Wallgren.

Snyder pleaded no-contest to the robbery, in which he was overwhelmed by a security guard and two bank customers. Teller Peggy Gutmanson and guard James Willis backed the Attorney, testifying that Snyder appeared "out of his mind" and "completely raving."

Haslett said his client suffered a severe head injury a month ago and has been "rootless, essentially wandering ever since, not knowing where he is or even what year it is." Police doctors said Snyder's head injury was "consistent with severe cranial fracture and contusion." The conditions could have been caused by Snyder being struck by lightning somewhere in the southeast part of the state, as he asserts.

**The Star Journal**

August 12, 2000

Ray Snyder's still alive!! Of course he would be, if he were in his twenties in 1979, he'd be in his forties today. At any rate I went through some phone books and found a Raymond Snyder living in Elm Grove, an okay suburb of Milwaukee and left a message with his wife. Said I was a medical history student, specializing in success stories of lightning strike survivors. She said, "Ray never talks about that," but that he might with me. I'm to call back tomorrow.

Meanwhile, driving home from Junction City at what by then was six forty-five, I decided to stop into Snyder's Country Inn, which was having Happy Hour. The bar was packed. Mostly yuppies, a couple of hot women, they and the guys mostly ten years older than me — I'll tell Bev Freneau about it. I went to the john and wandered around the place until I found the photos of the Inn's "founder's," Janice and Jason Terranova, aged about sixty-five in the photos (dated 1988) and both looking okay — Jason may have been a druggie but he was a stud-muffin too, cause he still looked good at retirement age.

Bartender had seen me very obviously checking them out, so back at the bar I asked if they were named Terranova, how come the place was called Snyder's. He didn't have a clue, said every new employee there asked the same question. He said the founder's grandchildren owned the place now, none of whom are named Snyder, and that Jason was dead a few years and Janice was an Alzheimer's vegetable at a local hospice. Very friendly guy. Half hour an hour later, he refilled my drink yet again for free and asked me out later in the week. Unfortunately, he's not dark, or slender, although he's good looking, muscled — wore a biceps tight shirt to show himself off — and red-haired. Sorry Kleinherz!

August 14, 2000

Now <u>this</u> is news! Talked to Ray Snyder yesterday on the phone. He was very circumspect at first. Wanted to know how I knew about him. I told him Dale Haslett who represented him, had mentioned his name to my father a while ago in my presence.

"Poor Dale, dying like that," Snyder said. I said I didn't know how. Turned out Haslett and his wife were in a massive car wreck in some tunnel in the Swiss Alps in which a fuel tanker truck caught fire and killed like forty people. "Dale saved my skin. Got me help. I owe my life to him," Snyder said. "So much for the good ending happily."

Took at least five minutes before Ray would talk about his old lightning injury. His memory of it was vague, and always had been, he said. He'd gained consciousness inside the flatbed of a pickup truck on Route 18 outside Fennimore, and the driver who'd stopped on the side of the road to urinate and who'd picked him up had noticed him staggering around the field with a bloody and blackened but already healing gash along his ear and head. He got Ray medical help at Madison, where Ray stayed a few days. Snyder said he'd lost his memory or it was totally screwed up by the injury. He did know his name, however, and he had some kind of non-photo driver's license from Milwaukee so he headed there. No one at the address listed knew him or of him. "I was missing big chunks of stuff that ended up making my adjustment really hard." Stuff like? I ask "Like who was President. Couple of wars. Every day stuff. All kinds of shit. It was terrible. Stuff five year olds knew, I didn't know." Snyder said that Milwaukee had looked familiar, but only parts of it. He had phoned a number for a Snyder, and said that the voice that answered seemed familiar but that the old woman said her brother Ray died forty years ago, told him not to bother her again, and then hung up. Snyder grew more confused, couldn't hold a job as he didn't know simple things that everyone else seemed to know. He was fired, lost his rental room, drank, got desperate, ended up on skid row, robbed the bank and went into the mental ward.

"Best thing that ever happened to me," Snyder said. "I met Janice there. My current wife. Janice was a De Paul Rehab volunteer. Ran a mobile library. We met, fell in love, and she got me work and a place to stay. I read books and newspapers and magazines and eventually I caught up with everyone else. We married and the rest is history."

I bit my tongue before I'd dare mention that his first wife was also named Janice.

But I gathered from all this that:

1) Jason Terranova and Ray Snyder had somehow switched at Ingoldsby. Jason was in 1979 and Ray in 1940.
2) Lightning was involved.
3) Jason knew what was he was doing, and may have intentionally made the switch. But not Ray. He had no idea what happened.

Leading to the logical question, what did Jason Terranova discover that I haven't so far?

August 18, 2000

"I'm afraid you can't take it out." Tonia Noonan said, and if it weren't that the book was stamped "For In-Library Use," I might have believed it was her own rule so she could keep me around. However, it was once again hot and nasty outside and cool indoors, so I sat at one of the writing tables of the little, old, admittedly handsome Fulton's Point Library, and perused <u>Portage County: A History</u> by Mabel Normand Freer, published in 1934, by — haven't you already guessed — the Portage County Chamber of Commerce.

However I hit pay dirt almost immediately, since the book had at one time not been so rare nor so restricted and among those who <u>had</u> taken it out was, drumroll here, please, on August 12, 1979 Jason Terranova, who'd signed his name.

I looked for underscored passages and there were plenty. So I went back to the beginning and concentrated. After an hour and two chapters of bluntly local boosterism, I came upon the following: "The Ingals family purchased this land in 1889 but didn't build on it for several decades. Possibly because it was long thought to be the site of an Indian Holy Place, and had accreted several tall tales. None of them more baffling or colorful than that of 'Injun Ralph'."

I searched for an index, found none, read on and on, another hour or more. At last my patience was rewarded halfway through the volume. I quote it in full:

> "Fulton's Point was a bustling trading spot along the route that would later become Lakeview Drive, connecting eastern towns like Milwaukee and Madison with western posts on the Missouri River, when Injun Ralph made his unexplained appearance.
>
> Injun Ralph was the name the townspeople gave him because of his Frontiersman costume of buskins, powder horn and moccasins. He insisted his name was Ralph Leninger, and when pressed, would offer eyewitness accounts of Chief Pontiac and other long-dead Indian Chieftains he claimed to have met and smoked peace pipes with on his foot wanderings through what he called Greater Louisiana Territory, and which he was astonished to see suddenly populated with steamboats, steam locomotives, and "many thousands of settlers."
>
> Like Rip Van Winkle, the by-no-means aged Injun Ralph — appearing to be less than thirty five years of age — had gone to sleep, hiding from a ferocious storm of lightning and thunder on what appeared to be the southern edge of what later became the Ingals property, and somehow slept nigh on forty years instead of forty winks, without any apparent worsening for wear. He assured all that Andrew Johnson, not Taft, was U.S. President, and he spoke English with a "lilting, yet distinctly more British than American accent."

Our Modern Rip adjusted soon enough, and he found gainful employment giving speeches about "America The Beautiful: As It Were" for Elks, Chambers of Commerce and varied Women's clubs. After some years of this activity, however, Injun Ralph encountered and then joined up with "Buffalo Bill" Cody and Calamity Jane's Wild West Show, travelling the Eastern Seaboard and to Europe.

Perhaps the oddest part of Injun Ralph's tall story was that it contained a disturbing instance of provable evidence. In the moment between his sudden awakening from a clap of thunder and his being catapulted into the year 1911, he claimed to have witnessed — not two feet away and very briefly in the blinding re-illumination — another person, male, young, looking astonished, wearing a checkerboard vest and porkpie hat, seated on a "tubular metal contraption" that Injun Ralph later recognized to be a bicycle. He had exactly described Wilfred Dix, a young man whose disappearance on the very day of Injun Ralph's appearance has never been resolved.

August 20, 2000

After a swim, and "tea" with not-bad butter cookies Celia made, I got Tony to walk with me back to the Gate House. He'd told me that he'd come in that night after me to retrieve his tux and cover me with a blanket, so I asked him upstairs, wondering what he could see of my time since I can see plenty from his. Turns out a lot, including the "Now What For Gay Rights?" cover story of <u>Newsweek</u> and recent edition of <u>The Advocate</u> and a copy of a book of gay short stories (<u>Men On Men</u>) both of which I'd found in Tonia's library and taken out especially for this purpose.

Having me tell him about gaylife today was one thing but actually seeing it all was another. First Tony was flabbergasted. Then he spent over an hour looking through it and I assured him he could come read them any time. Now I need something more substantial, not so much historical as sensible. Maybe like a practical guide to being queer. Who'd know that?

Nate the Gay Roommate would know.

**From:** HistoryKing78@aol.com
**Date:** Tue, 22 Aug 2000 12:30:18 EDT
**To:** snakecharming@juno.com
**Subject:** (no subject)

Greetings Snake Charmeroo. Long time no etcetera. Looking for Nate Smith. Old e-mail address stinks. What's he doing? What are you doing? Is your fiancee still hot for me?

•

**From:** Bufferzone@msn.com
**Date:** Wed, 23 Aug 2000 18:10:20 EDT
**To:** HistoryKing78@aol.com
**Subject:** (no subject)

Neal, you're just lucky I was cleaning house on that old moniker. Note new address is Bufferzone@msn.com. Dumped the old g.f. Have another rich, pretty one. Nate's new address is SalHepatica@aol.com. He asked Susan E. if you'd died. He lives in West Hollywood, works as talent agent for CAA has big Beemer & his own place. Heard you were in Jerkoffistan for the summer.

•

**From:** HistoryKing78@aol.com
**Date:** Wed, 23 Aug 2000 21:01:12 EDT
**To:** Bufferzone@msn.com, snakecharming@juno.com
**Subject:** (no subject)

Jerkoffistan is proving muy interesante. Thanks for the tips. Especially re Nate. More helpful than you'll ever know. I owe you a Dominos supersize with sausage and cheese in the crust.

August 22, 2000

In the Junction City Barnes & Noble, I figured out which guy behind the desk of the three there looked the most queer and asked: "What would I get for someone who needs to know like everything about being gay all at once?"

Wild haired Blondie with noseplugs walked me over to this big sex book, which he showed me inside was like a Dutch uncle and a history and an encyclopedia all in one. The drawings were really wild, some of them, the expected sucking and fucking and kinky stuff, but with blacks, midgets with whips. Woo! Will have to go slowly with Tony.

"I know this isn't for you," Blondie said, ringing it up.

"Oh, why not?" I asked, all innocence.

"Because you've already <u>done</u> it all," he said.

"In your <u>dreams,</u>" I replied.

"In <u>my</u> dreams, I've done it all <u>with</u> you!"

I had to laugh.


August 23, 2000

I've decided not to tell Celia anything about my plans and decided not to attempt to explain anything to her should my plans actually work. As for Bud, I'm not sure. He's one of those "scientific" guys and he'll eventually want to figure it out. Luckily, I now have the examples of Injun Ralph in Mabel's book about Portage County. In addition to his own stories and legends.

I feel bad about depriving them of Tony, however, because really that's what it comes down to, no? I'll make it up with Celia in hundreds of ways. With Bud of course I have the greatest way of all, I know what stocks to invest in, what fields to spread into. But I genuinely like the guy. Did from the beginning, and while I'm still not sure how straight he is, I really don't care. I do know that with Celia and Tony out of his hair, that Bud's little forays around Portage County with his own "round-heeled" women will end or get more serious. He might even decide to double-date with Celia and me.

Even so, in the last few weeks as the weather got cooler (for the most part) I've joined him as often as Tony does, playing tennis, a sport I'm coming to enjoy and which Bud excels at, and also in golf, a sport I'm less good and less interested in (Mark Twain called it "A good walk in the outdoors — ruined.") Tony doesn't do golf at all, and it's as social as it is athletic. So I'm trying to in advance "be there" for Bud when Tony's gone.

Meanwhile, me and Celia were "petting" so much the other afternoon in the chaise lounge that I came. I think she did too, without knowing what was going on. From being all soft she became suddenly totally rigid, then sort of convulsed, and pushed me away, jumped up and left me there while she went inside. After a while I took a swim.

But is that amazing or what?


August 25, 2000

Went to an attorney and had my will changed. For this to work, Tony too will have to change his will. Signing his estate over to me. As I'm signing mine over to him.

And if this doesn't work? If all that about Injun Ralph and Wilfred Dix and Jason Terranova and Ray Snyder is just bull, well, then my twin cousins Dean and Daryl, aged seven will be quite well off when they reach 18.

So now all I have to do is convince Tony and wait for a stormy day.

I'm guessing we'll both have to have our hands on that generator when the lightning hits!


*Here ends the journal provided by Fulton's Point Police*

# WISCONSIN STATE POLICE
Cold Case Department
Linklatter Mall, Bldg. E
Eau Claire, WI 54701
Detective-Sergeant Annabella Conklin,

To: Wayne G. King, Asst. D.A.
STATE of WISCONSIN, District Attorney's Office
Government Center, Building C
Madison, WI 53711

November 22, 2001

Re: Missing/Person Cold-Case, reopened as Case #324-01.

Dear Mr. King,

After a six month investigation by this office as per your request in May, 2001 we are able to enclose the following relevant documentation.

    A. Newspaper articles.
        1. *Junction City Intelligencer*, May 26, 1940.
        2. *Junction City Intelligencer*, December 12, 1940.
    B. Marriage License of Neal Bartram and Cecilia Nash-Ingals, April 4, 1941.
    C. Military Record of Neal Bartram, served U.S. CIVIL DEFENSE, July 9, 1942.
    D. *Junction City Intelligencer* Obituary of Neal Bartram, December 1, 1989.

# ❧ The Junction City Intelligencer ❧

*Morning Edition*      Sunday, May 26$^{th}$, 1940      *5 Cents*

# FIRE AT RENOWNED ESTATE
# INGALS & FRIENDS UNHARMED

## *Celebrated for its Architecture, Estate receives "Minor Damage" Residents & Rare Autos Unharmed*

### By Roger Pollets

Fulton's Point, WI— Tourists from Madison, out for a quiet country drive on Lakeview Drive, found amid blue skies, a cloud of black smoke, and drove to its source. They were stopped at the gates of the Ingals fortune heir's recently completed architectural marvel, known as Ingoldsby. Climbing the gates, they could see the main house on fire. Hugh J. Branch got over the gate and into the unlocked estate gate-house from which he was able to telephone local operator Minnie Drake, who called together members of the Volunteer Fire Department. When the fire truck arrived, Mr. Branch's wife Estelle let it in and told Chief Jackson that her husband and his brother Samuel had gone to the main house to see if any-one needed help.

By three-thirty in the afternoon, when they arrived, they were greeted by Chester A. Ingals and his house guests who'd managed to contain the fire in a section of the living room, saving the remainder of the Thurston masterpiece, one of the state's most famous houses. Also unharmed was the large garage containing Ingal's collection of expensive and rare automobiles.

Sheriff Acker said that Chester Ingals and his friends, Miss Cecilia Nash and Mr. Neal Bartram, both of Milwaukee, had been at the house for the weekend, Mr. Bartram aided Mr. Ingals in containing the fire. No servants were present on the property at the time of the fire. Young Moderns, the three were either used to fending for themselves, and/or preferred impromptu weekend trips to our district.

23-year-old Chester Ingals, glamorous heir to the Ingals Iron Works fortune, is a well-known figure in the state, as well as in Portage County, especially during the past two years when he engaged Charles Sigurd Thurston, protege of the controversial architect Frank Lloyd Wright and a figure in his own right, to design and build a large new estate on the southernmost sector of the Ingals property. Thurston's much-discussed estate was the height of the modern.

One story high, it was a rambling "ranch" style building with the most up-to-date conveniences, including a large

**FIRE AT ESTATE, Continued on Page 5**

## FIRE AT ESTATE: INGALS & FRIENDS UNHARMED

FIRE AT ESTATE, From Page 1

kitchen refrigerator, air-coolers throughout, built-in wireless sets and record players in many rooms, a sport regulation-sized swimming pool, and of course the separate, heated, ten-car garage for Ingal's conspicuous collection of automobiles, a building larger and more comfort-able than most Wisconsin homes. Utilizing rare woods from the east and south of America along with gold and aluminum trim, when completed, the estate at Ingoldsby was thought to cost an amazing four hundred thousand dollars!

An earlier three-story house built in 1907 on the property had been destroy-ed by freak lightning four years ago. Untenanted at the time, two servants sleeping nearby escaped unharmed. Part of the young heir's legacy, when he began building Ingoldsby, Chester Ingals often said that it was his "favorite place growing up."

**The Junction City Intelligencer**

---

## ∝ The Junction City Intelligencer ℘

*Weekend Edition*          *Saturday, September 14ᵗʰ, 1940*          *5 Cents*

---

# FIRE-DAMAGED ESTATE TO BE REBUILT / RESTORED

## *Complete Restoration of Fire-Damaged Estate to Begin Immediately. Town Receives Gift for "New Town Hall."*

### By Roger Pollets

Fulton's Point, WI — There was relief today with news that the architectural prodigy that brought us fame will be restored to its former glory. The restoration of the front room and the addition of new suites by the architect will be completed by Spring 1941, Ingals told The Intelli-gencer. At the same time the heir announced the engagement of the other two witnesses to the fire. Miss Celia Nash, Ingal's ward, of Milwaukee, grad-uate of The Eden School, and Mr. Neal P. Bartram, of Chicago, at North-Western University. The couple will reside at Ingoldsby, abroad, and elsewhere. As a gesture of re-commitment to our town, Ingals also donated $50,000 to build a new town hall to include administrative offices, a new Post Office and a restored Public Library on the spot of the former William Jeffers Pott Library.

**The Junction City Intelligencer**

# STATE of WISCONSIN
## PORTAGE COUNTY
**Department of Civil Licenses**
**Junction City Town Hall**
**Judge Martin Adams**
**1209 Old River Road**
**Fulton's Pt., Wisconsin**

Be It Known To All Persons!

That on This Date, April 4, 1941

**Mr. Neal P. Bartram**
residing at 1340 Lakeview Drive (Ingoldsby)
and **Miss Celia Nash**
of 1340 Lakeview Drive were

## Joined in Wedlock

by presiding judge

### Martin J. Adams

in a civil ceremony of

## Matrimony

after having passed in a satisfactory manner certain residence and health tests as required by certain regulations of the State and County, and now reside in full enjoyment of the civil responsibilities and benefits of that establishment.

| | |
|---|---|
| Witnessed by | Date of |
| *Chester A. Ingels* | *April 4, 1941* |
| And by | Date of |
| *Virginia (Bunny) Clarkson* | *April 4, 1941* |

ATTESTED TO by: *County Clerk, Nicholas G. Strath*

# STATE of WISCONSIN
## Governor's Office
### War Time Civil Defense
Jeffers Federal Building
Madison, Wisconsin
General Thurbert G. Kruger,

On this date: July 9, 1942

Mr. Neal P. Bartram
of 3430 Lakeview Drive a.k.a. Ingoldsby

Did Solemnly Swear to Defend to the Best of His Ability

## THE UNITED STATES OF AMERICA
and
## THE *SOVEREIGN* STATE of WISCONSIN

As a Ranking Member of The United States Civil Defense
With all the Privileges and Obligations of The Position
of
Portage County: Lieutenant Colonel

*Note: This Commission Allows Its Bearer to BEAR ARMS in public, to enlist or deputize for a period of no more than two days any other male citizen if deemed necessary and to make reasonable requests for material and other aid from any citizen of the county and state thereunder.*

signed                              witnessed

*Neal P. Bartram*                   *Chester A. Ingels*

Evening Edition —                                    — 20 Cents

# The Junction City Intelligencer

**** FRIDAY, DECEMBER 1, 1989 ****

# HISTORIAN / AUTHOR
# NEAL P. BARTRAM DIES

*CLOSE INGALS ASSOCIATE AND FRIEND
FOLLOWED HIS OWN PREDICTIONS
TO AMASS FORTUNE*

## By Kenneth Gregg

Fulton's Point, WI — Business associates announced the death yesterday of Neal P. Bartram, of heart failure. The noted historian and Professor, author of several books presciently warning of coming fiscal and ecological trends, was believed to be about 75 years old.

A Ph.D. graduate of Northwestern University and frequent Professor of American History and Politics at several University of Wisconsin campuses, Bartram is perhaps best known for his 1947 study,

*Re-Imagining the Future*, a text used by many influential think-tanks since.

While Bartram's early years are veiled, he was known to have been part of millionaire Chester Ingals' inner circle from the early days. Bartram wed Ingal's ward, Celia Nash in 1941, and became a consultant as well as a friend, steering Ingals out of the iron and steel business into new alloys, then into computer and microchip technology.

Bartram himself profited by following his own predictions. He leaves a per-

sonal estate valued in the hundred millions, and helped to endow several universities and libraries.

Prof. Bartram is survived by two children, Bud of Grosse Point and Tony of San Remo, Italy, as well as by several grandchildren. His wife predeceased him earlier this year.

Services to be announced.

**The Junction City Intelligencer**

That's all of it, Wayne.

Please note that the two newspaper articles differ substantially from those of the same dates enclosed in the journals provided by your office.

This office has spoken in person to various people mentioned by Bartram in his journals, including all those deposed by Sheriff Estes, who encountered Bartram daily in the summer of 2000. In addition we've traced the M/P's contacts with Mr. Kleinherz at the Intelligencer, and found M/Ps check-out slips at the main library in that city. A copy of his revised last will & testament is also on record. There is no question that Neal Bartram was active in Portage County during the summer months of 2000, and he was uniformly described as a slightly shorter than average, very hand-some, blond or light-brown haired male with light brown eyes and an excellent physique, aged early to mid twenties.

Unquestionably, according to various documentation we've found, only the most salient of which this office has obtained so far and enclosed for your perusal, Neal Bartram somehow also lived from approximately the spring of 1940 through December 1, 1989, dying around the age of 75 [*sic*].

Whatever really happened to the Missing Person Neal Percival Bartram, given all the evidence herein collected, this office cannot assess a finding of Homicide or Death by Foul Play.

I'm afraid it's back to you, Wayne — Happy Turkey day!

Det. Sgt. Anabella Conklin

# CONTEST FROM A DISTANT PLANET
## FOR ALL EARTHLING STUDENTS!

## SEND IN YOUR DRAWINGS / ARTWORKS

### WINNING DRAWINGS / ARTWORKS
### WILL BE INCLUDED IN AN UPCOMING REPRINT OF
### TALES: FROM A DISTANT PLANET

#### COMPETITION RULES

1. The competition is open to all students living on planet Earth.
2. The deadline is August 31, 2006 at midnight GMT. All artwork received after this date will not be eligible for the competition.
3. The artwork can be a painting, drawing, collage, photography, digital, or a reproduction of a three-dimensional sculpture. All artwork entries must be sent to our planet Earth address at: French Connection Press, 12 rue Lamartine, 75009 Paris, France. All Earthling artists who wish their original artwork to be returned after the contest must include a check, money order, or international reply coupons to cover the cost of postage. Any questions regarding the contest may be emailed to us at: infopress@club-internet.fr (no attachments, please).
4. The artwork has to illustrate or be directly inspired by at least one of the seven stories by Felice Picano in *Tales: from a Distant Planet*.
5. Each artist may submit one artwork for each of the seven stories.
6. In order to submit, the artist must complete the registration form available online at www.frenchcx.com or that can be sent to their address or faxed to their school. Only one artist per registration form, please.
7. All submitted artwork will be examined by a jury of three professional artists who will select one best artwork for each story. (By submitting their artwork, the artists agree to comply to the rules of the competition and grant all rights to French Connection Press for reproducing the winning artwork and for announcing their names to the press and media.)
8. The seven winning works (one for each story) will be featured in black-and-white in an upcoming reprint of *Tales: from a Distant Planet*. The Earthling winners will not only receive a winner's certificate, an autographed copy of the book, and a gift certificate—worth $100.00 (U.S. dollars) as honorarium for the reproduction of their artwork—but honorable mention in the book as: "Winner of The *Tales: from a Distant Planet* Artwork Competition."

Achevé d'imprimer en France par Hérissey en octobre 2005 (Évreux)
Dépôt légal : octobre 2005 - N° d'impression : 100210